*Nothing like a wedding to get a girl dreaming of happily-ever-after...*

Kessed Ling's best friend's big day is finally here. It's especially exciting because it's Kessed's chance to show her childhood crush she's not just a young bridesmaid, she's a full-grown woman—with red hot desires. But when her long-awaited prey barely blinks an eye at her, Kessed retreats right back into her deeply guarded heart. Doesn't matter that chivalrous Jasper Matthews steps in and offers a shoulder to lean on. Kessed is no longer in the market for a man, despite how unsettled the strong, silent groomsman makes her feel...

As a veterinarian, Jasper better understands a skittish filly than he does willful Kessed Ling. But when fate finds him playing ranch hand alongside the raven-haired beauty, Jasper realizes she's a woman running scared—and he's just the man to tame her. So with soothing words and bold kisses, Jasper sets out to show Kessed how good it can be between a man and a woman. Especially when the man is falling hard and fast in love...

# The Courage of a Cowboy

## Kristin Vayden

**LYRICAL PRESS**
Kensington Publishing Corp.
www.kensingtonbooks.com

Lyrical Press books are published by
Kensington Publishing Corp. 119 West 40th Street New York, NY 10018

All Kensington titles, imprints, and distributed lines are available at special
quantity discounts for bulk purchases for sales promotion, premiums, fund-
raising, and educational or institutional use.

To the extent that the image or images on the cover of this book depict a
person or persons, such person or persons are merely models, and are not
intended to portray any character or characters featured in the book.

Special book excerpts or customized printings can also be created to fit
specific needs. For details, write or phone the office of the Kensington
Special Sales Manager:
Kensington Publishing Corp.
119 West 40th Street
New York, NY 10018
Attn. Special Sales Department. Phone: 1-800-221-2647.

Kensington and the K logo Reg. U.S. Pat. & TM Off.
LYRICAL PRESS Reg. U.S. Pat. & TM Off.
Lyrical Press and the L logo are trademarks of Kensington Publishing Corp.

First Electronic Edition: April 2018
eISBN-13: 978-1-5161-0564-9
eISBN-10: 1-5161-0564-8

First Print Edition: April 2018
ISBN-13: 978-1-5161-0565-6
ISBN-10: 1-5161-0565-6

Printed in the United States of America

*For my husband, who walked me through all the various scenarios on how to be a large animal vet, even when the questions were a little silly. You're my love story, Harry, and each day is better than the last. And for my daughter, who wants to grow up and be a vet someday. I love your sweet and tender heart towards all our furry, and not so furry, friends. I love you.*

# CHAPTER ONE

"It could be worse."

Kessed narrowed her eyes at her best friend. "How exactly?"

Laken bit her lip, a sure sign she was fighting a smile—the traitor. "It could be too big?"

"Instead, it makes my boobs look like I'm about to have a wardrobe malfunction. At your wedding. Classy," Kessed replied with heavy sarcasm.

"Sterling won't mind." Laken lost the battle and started giggling.

"Why are you my best friend? Seriously." Kessed closed her eyes, pinching her nose with her thumb and finger. "Your wedding is tomorrow. How in the hell did we not get this dress sooner?"

"It was on backorder." Laken sighed, walking up to the three-way mirror and gently touching the creamy yellow fabric. "It really isn't that bad. I promise. You just look a little sexier than usual."

"For a family event," Kessed snapped.

"Wear stickers, just in case." Laken circled her chest area and smirked.

"I can't believe we're having this conversation. Whatever happened to the bridezilla disorder? You're immune? What is this?" Kessed sliced a hand through the air, popping her hip.

A few stiches snapped.

"Of course. So I can't move either. Fabulous."

"I'll see if they have anything else. You're the maid of honor, and if you're in a different dress, it won't be weird."

"Why are you so calm? You should be freaking out!" Kessed called after her best friend, who disappeared to the sales floor. "Hell, I'm freaking out." She sighed, wincing as the fabric bit into her sides as she tried to get a full breath. This was not going to work.

At all.

So much for stealing Sterling's attention. She snorted. Yeah, she'd steal it all right, just not the way she wanted. Biting her lip, she glanced to the floor. It had been a constant struggle from day one.

Sterling was Laken's brother. A marine, hard-core, fit, and a smile that could make a girl forget her name. But he'd never seen anything past the *friend zone* with Kessed; rather, he'd pestered her, teased her about being in love with him—which was too accurate for comfort—and then left to go and save the world, again.

His love was the military; it was his mistress and addiction.

And Kessed didn't know how to compete with that.

"What about this one?" Laken strolled into the room, holding up a midnight-blue gown.

"It's blue," Kessed stated as she took in the shimmering fabric.

"You're so observant. Yes, it's blue. Which is one of my other colors. Yellow, blue, and gray. You can get away with wearing blue as the maid of honor. Now try it on. Hurry. I've got other things to do than argue with you, and I'm about fifteen minutes from flipping the switch to the bridezilla you're fearing," Laken replied with a grin.

"You can't threaten me like that then smile. It totally voids your attempt." Kessed sighed with contempt and took the dress into a private room. "Wait, I think you might need the Jaws of Life to get me out of this thing, if the zipper hasn't already popped loose."

"Dramatic much? Seriously. Chill. Hold on—sit still for crying out loud!" Laken scolded but pulled down the zipper, and Kessed breathed deeply, thankful for small blessings.

"Air." She sighed longingly.

"You sure talk a lot for being oxygen-deprived," Laken shot back.

"It's a talent."

"Or a curse."

"For you."

"Are you ever going to stop talking?" Laken asked in an irritated tone.

"Shh, I'm changing." Kessed tried not to laugh as she imagined Laken's reaction.

Laken muttered, "Pain in my ass."

"All the best maids of honor are!" Kessed replied, slipping into the new dress. It flowed freely, accentuating each curve of her almost nonexistent hips, and showing off the swell of her breasts without making them indecent. The blue hue highlighted her jet-black hair, giving it a bluish sheen that made her hazel eyes almost navy-tinted. "Whoa."

"That good?" Laken asked from outside the door.

"I'm never taking it off."

"I'll take that as a yes." Laken waited a moment. "Do I get to see it, or are you going to just stare at yourself all day?"

"Stare," Kessed answered, turning to see the back.

"Gah, killing me over here!" Laken banged on the door.

"Shh, I'm having a moment."

"Really? Hello? Bride over here. Out. Now!"

Kessed grinned, opening the door and watching as Laken's eyes widened then squinted with the power of her smile. "Yes!"

"Amazing, isn't it?"

"Breathtaking. Sterling's jaw will hit the floor."

"That will be interesting."

"For both of us. I'm so good. Damn, I impress myself. I picked it out, you know." Laken walked a circle around Kessed, studying the dress.

"Full credit given."

"Thank you. Now quick, change. I gotta go and meet Cyler at the ranch. And you have a shift starting in a half hour."

"I know. I know." Kessed offered her back to Laken, who unzipped the dress with a soft touch, and soon Kessed was hanging it back up, studying it longingly.

"Did you apply for the management position?" Laken asked, pulling her back from her thoughts.

"Yes! I'll find out in a few weeks when the position opens. It would almost double my income because of the increase in hours."

"Call me when you know," Laken requested.

Kessed pursed her lips. "Yes, because that's what best friends do. Interrupt the other one's honeymoon. As if you're going to want to get out of bed."

"It's Hawaii. We'll be getting out of bed."

"To have ocean sex," Kessed called back, opening the door.

Laken blushed, grinning. "It still counts because we're technically out of bed."

"And we're done. Don't want to know." Kessed held up a hand and walked to the front of the store.

"You started it."

"And I'm ending it."

"Wait, where's the dress?" Laken paused.

"Shit." Kessed ran back to the dressing room, grabbed the dress, and caught up. "I'll take care of this. You head back home. I'll call you later.

You know what? Scratch that, I'll see you at eight a.m. sharp tomorrow. Enjoy your last night as Laken Garlington. Tomorrow you're Laken Myer." Kessed reached out and pulled her friend into a hug, careful not to wrinkle the dress she held between them.

"I can't wait," Laken breathed.

"Fine, go. Don't let that handsome cowboy of yours wait. He'll blame me."

"He always blames you."

"Yeah, well... he's usually right."

"True story."

"I'll be at the ranch at eight on the dot. I don't want to drag your ass from bed, so do me a favor and save me the trouble. Set an alarm," Kessed insisted, walking to the door.

"As if Cyler would let you in the house."

"I have a key."

"Damn, you do...." Laken snickered, pausing. "That would be funny."

"For you. I'd be visually violated. Cyler's got a nice ass, but I don't exactly want to see it in all its naked glory."

"Whatever." Laken lifted a hand in surrender. "By the way, thanks for housesitting. I'm glad someone will be at the ranch. Margaret—"

"That horse is spoiled."

"With love! And sugar. Don't forget to give her some, okay?"

"Gah, fine. And I'm happy to housesit for you while you're gone. Just as long as you swear the only animal I have to care for is the horse." Kessed leveled a stare at her friend.

"Pretty sure any other animals would suffer a fate worse than death if you had to take care of them," Laken teased. "But I know Cyler is really glad you'll be there. With him getting the ranch back up and going, he didn't want it left alone the whole time we were gone. Even if the steers aren't arriving till a few weeks after we return, he was still all uptight about it."

"Men." Kessed shrugged.

Laken gave her head a quick shake. "See you. Be good, and I'll be waiting to see your bright and shining face in the morning!"

Kessed waved. "I won't be bright, and I won't be shining. I'll be grumpy and demanding, but I will have coffee...."

"Then we're still set."

Laken walked out the door, and Kessed watched her friend leave. Tomorrow would be a huge day for sure, and it was long overdue.

While Cyler and Laken hadn't let grass grow under their feet, they'd also had a harrowing year. Cyler's father had died not three months ago, and the grieving process had been difficult for both of them. Though Jack,

Cyler's father, would always get credit for bringing the two of them together, it had been hard on Cyler, finally forgiving his father only to lose him.

But that was history, and Cyler and Laken's future was beautiful, and they did a great job focusing on that, rather than the pain of the past.

As Kessed glanced at the garment bag, she sighed in relief. Maybe miracles did happen—finding a quick replacement dress was proof. Now if she could only conjure up another miracle....

That maybe, just maybe, Sterling would, for once, see her.

Really see her.

Tomorrow would tell.

# CHAPTER TWO

The wedding day dawned without a cloud in the sky, the crisp fall air promising to warm up nicely by afternoon. Kessed had spent all morning helping Laken prepare for the big day and chasing Cyler away. Stubborn guy, he was relentless in trying to sneak a peek at his bride.

Of course, he might just have been doing it to piss Kessed off, too.

They'd had a true love/hate relationship from the start. Of course, to Cyler's credit, Kessed had told him she wasn't afraid of prison if he hurt her best friend.

*But that's what friends did, right?*

"Kessed, what time is it?" Laken asked, pulling Kessed from her thoughts.

"Almost noon. Are you hungry yet?"

"Yes, and no. Why in the hell am I so nervous? Seriously!" Laken sighed, sitting down on the bed, earning a glare from Kessed when she sat on the corner of the veil.

"It's a big deal, and it's perfectly normal to be nervous." Kessed gently tugged the veil from under Laken's ass and set it aside. "Pizza?"

"No! Sorry. I mean, no thanks," Laken corrected, taking a deep breath. "How about something that won't sit in my stomach like a rock."

"Hamburger?"

Laken glared. "What is it with you and fast food?"

"It's my love language." Kessed shrugged.

Laken shook her head. "What about a salad? You know, something that won't make me all bloated?"

Kessed giggled. "Fine. As long as I don't have to order a salad."

The rest of the afternoon passed in a whirl of activity till they were finally on their way to Suncadia Resort. Laken was quiet most of the thirty-minute drive. They were scheduled as the last to arrive. The rest of the bridal party as well as the groom's party were supposed to be at the resort in the early afternoon to finish the setup.

The resort was situated between the Cascade Mountains, with big blue sky meeting rugged peaks and green trees, broken up by flowing streams in the distance. It was lovely and made it easy on the guests, having the venue as their hotel.

As they wound around Bullfrog Lane, they entered the dense forest that led to the conference center that doubled as the wedding site. Cars were lining up in the parking area, signaling that the time was getting close, and Kessed's stomach leapt in anticipation and nerves.

"You okay?" she asked Laken, who gave her a slight smile in return.

"Yeah, I'm ready for being married. The wedding I can survive," Laken teased.

Kessed reached over and held her hand. "It will be fine. Sterling's here. He's giving you away. It's going to be amazing," Kessed assured her.

"I know. Let's do this."

As they walked to the venue, Kessed watched as the door swung wide, revealing emerald-green eyes and a dove-gray suit.

"Ladies, I'm here to escort you to your dressing room and protect you from the prying eyes of the groom." His grin widened, and Kessed gulped slightly. *Who the hell is he?*

"Thank you." Laken answered but Kessed didn't miss the way she glanced around the hall, apparently, for Cyler.

"Stop it. You're worse than he is." Kessed groaned, tugging on Laken's arm.

"Kessed, right?" the stranger asked.

"And you are?" Kessed held out her hand, unable to stop the suspicious pinch in her forehead. Hot or not, she didn't like it when people had an advantage over her.

"Jasper Matthews." He nodded kindly, grasping her hand with his warm one and shaking it.

"So, *you're* Jasper? Nice to put a face with the name." Laken's face lit up with familiarity.

Kessed glanced to her friend, arching a brow as if to say "*How do you know, and I'm still in the dark?*"

"Yes, ma'am. I'm honored to be a part of your special day."

Kessed narrowed her eyes in suspicion. *People, especially grown men, don't say* ma'am, *do they? And who is he, and how does Laken know about him but I don't?*

"So, you're taking over for Vince?" Laken asked as they started to walk down the hall.

"Yeah." He turned to Kessed. "My uncle is the vet around here but is retiring. I'm taking over. He's all but done, and so I'm swamped."

"Oh, so you know Cyler from..." She let the question linger.

"I grew up in Ellensburg. We played football together in high school and got into more than our share of trouble." He winked, his chestnut hair distracting her with the rich color and the way it appeared so soft.

*Easy girl. Think of Sterling.*

Kessed wanted to roll her eyes. "Sounds fun."

Jasper paused in front of a door, knocking once. Kessed heard a few squeals before the door opened, and several of their other friends enveloped Laken in hugs.

"That's my exit cue." Jasper chuckled. "But, Kessed, if you wouldn't mind, I think Cyler wanted to speak with you."

Kessed patted Laken on the back and walked off with Jasper, her tension slowly releasing. *Why am I so uptight?* It wasn't her wedding, but Laken was closer than a sister and, well... she wanted it perfect.

"A vet, huh?" Kessed asked, making conversation as they strode down the hall and out into the sunshine.

"Yup. What do you do for a living?"

Kessed groaned inwardly. It wasn't that she was ashamed of her job. She served coffee! She saved lives! It just didn't sound grown-up, and twenty-four was plenty grown-up. "I'm a barista at Starbucks."

"This is going to be the start of a beautiful friendship. I can feel it." Jasper nudged her with his elbow, and she released a pent-up breath.

"Coffee?"

"It's survival."

"I know how you feel," she answered as Cyler waved them down.

He was already in his tux, his light brown hair cut with a hard part that made him look like a cross between Scott Eastwood and David Beckham.

"Kess, so don't tell Laken because she'll kinda freak, and I don't want her to deal with this today, all right?" Cyler held his hands up in defense as if he was expecting a blow.

"Shit, what is it?" Kessed asked, glaring at her best friend's almost-husband.

Basically family.

Cyler sighed. "The livestock broker emailed me this morning, and I guess there's an issue with the timeline of delivery."

"Meaning?" Kessed prodded.

"Meaning that the steers might not be on schedule. They might be early," Jasper clarified, tucking his hands in his suit pants.

Kessed sent him a wary glance. "I don't know anything about cows."

Cyler choked back a laugh then sobered when she glared. "Don't worry, I'm well aware of that. Chances are I'll get it all sorted out, and it won't be an issue, but since you're housesitting while we're gone, I wanted you to be aware."

"So, it won't happen?" Kessed asked, nervous.

"Nope. But if it does, Jasper will be on deck to help you." Cyler gestured to his friend, who smiled widely.

"It looks like we should probably get to know one another, just in case," Jasper replied with a grin.

Kessed wanted to roll her eyes. *Is that a line? If so, is that the best he can do?*

"Let me get your number—"

"I don't think that will be necessary. I mean, if the worst happens—"

"Kessed, a few steers are not *the worst* that can happen," Cyler interrupted.

She glared. "For you. Be thankful I like your damn horse. Anything else is on its own."

Cyler chuckled. "You'll be fine. You're tougher than you think."

"Damn straight, I am," Kessed replied.

"So, since that went so well…" Cyler sighed heavily, rocking back on his heels. "Jasper, how's my almost-wife?"

"Say nothing." Kessed pointed to Jasper, and he lifted his hands in surrender.

"I'm saying nothing." Jasper arched a brow then turned to her. "Happy now?"

"Yes," Kessed answered. "*You*? You I'm not so happy with." She pointed to Cyler. "You get forever with her. You can wait an hour. It's worth it."

"Oh, I know it's worth it. But it's so entertaining to see you get all bent out of shape."

"Pain in my ass," Kessed replied.

"Ah, someone called my name?"

Kessed froze, her body tingling with awareness at the sound of the familiar tone of Laken's brother, Sterling.

"Yup, Kessed was just complaining—"

"About Cyler." Kessed finished, glaring at Cyler.

"Ah, and here I thought she reserved the sweet talk for me." Sterling winked at her.

Kessed's insides fluttered, and she took a silent breath. "What can I say? My heart beats for you, Sterling." She spoke with sarcasm and added an eye-roll for good measure, even though the words were too close to the truth for comfort. But that was the way of it, the give and take, the teasing and banter that only danced around the truth...

But never actually landed on it.

"That's what I love about you, Kess—your sarcasm. Like the sister I never had."

"Your sister is the one getting married," Kessed reminded him dryly.

"The other sister, the one I didn't like," Sterling articulated with a joking grin.

Yet even as he said it, Kessed died a little inside, because it reminded her of the truth.

He didn't see her romantically.

At all.

"I'm off to go check out the other bridesmaids. I'm in town for two more days on leave, then I'm gone. Let's see what trouble I can get into." He winked at the group, then left.

A cricket chirped in the distance.

Cyler cleared this throat. "Well, that was awkward."

Jasper whistled lowly.

Kessed glared at them both then groaned. "Tell me it wasn't that obvious."

Cyler glanced to the ground.

But Jasper met her gaze with a direct one of his own. "He's as dense as concrete. You can do better." He shrugged then patted Cyler on the shoulder. "I'm going to go and check on the dance floor setup."

Cyler nodded, and Jasper turned to Kessed. "In case you're interested in someone who doesn't have their head up their ass, you know where to get my number." With that, he strode away.

"You could do worse," Cyler spoke softly. "He's a good guy, Kess. And you should have seen the way he looked at you when you weren't paying attention."

Kessed turned to him. "Sterling will come around," she said mostly to convince herself.

"But what if you can do better?"

"What if I don't want to?" Kessed replied.

"Then I guess that's your choice. Even if it's a really bad one. I mean, Sterling's going to be my brother-in-law, and I know I'm going to sound like a sap—blame Laken—but I know what it's like to have your love shoved back in your face. It sucks. Don't willingly subject yourself to that when it's not necessary."

Kessed glanced to the grass, a frown puckering her brow. Cyler spoke from experience. The rift between his deceased father and himself was because Cyler's fiancée had made a successful play for his dad. It had taken years before Cyler would even talk with his father, and that was largely due to Laken. So Kessed didn't doubt that Cyler knew what he was talking about, but that didn't change anything—for her.

*Because how do I let go of the one thing I've always wanted?*

"Just think about it." Cyler placed his hand on Kessed's shoulder.

With a single nod, she walked back to the dressing room, forcing a happy face.

It was Laken's day, and come hell or high water, she was going to do everything in her power to make it perfect for her.

A short time later, Kessed waited for the music to sound then took measured steps down the white runner toward the bridal arch. The gentle breeze swept through the pines, accenting the string quartet perfectly. Her gaze shifted to the groom's party, but she averted her gaze before she made eye contact and focused on each step till she held her position as maid of honor.

Kessed's eyes watered as Laken walked down the white, rose petal–lined aisle. Laken's gaze was locked with her almost-husband. The intensity between the two of them made the fall air even warmer, and Kessed glanced away, feeling intrusive for even watching. Her eyes scanned the audience for a new target then shifted to the lineup behind Cyler before landing on Sterling. The dove-gray suit brought out the steel color of his eyes, giving her a shiver of attraction that she tried to cover with a deep breath.

Sterling met her gaze, grinning kindly—the sort of grin he'd give his kid sister. Kessed groaned inwardly, both irritated and disappointed at once.

*Seriously.* Her dress fit like a glove, her hair cascaded down her back like a thick waterfall, and she'd worked out for a month to get toned for this occasion! *The least he can do is notice, dammit!*

But that was always the case with him. He noticed but never really *noticed.*

Irritated with Sterling, she glanced past him. Startling green eyes met hers, and she suppressed a groan.

Of course, *he'd* notice. It wasn't that she wasn't attracted to Jasper. It was just that he wasn't Sterling.

Kessed brought her attention back to Laken and Cyler, watching as they repeated their vows after the minister. Cyler's blue eyes never left Laken's, his words tight with emotion, and Kessed was overwhelmed with the thrill of joy for her best friend.

She'd found her soul mate, her one and only.

*Her lobster.* She grinned, thinking of all the *Friends* reruns they'd watched together over the years.

Soon the ceremony was over, and as Cyler pulled Laken in for a less-than-PG kiss, Kessed's eyes brimmed with warm tears of joy. When Cyler finally let Laken come up for air, she turned to face the guests with her husband to the sound of enthusiastic applause as the minister announced them as Mr. and Mrs. Myer.

After Laken and Cyler walked down the aisle, she held her breath, waiting for Sterling to offer his arm. Heart pounding, she bit her lip as she wrapped her arm around his, hazarding a glance at him as they exited the front.

The rest of the evening flew by in a blur of activity that was peppered with highs and lows; regrettably, the lows being about just one thing.

Sterling *still* hadn't noticed her.

Or if he had, it wasn't the kind of notice that she'd wanted. He'd taken his turn twirling her around the dance floor, his grin as devastating as ever, set against his tanned skin and bleach-blond hair. But his gaze kept straying, as if he was never fully comfortable in a crowd, but always aware, always vigilant.

It was both comforting and annoying. But old habits died hard, and well, he was a marine after all.

When their dance ended, he took her to the edge of the floor and tossed a quick smile over his shoulder as he walked off to find another partner.

"You want to dance?"

Kessed turned to Jasper, not for the first time noticing the brilliant green of his eyes and single dimple on his left cheek as he smiled. But there was no spark. "Thanks, but I think I'll go and check on the getaway car."

"Need help?" he asked.

"Persistent, aren't you?" Kessed asked, grinning in spite of herself.

Jasper shrugged slightly. "I've been called worse."

Kessed nodded. "Thanks for the offer, but no thanks. I'll let you know if I'm interested." A twinge of guilt twisted her gut, but she held fast. The last thing she needed was a guy who wouldn't take no for an answer.

Jasper shook his head once. "I understand. You know where to find me if you change your mind." He gave a shy smile and walked away.

*Why can't I be attracted to someone like him?*

*Why does it have to be Sterling?*
Leaving Kessed to wonder...
Maybe it wasn't Jasper.
Maybe it wasn't Sterling.
Maybe it was her.
And maybe that needed to change.

# CHAPTER THREE

Jasper wiped his hand down his face. "Shit." Well, life was about to get really interesting. He narrowed his eyes at his phone, re-reading the text. The apology, really. To think he'd actually volunteered for this.

*Ha. That was a mistake.*

One he was paying for dearly.

He unlocked his phone and quickly replied...

Sure thing.

...when it was anything but. Oh, he could handle the cattle. In fact, give him a raging bull or a pissed-off stallion any day. It was *she* who had him concerned. Ever since the wedding, he'd steered clear, trying to keep his distance, and that wasn't exactly easy when they lived in a small town like Ellensburg, Washington. She'd been clear she wasn't interested, and he hadn't pushed it. But navigating around her wasn't easy when she worked at the only Starbucks in town. He'd always been unapologetic about going after what he wanted in life, but he wasn't the type to force the issue either. Kessed struck him as the kind of person who knew her mind, and if she wasn't interested, she was exactly that. He could respect that, was trying to respect that....

But all his efforts to avoid her had been in vain.

Cyler and Laken had decided to reestablish the ranch, which meant they needed cattle. They'd arranged for their new herd to arrive shortly after they finished their honeymoon.

Except there had been a mix-up, and the cattle were being delivered almost a month early. The only person on the ranch was Kessed—beautiful, stubborn, and animal ignorant. He could only imagine what she'd do when two stock trailers arrived.

He sighed a deep breath and slid his phone in his pocket. After reaching for his keys, he shut the door behind him, not bothering to lock it. If someone wanted to break in, they were welcome to his old laptop and microwave. That was about all they'd get. Plus, living so far out in the sagebrush meant that the biggest threats were snakes and cougars, not thieves.

His old Ford F-250 roared to life, the diesel engine growling as he accelerated down the dirt road, thankful for the twenty minutes or so that he'd have to think before he arrived at the Elk Heights Ranch. Hopefully, Kessed wouldn't think he was being persistent, but rather, she'd understand that he was helping out an old friend.

She'd made it abundantly clear at the wedding that her heart belonged elsewhere. Fleetingly, he wondered why she held on so hard to someone who clearly didn't feel the same way. Sterling. He remembered the name. He seemed like a good guy, but distracted, restless—bored. Cyler had said he was a marine, and that made sense. Even at the wedding, Jasper noted how the man's eyes never stopped scanning the crowd, looking for threats. It was a way of life.

A coyote ran across the road ahead and then ducked over the ditch, pulling Jasper's thoughts back in line. If Cyler was correct, the bull wagons should arrive in two days, and that gave him only forty-eight hours to finish all the repairs to the fencing Cyler had planned on taking two weeks to accomplish. Good Lord, this was going to *suck*.

At least his friend wasn't just calling in a favor; he was paying him too. But Jasper knew he'd have done it anyway. Loyalty was loyalty; it didn't require reimbursement, but in this case, it sure would be appreciated. This was going to take quite a bit of time out of his work schedule, and already the appointments were starting to line up. What he needed was an assistant.

The hills rolled in the distance as the late fall heat burned into an Indian summer. And soon he was pulling into the drive that led to the Elk Heights Ranch. Sure enough, there was a bright blue hatchback parked in the circular drive, and he could only assume that meant Kessed was home.

He threw his truck in park, half-thankful that his loud engine would at least give her a heads-up that he was there. As his boots hit the gravel of the drive, the front door opened. Kessed gave a small wave, her dark hair pulled back in a messy bun, and her dark eyes unreadable.

Damn, she was even prettier than he remembered. He put one boot in front of the other and walked to the porch. "Morning."

Kessed opened her mouth, as if about to stay something, then paused. She took a deep breath and opened the door wide. "Coffee?" she asked.

Jasper exhaled a sigh of relief. "Always."

"I'm pretty sure we're going to need it," she replied, closing the door behind them.

Jasper studied the house. It had been a long time since he'd been inside. He and Cyler had been friends in junior high and high school, but they'd lost touch during college, as was easy to do. The house looked much the same, save a few different decorating touches that updated the cozy home.

"Kitchen's this way." Kessed stepped in front, leading down the hall.

He almost told her that he was more than aware where the kitchen was but held his tongue. Rather, he simply appreciated the view she presented, trailing his eyes down her slender shoulders to her rounded ass, which filled out her jeans in a way that made his blood surge to his lower regions. Clearing his throat, he glanced away, trying to keep his body in line.

"So, I'm assuming Cyler spoke to you?" Jasper asked, distracting himself from the sway of her hips.

"Yeah." She glanced over her shoulder as they walked into the kitchen. She pulled out two mugs from the shelf above the coffeepot. "He called last night—rather, Laken did then handed the phone to him so he could explain. Seriously. As if I know what in the hell I'm doing." She gave an exasperated sigh and filled the two cups.

"That's where I come in." Jasper gave her a polite smile, taking the mug as she offered it. "Cyler emailed me a list of the necessary repairs and preparations. I'm going to need a little help from you, but I'm pretty sure I can handle most of it on my own. I'll just be in your hair a bit during the process." He took a slow sip of coffee, its bitter and bold flavor a familiar taste that helped release some of the tension he held.

"Oh, so you don't need me?" Kessed's dark brows furrowed. "Cyler said that there was, well, in his words, 'a shitload of work,' and I needed to get my ass out there and do something productive. But really, it was just Laken telling him to say that. I didn't take offense. I'll just poison his coffee next time he stops in the shop." She arched a brow wickedly, grinning.

Jasper glanced at his coffee, regarding it suspiciously.

"Kidding! Gah, you guys are all so serious." She threw a hand up in irritation and walked toward the back door. "Are you going to show me what we need to get started with, or what?"

Jasper regarded her for a moment then took a long sip of coffee, drawing it out just to ruffle her feathers. It worked, and her dark brown eyes narrowed before she arched a dark brow.

"Sometime today."

Jasper just nodded, taking slow steps to the door, chuckling when she growled lowly and walked outside, her steps overly loud as if conveying her irritation.

He fought a chuckle, watching her stomp off toward the barn. *Well, this is shaping up to be far more fun than I expected.*

Just to piss her off, he headed for his truck. She was opening the barn door when the truck's engine roared to life, and she gave a little jump as if the noise startled her. He drove down the gravel road toward the barn and reached over, opening the passenger door. "What are you waiting for? Let's go."

Kessed glared then closed the barn door and hopped in the truck. "You could have told me."

"And miss the cute little stomp-off you did? Never."

"I didn't *stomp off.*" She narrowed her eyes.

He started down the dirt road that led behind the house and along the property. "Sure."

Kessed sighed. "If I did, it was just because you were being extremely slow."

"It was fun."

Her eyes shot to his face. "You did that on purpose."

"Yes."

"Why?" she demanded.

"It amuses me," he answered, meeting her gaze for a moment, grinning.

"Jackass," she muttered under her breath.

"Pain in the ass." Jasper coughed the words, earning another glare.

They went over the bumpy and overgrown road, his truck handling the rough terrain well. "Over there is one of the areas that Cyler said needed repair." Jasper drove a few feet closer then put the truck in park, not bothering to turn it off as he slid from the driver's seat and walked around the front.

Kessed followed, her tennis shoes no match for the cheatgrass and sagebrush. She hissed a few times, probably from the weeds poking through, but Jasper was focused on the fence line.

"Well, I guess it could be worse."

"That only means it could be a lot better," Kessed said and walked up beside him. She reached down and pulled the prickly seeds from her shoes.

"Observant."

"I try." She stood up and gave him a wink.

He smiled. "This barbwire needs to be replaced… and these fence posts"—he rocked the wooden post in its hole, noting how loose it was—

"need to be reinforced, if not completely replaced as well. The question is how much of the ranch is in this condition." Jasper asked the question mostly to himself.

"Well, I guess we're going to be driving around a lot today." Kessed took a deep breath and marched toward the truck.

"Do you have to work later?" Jasper asked, heading back to the truck as well.

She glanced over her shoulder. "Nope. They actually cut back my hours a bit, so I'm free for the next three days. I'll work all weekend—which sucks—but a job is a job." She shrugged and climbed into the truck.

Jasper nodded, and soon they were driving down the road once again. Kessed was a dangerous distraction, and the prospect of spending the whole day with her was both exciting and alarming. Even as he tried to keep his eyes on the road or the fence line, searching for weaknesses, out of the corner of his eye he'd see her tuck a wisp of hair behind her ear or watch her face light up in a smile.

"Are you usually this quiet?" Kessed asked a few minutes into their journey.

"Nope," Jasper answered, keeping his eyes trained on the road, then the fence, then back to the road.

"So, I'm just lucky?" Kessed teased.

If he didn't know better, he might have thought she was flirting.

Good thing he knew better.

"Yup."

She sighed. "One-word answers are your favorite, huh?"

"Yup."

"Gah! You're killing me!" Kessed leaned her head back against the seat.

Jasper chuckled. "You're easy to mess with."

"I'm impatient."

"That too."

"Well, you're irritating. And silent."

"Odd how you put those two together."

"Odd how you make it work!"

Jasper nodded, enjoying the banter, the push and pull, the give and take of a worthy sparring partner. "You're something else, Kessed. But you're fun." He gave her a quick smile then pulled over slightly and left the truck to check on another length of fence.

The passenger door shut, and soon Kessed was marching beside him. "Glad I can entertain you," she remarked.

"You do. But it's not just that." He shrugged then bent down, studying the rotting fencepost. "We'll need to replace the ones like this with the T-posts."

"T-posts?" Kessed echoed.

"Yeah, the metal posts. They'll be stronger and easier to install than the wood ones. They aren't as rustic, but I'm pretty sure Cyler isn't into the aesthetic appeal of the fence line." He gave a short laugh.

"Laken might," Kessed dared, arching a brow.

"If Cyler takes Laken out this far, they won't be looking at the fenceposts, if you know what I mean." He dusted off his hands from the dirty wood and walked back to the truck.

"You can keep comments like those to yourself!" Kessed called out as he got back in the truck.

He chuckled, waiting for her to climb in. "And here I thought you wanted me to talk more."

"I changed my mind."

"You're a woman. I guess it's your prerogative."

"Damn straight it is," she muttered, and he snickered in response.

Jasper searched for a place to turn the truck around, and soon they were heading back to the ranch. "I'm going to go check the north side. Do you want to come with me or do you have something else you need to do?" he asked as the house appeared on the horizon.

"Getting tired of my sparkling conversation?" Kessed teased with a smile.

"Nope."

"Then I guess I'll tag along."

"Would you mind tallying a few things for me?" He picked up his phone and quickly entered the passcode. "Can you open the note app and make a list for me?"

Kessed took his cell and tilted her head, waiting. "Ready when you are."

"T-posts, fifty." He narrowed his eyes as he thought. "Next, barbwire. I'll need at least a thousand feet."

"Whoa," Kessed remarked as her fingers tapped.

"Remember, it's not just one line. It's two. I've got to double everything. The last thing Cyler wants is to come home to his cattle free-ranging outside the range."

"Noted." Kessed nodded. "Next?"

"Gloves, boots, and nails."

"Got it. What kind of boots?"

He glanced over to her, watching her eyes flicker from his boots and back to his face. "Women's."

He stifled a grin at her confused expression.

"Huh, I didn't take you as playing for that team." She blinked.

"I don't. The boots are for you, which reminds me…. What size?" Her confused expression deepened. "Me?"

"You're like a magnet for cheatgrass in those shoes. And if you're going to help out, like you said you would, then you're going to need some boots."

"What if I already have boots?"

"Then you should have worn them."

"Well—"

"Do you have boots?" Jasper asked.

"No."

"Then why are we having this conversation?"

"Because… you just assumed. You didn't ask."

Jasper paused, both seeing her point and disregarding it at the same time. "Do you have gloves?"

"Snow gloves?" Kessed asked, her tone hopeful.

Jasper closed his eyes for a moment, shaking his head. "I'll take that as a no." He turned down the north road and continued searching the fence line.

"What kind of gloves?"

"Work gloves."

"Oh."

"Yeah, your hands are used to coffee, not rusty barbwire."

"There's nothing wrong with coffee," Kessed replied defensively.

"I don't remember mentioning that there was." Jasper turned to her, putting the truck back in park.

"You implied it."

"You're oversensitive. The world needs coffee, woman. Be proud of your service to mankind." He gave her a serious nod.

"You're patronizing me." She glared.

"Nope. Coffee is proof God loves us." He nodded once and left the truck, starting toward the fence.

If his memory served correctly, there was a creek that flowed through the pasture just ahead. It would be low this time of year, but he wanted to make sure it was still a viable source of water for the cattle. Cyler had mentioned it, but it needed to be double-checked.

As before, soon Kessed was beside him, and they walked up the road a bit. Jasper paused here and there, studying the condition of the wire. "I'm thinking this side is in better shape than the west. That's good."

"Do you think we can get it done in time?" Kessed asked, the first sign of uncertainty in her tone.

Jasper regarded her. "It will be close, but I think we'll manage."

"But what about your vet stuff?" Kessed asked, her dark eyes searching.

"I'll just rearrange things a bit. It won't be easy, but all of it needs to get done. I'll find the time." He shrugged, closing the conversation, and walked toward the sound of the water.

"Why?"

Jasper turned, noticing that Kessed hadn't followed him, but stood with her arms crossed. "Why what?"

She stepped toward him. "Why put your own career on hold to take care of someone you knew from high school?"

Jasper slipped his hands in his pockets. "Why not?"

"Because it's..." She paused, biting her lip as she thought.

Jasper watched with a hungry interest that he forced down as he focused on his words. "Sometimes, when you help someone out, it's not a reflection of their character, but your own. But in this case, Cyler's a good man— always has been. He asked me for help, he's paying me to help, and I had volunteered long before I knew this was going to be an issue. I'm not backing out now just because it's an inconvenience. Sometimes that's just the breaks. You work with it, you get it done, and you move on."

Kessed glanced to the road.

"If we're being honest... why are you here? You said yourself you don't know anything about this, yet here you are, walking through the prickly grass, tolerating my company, and planning to help out tomorrow as well. Why?"

Kessed sighed. "I see your point."

Jasper nodded then turned back to the creek.

"So, do you need me to remember anything else?" Kessed asked.

"Just those things for now."

"I'm a size eight," she remarked as she stood beside him, looking across the vacant pasture, the wind gently blowing the rye grass. The water bubbled through the pasture, making a lazy carving in the basalt and dirt.

"Maybe you need to write that part down." Jasper slid a glance to her, a slight grin teasing his lips.

"And here I thought I was done."

"No rest for the wicked." Jasper winked, then headed back to the truck.

"And if I get boots, I want red ones." Kessed spoke from behind.

Jasper paused, turning to face her. "Red?"

"Yup."

"Anything else while we're being specific?" Jasper arched a brow.

"Nope. Just red. Size eight."

"And I'm sure you're writing that down."

"Of course. It's my job."

"Right." Jasper wiped his hand down his face. "Let's get going."

"They do have red cowboy boots, right?"

Kessed's question followed him to the cab. He waited till she got in before answering.

"Yes. I think. Honestly, I've never bought red ones. I'll ask Harper." He put the truck in gear and headed back toward the ranch.

"Harper?" He felt Kessed's gaze on his face, but he ignored it, hoping to tease her a bit.

"Yeah, she'll know. She was a rodeo queen in high school, and ever since then, she's been a fan of whatever bling she can add to her gear."

"Oh."

He could see from the corner of his eye that Kessed glanced away and stiffened.

"Girlfriend?"

*As if you'd care?* "Sister," he answered, flickering his eyes to study her face.

"Oh." She shrugged, as if not concerned, when her previous posture had suggested the opposite.

"What about you?" Jasper asked, using the topic to learn a bit more about the woman beside him.

"What about me?" She crossed her arms, almost defensively.

"Do you have any brothers or sisters?" he asked.

Her brow furrowed a moment before he glanced back to the road.

"Oh, no, actually."

"What did you think I was going to ask?" He could guess, but wanted to hear her say it.

"If I had a boyfriend, which you know the answer to."

"I suppose I do."

"Gah, could this be more awkward?" She sighed and turned toward the window.

"I'm not feeling awkward."

"Yeah, well, you should."

"Why?"

"Because, well… the wedding… and…"

He could see that beneath her olive-toned skin, she was burning red. He bit back a grin and debated whether to push her further or take pity.

He decided to push. "Sterling—that's his name, right?"

"Seriously, you even remember his name. I was wrong. It can totally get more awkward." She covered her face with her hands, groaning.

"Happy to do what I can."

"Can I just walk home?" she asked, unveiling her eyes.

"Nope. This is way too much fun."

"You're such an ass!"

"Me? Me?" Jasper turned to her, shocked.

"Yes, you! Because, because... gah! Okay. Never mind."

"Whatever you want," Jasper conceded, holding back a grin at her obvious discomfort.

"It doesn't matter anyway. I'm completely nonexistent to him. Well, so maybe not nonexistent, but not enough. And you know what? That really sucks." She sighed.

Jasper opened his mouth then closed it. Oddly enough, he knew what she meant. It did suck. The irony was that *he* felt that way because of her... and *she* felt that way because of another.

But what could he say?

He simply pulled up next to the house, and before he could think of anything, Kessed was out of the truck and stomping toward the house.

"Well, that could have gone worse."

*And it certainly could have gone better....* He finished the thought and turned the truck around and down the drive. Kessed didn't need him pestering her further. She needed time, and he could give her that. He had a list, and belatedly, he glanced to the passenger side seat and felt a mixture of relief and disappointment when he saw his phone waiting for him. Relief, because then he wouldn't forget anything he needed, but disappointment, too, because that took away his excuse to ask Kessed for it. Oh well, he'd find a reason soon enough.

A smile spread across his face, and he picked up his phone.

After dialing the number, he smirked when his sister answered.

"Hey, darling.' So, I need your help...."

# CHAPTER FOUR

Kessed stretched her toes, twisting her ankles as she slowly woke up. Sunlight was streaming through her window, and a smile teased her lips, till she remembered.

Today, she was supposed to help Jasper.

Damn.

It wasn't that she didn't like him.... It was that... well, he liked her. At least she thought he did.

At least that was the impression she'd gotten. *Am I wrong? Am I making this more than it should be?*

THIS was why she wasn't excited about spending the day with him! He was impossible to read and knew way more about her than she knew about him—putting her at a distinct disadvantage. Yesterday had been pretty relaxed until he'd brought up Sterling's name.

*How in the hell does he even remember it?*

It was insane, yet there it was, the elephant in the room that she carried around with her whenever she was with Jasper.

And based on her volunteering yesterday, she was going to be around him a lot.

The day already sucked, and it wasn't even 7:00 a.m.

Reluctantly, Kessed slipped from the guestroom on the ranch and padded down the hall toward the kitchen, the heavenly scent of brewing coffee calling to her before she'd even crossed over the threshold. "At least you're always predictable," Kessed mumbled as she poured herself a cup.

The steam swirled around her face, and she took a small sip before her lips bent into a smile. After another tentative sip, Kessed walked to the breakfast nook, studying the landscape through the wide picture window.

The sun was fully up, casting a warm glow across the autumn-kissed terrain. Yet, her mind wandered back to Jasper. She glanced to the wall clock and guessed that he'd be there shortly. The clock in the hall chimed seven, and she took a deep breath and padded to the bathroom.

Before seven thirty, Kessed was back in the kitchen, dressed and teeth brushed, her hair piled into another messy bun. Why not? It wasn't as if she were trying to impress Jasper.

The very opposite.

As soon as she took the last bite of cereal, a rumbling sounded from outside, signaling Jasper's truck. Not a minute later, a knock sounded. "Come in!" she called as she walked toward it as it opened. "Hey." She waved Jasper inside, studying the two plastic bags he held.

"Mornin'," he mumbled, as if groggy.

"Still asleep?" Kessed teased, not able to resist the chance to harass him. As they moved into the kitchen, she picked up her coffee mug, using it as a distraction. His hair was tousled, his expression less guarded, and it had a strange effect on her heart.

"Almost." Jasper yawned, setting down the two sacks. "Had a breech calf last night. It turned out all right, but not until after taking as long as possible."

"Sounds fun."

"Believe me, it was anything but." He sent her a quick glance. "But it's always worth it when you watch them stumble and stand, alive and well." He slipped the plastic off and revealed a boot box. "See if they fit."

Kessed set her mug of coffee down, a smile crossing her lips even as she tried to tamp it down. "So, you found red?"

"Did I say that?" Jasper asked as he leaned against the wall.

"Well, no. I'm just assuming." She hesitated.

"You know what they say about assuming things—"

"Yeah, yeah..." Kessed waved him off dismissively and set the box on the table. She lifted the lid and the paper that covered the contents. A wide smile broke across her face as she took out one bright cherry-red boot then another.

"If they don't fit... lie," Jasper spoke, and Kessed glanced to him then, his wide smile full of amusement.

"They don't fit." Kessed arched a brow.

"You haven't even tried the damn things on yet," Jasper replied, his tone beleaguered.

"Don't swear at my boots."

"Ah, you like them then?" His grin widened, and her heart did a strange thump in response.

Turning away quickly, she replied, "No, I love them." She set them down on the floor and slipped one of her feet inside. The soft leather hugged her calf through her skinny jeans and wrapped around her foot like a glove. "I'm beginning to understand why people wear these so much. Wow, they are comfortable." She twisted her foot to get a better view. Leather detailing wound around the top, making a feather-like design that continued down the boot to her toe.

"Try the other one on. I bought heels so you're not so short," Jasper remarked, and Kessed expressed her irritation in a glare.

He lifted his hands in defense. "Just saying."

"I'll let it slide since you brought them."

"Lucky me."

"No one in this room is lucky, or getting lucky, or anything of the sort."

"That spiraled quick. Should I be concerned? I mean, my mind wasn't even going there, and yours was... hmm... What does that say about you?"

"I'm ignoring you now."

"If you were ignoring me, you wouldn't have to tell me."

"Can you just show me what's in the other bag while I walk around in my amazing boots and pretend you're not standing there?"

"And here I thought that I'd be getting a thank you," Jasper replied under his breath, just loud enough for Kessed to hear.

She stopped her pacing, sighing. "Thank you."

"Was that so hard?" Jasper asked as he pulled out a set of leather work gloves and handed them to Kessed.

"Yes. Yes, it was."

"At least you're honest."

"Always. So, gloves. Thank you."

"Gratitude right away? Wow. You learn fast."

"I've always been quick on the uptake. What's your excuse?" Kessed asked irritably.

"Didn't know I needed one." Jasper chuckled, shaking his head.

"So how much do I owe you for the boots?" Kessed asked, rocking back and forth on her heels.

"Time. Sunup to sundown. It's going to take that long to get this place set up." Jasper let out a sigh.

"Sounds good. Will work for boots." Kessed nodded.

"Not surprised."

"Enough talking!" Kessed made a slicing motion with her hand. "What do we need to do first?" she asked.

Jasper grinned, rubbing his chin with his hand. "First, we need to check the barn for a post pounder."

"Do I want to know?"

"I'll show you. But before we head out, go and grab some old sneakers to put in the back of the truck. Your boots will need to be worked in, and you might need to switch them out later today."

"I don't want to take them off." Kessed narrowed her eyes.

"Your blisters, not mine," Jasper replied, opening up the screen door and pausing.

"Fine. I'll meet you out there." Kessed tossed her gloves onto the table and ran back to her room, picking up the sneakers from yesterday. As she made it back to the kitchen, she swiped her work gloves from the table, knocking down the boot box. The lid went sliding across the floor, and a piece of paper floated down to the floor.

Kessed picked up the lid and started to crumple up the paper, pausing when she noticed it was a receipt.

For the boots.

The very expensive red boots she was wearing on her feet.

Dear. Lord.

Blinking, she glanced from the scrap of paper to the door, then back, a slow smile teasing her lips. It had been a long time since someone had done something nice for her... without trying to take credit. Yet suspicion crept in.

There was always a catch.

A reason.

People didn't just do nice things, not expecting something in return.

The receipt crinkled in her hand as she balled it up then strode to the back door.

"Hey, Jasper." Kessed jogged toward the barn, waiting for him to answer.

"In here." His deep baritone carried across the drive.

Kessed tried not to notice the way her beautiful new boots crunched on the gravel, or the way they made her stand a bit straighter due to the square heel, or the way she felt like a badass just wearing them. "You didn't mention that these boots were three hundred dollars. What are you trying to pull?"

Jasper straightened, a confused expression marring his otherwise perfect face. "Say what now?"

"These boots? I saw the receipt. Why in the hell would you pay that much? What's in it for you?" Kessed stood her ground, waiting, watching.

"I thought we agreed that your time was payment for the boots?" Jasper replied, opening the door to a storage room in the barn. "I'm not complaining. I can't see why you are." He ignored her question, disappearing into the dark room. "Damn, it's darker than the inside of a cow. You have your phone?"

Kessed paused then took out her phone, switching on the flashlight app. "Here. And I'm not complaining, but I don't want to be naive either. People don't spend money unless they expect something in return."

"Shine it over there, yeah. Thanks. And uh... you do realize you're talking in circles, right? What am I missing in this conversation that somehow makes sense to you?"

"You can't buy me."

Jasper slowly turned, his expression fierce, hurt. "You think I bought those boots to get you in bed with me?"

Kessed stepped back, her hackles rising. "Well? Did you?"

"Sweetheart, I've never had to resort to any sort of bribery to get a woman in my bed, if you get my drift. And I'm pissed that you'd think so little of me. Damn." He shook his head.

"Is it wrong to ask?" Kessed defended herself, hating that she felt ashamed for asking.

"No. But it sucks that I can do something nice for you, and you immediately think it's something underhanded. You know what? Enjoy the boots. I think I'll work better alone." Jasper shook his head and stomped back into the dark hole, the flashlight now pointed at the ground.

Kessed narrowed her eyes. "Two can play that game."

"What game!" Jasper roared, stomping back out from the blackness. "I'm not playing anything, sweetheart. I hate to break it to you, but I'm pretty simple. What you see is what you get. If I had a plan or pretense, I'd probably last about five minutes before I'd have to just lay it out. That's who I am. Take it, leave it, but don't insult it," he grumbled then stalked off to another corner of the barn. "Damn posthole pounder."

Somewhat defused, Kessed sighed. "What's the damn thing look like?" she asked, walking toward Jasper.

"Not sure if I want to tell you. Won't you just twist it?" He spoke tersely.

"Now you're being an ass. I didn't call you an ass. I asked if you were one. Which, by your own definition of self, if you were, you'd be compelled to tell me. So, don't be the ass."

Jasper dropped his chin to his chest. "You're insane. You know that?"

"Yes."

He sighed. "At least you're honest. Fine. It looks like a really long metal pipe that has handles on the sides, and it's closed off on one end."

"Was that so hard?"

"It didn't have to be, yet you made it that way," Jasper mumbled.

"Heard that."

"Don't care."

Kessed bit her lip, trying not to smile. Her eyes scanned the semi-dark barn, and she walked over to Margaret, Cyler's mare. "Hello, beautiful."

The chestnut mare nodded a welcome, nickering. Kessed stroked the soft velvet of her muzzle.

"Distracted much?" Jasper asked, but his tone held a hint of humor.

"Yes. Deal with it."

He chuckled, and Margaret bobbed her head, gently shoving at Kessed. "I know you want a treat. You're going to have to be patient. I need to find something first."

Margaret stomped her foot, and Kessed gave her a pat on the neck before she went around the mare's paddock, looking for the posthole... thing.

All sorts of farm implements lined the walls of the barn. To Cyler's credit, they were mostly organized, but it didn't help that she had no idea what the method was to the organization. As she scanned the various tools for one that fit Jasper's description, she saw a rusty metal handle lying in the corner. Walking over to investigate, she narrowed her eyes in the dimly lit barn. "Hey, is this it?"

Jasper's footsteps grew louder as he walked over to where she pointed. "Yup. Good work. Let's get moving—unless you have more questions?" He arched a brow in challenge.

"I'm good." Kessed shrugged, noncommittal.

"Sure you are." Jasper pursed his lips but slung the tool over his back and headed out into the sunlight.

Quickly, Kessed ran to the tack room, snatched a sugar cube, and extended her palm to Margaret, who greedily lipped it from her open hand. "I always keep my promises," Kessed whispered, touching Margaret's cheek tenderly, then jogged out the barn door.

Jasper's pickup roared to life, and Kessed hopped into the passenger seat. "Ready?"

"Waiting on you, sunshine."

After setting her phone in the cup holder between them, she turned to Jasper. "So, fence posts today, huh?"

"Yup." He nodded, not turning toward her but keeping his eyes toward the dusty road.

"Care to elaborate?"

"I would think it's pretty self-explanatory." Jasper gave her a quick glance.

"Humor me."

He sighed. "We need to hammer the T-posts into the ground to replace the rotting or pulled out wooden ones."

"Sounds easy enough." Kessed shrugged.

Jasper chuckled. "For you. You're not the brawn in this business." He eyed her up and down before turning his gaze back to the road. The truck lurched to the left as they went over a pothole.

"I'm the brains?" Kessed guessed, her grin widening.

"Sure. Let's say that." Jasper twisted his lips as if holding back a laugh. "Although, to be fair, you were the one who had no idea as to what we were even doing, so..."

"Not my area of expertise."

"I'll say."

"I'll be the beauty then." Kessed shrugged, her gaze falling to her red boots. Yep, she felt like a cowboy princess, even if she didn't have the first clue as to what a cowboy princess even did.

"Well, of the two options... that's probably the closest you'll get," he jabbed.

"Ha. Funny." Kessed arched a brow.

They rounded a hill and pulled up to where they'd started evaluating the fence yesterday. The brakes squeaked softly as the truck came to a stop, and soon Jasper was pulling long metal posts from the truck bed while Kessed watched from the fence line.

"Kessed, why don't you go and start pulling those posts out and laying them beside the broken wooden ones. Think you can handle that, sunshine?"

"Wait, no. That's not going to stick. I don't answer to sunshine, *slick*." She accented the last word threateningly.

"You're so uptight. Seriously, you need to loosen up... sunshine." Jasper turned away, but not before Kessed spied the beginning of a grin.

"Pain in the ass," she muttered, but walked to the truck. One by one, she laid out the green metal posts on the dirt with the white tip facing away from the broken fence.

Jasper filled the air with the pounding sound of metal on metal as he drove a post into the hard, sunbaked earth.

"Is that all for this round?" Kessed asked as she dusted her hands off.

"Yup, the easy part is done," Jasper replied, his breathing heavy from the manual labor.

Kessed watched as he lifted the steel pipe, holding it over the metal post. His hands gripped the side handles and slammed the pipe down over the metal post, the closed-off end of the pipe acting like a hammer and driving the pole into the ground.

After the second post, Jasper wiped his face with his black T-shirt, then stretched, pulling it completely off and tossing it toward her. She blinked, trying to pretend she wasn't impressed by the way his back muscles bunched with each movement or the way his broad shoulders tapered down to a *V* that she hadn't ever seen on someone other than in the movies.

*Hot damn.*

"Catch," he said belatedly, but Kessed had already reached out and caught the shirt. "Toss it in the truck for me? And can you get me a bottle of water? I put a whole case in the back of the cab." He turned back to the fence line, picked up another post, and as Kessed walked to the truck, the sound of metal on metal pounding filled the canyon once more.

Sure enough, in the back of the quad cab was a huge pack of bottled water. Kessed pulled out two and turned toward Jasper, watching with fascination as his shoulders bunched with each pound. His arms were all hills and valleys as his biceps narrowed to his elbows only to grow into forearms that had somehow escaped her notice before now. His skin held a slight tint of a tan, telling her that he worked like this just often enough to keep from what would surely be an impressive farmer's tan. She measured her steps, enjoying the view but not wanting to risk being caught. As Jasper finished up the third post, Kessed closed the distance and held out the bottle of water.

"Thanks." He twisted off the cap and downed the liquid in less than ten seconds.

Kessed stepped away, keeping a safe distance. It was unnerving, the unexpected attraction she felt toward Jasper. As he turned back to her, the feeling of apprehension grew.

"Is there anything else I can do? I'm kinda bored just standing here," she lied. Watching him was anything but boring.

Jasper frowned. "Sorry about that. Hmm…. Why don't you take the truck and drive on ahead? You can lay out the posts for me and then swing back and pick me up."

"Sounds good." Kessed nodded then caught the keys as he tossed them toward her. "Same places we went yesterday, right?"

"Yup. Just don't forget about me, 'kay?" He gave a quick wink before pounding back on the post.

Kessed all but fled to the truck, then pressed on the gas a little too heavily in her rush to get away. The tires kicked up dust, and she saw Jasper pause and watch her from the corner of his eye as she drove down the road.

With each moment that passed, her body relaxed a bit more.

*Sterling.* She wanted Sterling. Not Jasper. Sterling—her best friend's brother. She'd loved him as long as she could remember.

Yet as she pulled up to the next line of broken fence, she had the sinking suspicion that this unwanted attraction she felt for Jasper was only the beginning.

This was going to be a long few days.

# CHAPTER FIVE

*Like a bat outta hell.*

Jasper bit back a grin as he turned to the next fence post. If Kessed had driven away any faster, she'd have left rubber on the gravel road. He'd thought she was studying him, but her need to flee the scene confirmed his suspicions. But more than that, it told him what she wasn't willing to even admit to herself.

She was afraid.

Kessed... brave, bold, unreserved, and louder than Fourth of July fireworks—was scared.

Of him.

Okay, so maybe not only him, but certainly of what he represented.

Something she couldn't control.

It was amazing how people and animals could be so different, yet so alike. Kessed was a skittish filly—proud, brave, and stubborn. Yet like any filly, a soft hand, a kind word, and slow movements were the key to winning over the foal's affection. He had a strong inkling that she'd be the same.

And would probably punch him in the throat if she ever knew he'd compared her to a horse.

He grinned at the idea.

She was such a contradiction, one that had him puzzling late into the night. She was already in his blood, and he had no intention of letting her out. With a sigh, he glanced at the empty water bottle, wishing he'd asked Kessed to leave a few for him. But it was useless to wish, so he picked up another T-post and started slamming home. The earth was rock-hard and full of hunks of basalt to boot. By the end of the day, he'd be aching, and tomorrow would be pure hell. It had been far too long since he'd worked on fences, and his body's protesting was proof.

As he picked up the last post, he sighed in relief as he heard the pickup approaching, this time much slower than when it had taken off. He forced himself to hold back a knowing smile.

It sounded stupid, even to himself as he thought it, but he loved watching her drive his truck. As if something as simple as that mattered, but to him… it did. After the last pound, he dusted off his gloved hands and turned.

Kessed lifted a hand in a wave, a rueful grin on her face. "All right, boss. I'm done with the posts. You ready?"

Jasper shook his head. "Not yet. We gotta fix this break in the fence. You have your gloves?"

Kessed paused, tilting her head. "Yeah?"

"Grab them. And I'll get the barbwire from the pickup. There's a fence stretcher in the back too. Cyler said he broke the other one, so I bought a new one yesterday."

"Fence stretcher?" Kessed called out as she opened the cab and grabbed her gloves.

"You'll see."

"I'm sure about that."

Jasper grinned then lifted the roll of wire, careful to carry it away from his jeans. Damn stuff would shred his denim faster than he could blink.

"I'm going to take a wild guess that this is the fence stretcher?" Kessed spoke with dry sarcasm.

He didn't bother to even turn around. "Yup."

"Way to double-check."

"I trust you. Also, it's literally the only other thing in the pickup aside from barbwire and T-posts." He set the roll of wire on the ground and took a knee. Picking up one end of the torn fence, he bent it back on itself and then tied the tail, wrapping it around itself several times to make a loop.

"Here you go." Kessed set the stretcher beside him.

"Thanks. Hold this for me?" He held out the looped end of the wire for Kessed, and she grabbed it.

He stood up and moved down about ten feet then picked up the other loose end and repeated the process; only this time, he threaded a new line of barbwire through the hole and connected the two. After unraveling several loops, he walked over to where Kessed waited and picked up the fence stretcher and then the end she was holding.

"Thanks. Oddly enough, it's just easier if someone holds the end. Damn things disappear in the sagebrush."

"No problem," she mumbled, her expression curious as she watched. He placed the end Kessed had held into the end of the fence stretcher and pinched it tight. In quick work, he connected the edge of the new barbwire fence into the other end then started working the ratchet. With each click, the wire grew tighter till the line was mended and no longer resting on the ground. He was cautious not to pull the line too tight. He had a scar on his right cheek from when he'd created too much tension, and a rusty part of the old wire had snapped; it had flown up and caught the side of his face, leaving its mark. He'd learned his lesson and hadn't had a repeat of it since.

"Hold this now." He handed the stretcher to Kessed and used his free hands to wind the other end of the new barbwire around the tight line. He pulled a set of plyers from his pocket and clipped it. "That should do it."

After taking the stretcher back from Kessed, he released the ends, and the wire bounced, holding its tautness.

"Nice work." Kessed said and dusted off her jeans.

"I aim to please." Jasper stood as well then arched his back. He turned to Kessed and chuckled as he caught her staring. Belatedly, he remembered he still wasn't wearing his shirt, and a surge of pleasure hit him, knowing he was making her uncomfortable. "One down, a hundred more to go."

"I think we need to rethink this. It's going to take too long. How do you use this thing? If you can do the fence posts, I can use... that." She pointed to the stretcher.

"You think you can handle this?" He held it up, a little closer to his body than necessary, watching as she avoided looking at the tool.

"I can deal with you. I can manage some barbed wire and... that."

"Fence stretcher."

"Whatever. I can do it."

"See this scar?" Jasper pointed to the small linear white mark on his right cheek as she leaned in. "That's from pulling the fence too tight. The damn thing was rusty too. Had to get a tetanus booster."

Kessed hissed then shivered. "I hate needles."

"I hate lockjaw more," Jasper replied. "But if you want to give this thing a go, you'll probably be fine. You'll have to pull it pretty tight, and I don't see you doing that too easily." He glanced down at her biceps, arching a brow to tease.

"I'm small but mighty." Kessed lifted an arm and flexed.

"Your mouth gets more exercise talking than those little chicken wings you call arms. Which is why you'll be just fine."

Kessed glared, but he ignored her. "Let's get to the next area and, if memory serves correctly, it's a smaller break. It shouldn't take too long to pound the T-posts, and I'll let you get a go at the fence."

"Deal. Hurry up. Daylight's burning," she commented over her shoulder as she walked to the pickup.

Jasper rubbed the back of his neck, amused. *Damn if that woman isn't as flirtatious as she is prickly.* "Keys?" he called out.

"In the truck," she replied as she hopped in.

Soon they were pulling up to the next break. And just as he remembered, only a few posts were left to replace. The ground was a softer, sandier variety, so the work was done in a few minutes. When the time came, Kessed huddled down beside him, and he took her step-by-step through the process, reminding her to not overwork the tension. To her credit, she held back whatever smart comments she could have made, and when he coached her through the second break, she fixed it with only minimal help.

"I think the boots are wearing off on you," he remarked as she grinned proudly at the mostly taut fence line.

"Maybe. Or maybe I'm just naturally awesome. I'll let you figure that out." She shrugged a shoulder and walked back to the truck.

As the sun started to hit its crest in the sky, Jasper finished the seventh section of fence and waited while Kessed stretched the wire, by now, like a pro.

"You about ready for lunch?" he asked, heading to the pickup to fish out another water bottle.

"Starving!" she called out then hissed. "Damn."

Jasper tossed the water bottle back in the truck and started back toward her.

"What's up?" He knelt beside her and saw the blood.

Kessed bit her lip as blood trickled down her forearm toward her elbow. "I snagged myself reaching across. But I guess that's better than it snapping and smacking my face, right?"

"That damned wire will slice right through you, honey," he murmured as he took her arm in his hands. "Hold on, I have a first-aid kit in my truck. Don't touch the wound. You've been messing with rusty wire all day, and that won't do you any favors." He paused. "You did snag it on the new stuff, right? Not the old line?" He waited for her nod then finished his trek to the pickup.

After pulling his kit from the dashboard, he crossed the short distance to where Kessed waited.

"It's not that bad."

"Nope, it's not. But you still need to patch it up." Jasper used a softer voice, the one he used around injured animals—purely out of habit.

He quickly put on his latex gloves and wiped the cut clean. "Whoa, girl. You did a number on yourself." He studied the long laceration that started where her glove ended and headed toward her elbow.

"Go big or go home," Kessed replied through clenched teeth.

"You all right? You're not going to pass out on me, are you?"

"No! I'm fine, just... don't like blood. My blood. I'm okay with other people's."

"Heartless, are you?"

"Not fair. Be nice. I'm injured."

Jasper chuckled, applied antibiotic ointment, then placed the gauze along the line of her cut and taped it to her skin. "I am being nice, see? I fixed you right up." He patted her head teasingly.

"Not one of your regular patients." She slowly stood.

"True. They talk less." Jasper leaned forward and finished twisting the barbwire then made it nice and tight.

"Thanks." Kessed's softer tone surprised him, and he picked up the fence stretcher and glanced at her.

"You're welcome." He shrugged. It wasn't as if he'd done something important. "You ready to go eat?"

"Yes, a million times *yes*," Kessed replied in a pathetic tone.

"Whine much?" Jasper goaded as he tossed the stretcher in the back, counting the remaining T-posts. At this rate, they'd be done by evening.

Thank the Lord for small favors. That meant that tomorrow he could fit in at least a few appointments.

"Where to?" Jasper asked as he turned the pickup around.

"I get to pick?" Kessed eyed him, and he had the sensation of walking into a trap.

"Within reason," he added carefully.

Kessed arched an eyebrow in amusement. "Don't be so suspicious. I say McDonald's."

Jasper relaxed. "Oh. Sounds good."

"But don't judge me when I order." She pointed a finger at him.

Jasper lifted a hand in defense. "Swear, I won't. I have a sister, remember? Besides, there's nothing more irritating than a woman who orders a salad then eats all your fries, you know what I mean?" He shook his head as he drove past the ranch house and toward the main road.

"Trust me, it's worse when you order the same thing as the guy, and his ugly eyes judge every bite you take. This one time, this guy actually said, 'Do you know how many calories are in your meal? That's a lot of miles you'll need to run.'"

Jasper winced. "Is he still alive?"

"Barely. Only because I gave him a head start. You know, since he said I needed to run, it was only fair I had something to chase." She arched a brow to match her evil grin.

"Remind me never to piss you off."

"You already have—many times—but you haven't messed with my food so you're safe… so far."

"Noted."

Soon they were pulling up to the old McDonald's down by the freeway. "Drive-through or inside?" Jasper asked as they pulled in.

"I'm a wreck. Drive-through. I'll just get dirt in the restaurant, and they'll have to alert the food inspector." She glanced down then dusted off her jeans.

"Yes, because no one in Ellensburg gets dirty from working outside. And those people certainly don't go to McDonald's." He cut her a wry glance but pulled up to the speaker, lowering his window.

"Are you done?" She gave an impatient glare.

"No, just on pause."

*"Welcome to McDonald's! Order when you're ready!"*

Jasper raised his eyebrows, waiting.

Kessed leaned across the cab toward the window. She placed a hand on his thigh, and heat burst through him. Sunshine and warm earth saturated her skin, fragrancing the air around her. "Hi, I'd like the Double Quarter Pounder with cheese, super-sized, but I don't want the drink. I'd like a chocolate milkshake instead. And can I get an extra order of fries? Small? And an ice water. Large."

As she spoke, her nose crinkled slightly, and she tilted her head like a curious little bird, yet his greater focus was on her hand, its warmth seeping into his skin. He prayed she'd not look down and see the current state of his body. That would be a fun explanation, one she'd probably not appreciate. Then as quickly as it happened, she was gone.

Immediately, he missed the contact. *Leave it to me to find the one woman who drives me crazy—in every sense of the word—and have her be in love with another man.*

Damn, fate was a cruel bitch.

"Jasper?" Kessed stage-whispered.

"Oh, same for me." He glanced at the screen and nodded his approval. *"Thank you, please pull forward to the first window."*

"Not a word," Kessed warned.

Jasper turned to her, her almond eyes wary. "Chocolate is my favorite too."

Her expression relaxed slightly, just enough to take the edge off. "The vanilla isn't bad, but my favorite is when they mix the two. But they get cranky if you order half-chocolate, half-vanilla." She hitched a shoulder.

"If you tell me you save the small fries for your milkshake, I might kiss you. Fair warning." He turned to the first window, not waiting for her reaction.

He handed over his card then took the receipt before pulling forward.

"My purse is at the ranch, but this is my usual order, so I know what I owe you. Don't worry," she replied hesitantly.

He noticed how she hadn't responded to his previous statement but let it slide. "I'm not worried about it. If nine dollars breaks me, then I have bigger issues to address."

"Stop being so nice. It's killing me," Kessed groaned.

Jasper took the bags handed to them and set the milkshakes and waters in the cup holders. "You make no sense."

"I'm a girl. I don't need to."

"You know, Harper has said the same thing to me more times than I can count. But she usually only says it..." He let the words linger as he pulled out of the drive-through and back onto the road that would lead back to the ranch.

Kessed took a sip of milkshake, then asked, "Well, are you going to finish your sentence?"

"Nope. I decided not to."

Kessed sighed. "That's really frustrating."

"I'm a man. I don't have to finish my sentence if I don't want to," he retorted, pinching his lips together to keep from laughing at Kessed's irritated expression.

"You win."

"I love hearing that." He lifted his own shake and took a long sip. Thick, cold, and sweet, it was the perfect antidote to hard work.

"So, how are we doing as far as time? Do you think we did well this morning?" Kessed asked as she unwrapped her burger. As she took a bite, she moaned softly.

Jasper choked on the milkshake.

"You okay?" she asked around the bite.

He nodded his head as he coughed then took a long drink of ice water. "Wrong tube."

Kessed reached into the bag and fished out his burger. She opened the carton and offered it to him.

"I'll wait. I've tried eating it while driving, and I almost hit a fence. The ketchup slimed my wheel, and I slipped. I learned my lesson," he replied, trying to ignore the way his body was humming with awareness.

"Let's stay away from fences for the moment." Kessed put his burger back into the bag took another bite of her own, moaning softly again.

Even as he steeled himself against it, the effect on his body wasn't lessened. She was playing every string perfectly, and he couldn't help his reactions. Clearing his throat, he turned on the radio, anything to drown out the soft pleasurable sounds coming from this woman.

"Good song." Kessed nodded with the music, a grin on her face as he pulled into the ranch's drive. The music worked, and as she took another bite, he barely heard her enjoyment, and his body cooled—but only slightly. He bypassed the house and headed toward the next area that needed to be addressed. As he put the truck into park, the radio cut off just as Kessed finished her burger.

He almost sighed with relief then grabbed his burger bag and went to the back of the pickup. He let down the tailgate and set his food on the back then went around to get his drinks.

Kessed followed, and soon they were sitting on the back of the truck, the hot sunshine beating down on them even as a cool breeze wound its way through the canyon.

Jasper took a bite, savoring the flavor of the beef, when Kessed dipped a fry in her milkshake, and though it was much softer than before, she made a soft moan of delight.

"Can you please not do that?" Jasper asked, closing his eyes. When she didn't respond, he hazarded a glance.

Her dark brows were furrowed. "What am I doing?"

*Ah, hell no.* Jasper rubbed the back of his neck. "It's uh… distracting when you"—*moan with pleasure, show me what you'd sound like in my bed, sound satisfied*—"hum."

"I hum?"

"Yes." *No.*

"Huh, sorry." She blushed, dipped a fry. Then blessed silence.

Jasper took a deep breath, took another bite, and soon finished his burger, grateful for the silence—for a minute. Till the silence was too… silent.

"What gives?" He turned to Kessed as he dipped one of his own fries into his chocolate shake.

"I'm being quiet! What am I doing wrong now?" she asked, her eyes narrowing.

"You're too quiet."

"You're impossible." Kessed jumped off the tailgate.

"That may be, and I might not have known you for a long time, but I think I have a pretty strong grasp on your nature, and that nature doesn't include silence."

Kessed glanced away, shuttering her expression. "Nothing."

Jasper glanced heavenward. "Nothing never means nothing. I got all day, Kess."

"It's nothing I want to talk about," she amended, her expression walled.

"Why?" he asked, regarding her.

"Because, it's... not important." She walked out a few steps.

"That usually means that it is, or at least *was* important," he added.

Kessed paused. "If I tell you, will you leave me alone?"

"Nope. But I'll stop pestering you about this." He shrugged.

"Fine." She took a few steps back toward the truck then paused. "I did the whole humming thing a lot when I was younger, and I got teased. Okay? It wasn't bad. It just made me a little insecure about it, and well, Laken was fine, but Sterling—" She cut off her words. "It's just that it was something I was—I *am* sensitive about."

Jasper set his cup down. "Honey, I'm sure you were just a little bitty thing—"

"I was a sophomore in college, Jasper. Not young."

Jasper nodded. "I see. Well, then I think I better clear something up." He took a deep breath. "Because I'm betting there's a little bit of confusion on your end." He took another fry, dipped it in his shake, and walked over to Kessed, offering it.

Her chocolate eyes narrowed, but she accepted it.

"Eat it. Enjoy it. The only reason I said it distracted me was because I know that you don't look at me the way I look at you, and quite honestly, hearing that sweet little moan from your mouth makes whatever self-control I have disappear. So, it's not that I don't like it, Kess. It's that I like it a little too much."

Holding his breath, he waited for Kessed to move, to react. A slow smile spread across her face. She squinted her almond eyes as she blushed slightly under her tanned skin.

"Too much, hmm?" She glanced away, almost shy.

"Almost embarrassingly so. Now that I've fully blown my cover, I think I'm going to start working on that fence." He nodded once and turned back to the truck. His face burned from his blunt statement, but he was glad he'd set the record straight. His anger burned against Sterling. The guy probably had no clue he'd hurt Kessed's feelings, but that didn't stop Jasper's irritation toward him.

A hand grasped his, and he paused, surprised and slightly startled.

"Thank you." Kessed glanced up, giving an uncertain smile as she studied him, her brown gaze holding him captive.

He simply nodded, watching in disbelief as she slowly traced her hand up his arm before resting her palm on his still bare shoulder. When he didn't move, she gave a slight eye-roll of irritation and moved her hand to his neck, pulling him down where she met his lips, kissing him softly.

Jasper leaned into the kiss, but only somewhat, letting Kessed lead. Lord knows, he'd willingly follow. Her lips slowly shifted over his, and he caressed her lower lip with just the slightest tip of his tongue. She tasted like chocolate and salt—of course she'd be his favorite flavor.

As soon as the kiss started, it ended, and Kessed released her hold, stepping back. Her eyes were wary but not guarded like usual, and with a shy smile, she walked by him toward the fence.

"Hurry up, cowboy. We don't have all day."

# CHAPTER SIX

Kessed wrapped the last wire around the line and took off the fence stretcher. They'd all but finished the repairs and not a moment too soon. The sun's arc was just above Rattlesnake Mountains, which meant it was at least six in the evening. She gave a covert glance at Jasper, who was loading the barbwire into the back of the pickup. He hadn't mentioned the kiss, hadn't even treated her differently. They'd worked all afternoon, talked, mended more fences than she cared to admit, but nothing about the kiss.

And honestly, she didn't know if that was a good or bad thing. Part of her was thankful that he hadn't mentioned it; she didn't quite know what to think of it herself. It was utterly impulsive, but she wouldn't go back and do anything differently—except kiss him again.

Which was all sorts of crazy. She wasn't in love with Jasper.

Hell, she wasn't sure she even liked Jasper.

So maybe she liked him a little.

He was a pretty amazing kisser, even if it was just a short kiss.

Right away, she'd known if she didn't end the kiss, she'd be in too deep to step back before it turned into something more.

"Waiting on you, sunshine!" Jasper called out, and she gave a rueful grin as she stood, her knees protesting. But her boots never once made her feet ache, in contrast to what Jasper had told her to expect.

"Impatient?" she yelled to Jasper, who'd just started the truck.

"As a general rule, no," he answered as she paused by the open passenger door.

Kessed quickly placed the fence stretcher in the back then hopped in the front. "But?" she inquired.

"But I just got a phone call from Monson Ranch down the way. There's a heifer in labor. It's her first, and well, it's breech. I gotta head over there and take a look."

"I thought you were working with the other guy, Vince?" Kessed asked.

"Yeah, but his shoulder got injured this past summer. A bull pinned him against the rail. Dislocated it and broke a few ribs. Calf-pulling isn't something he can do. Plus, he's all but retired." Jasper's stomach growled loudly, and Kessed giggled.

"Hungry?"

"You have no idea. But I'm not going to get to pick up anything till after I see the calf." He turned toward the house and slowed to a stop.

Kessed nodded. "Well, have fun?"

"You know it." He gave a wry grin.

Kessed slid from the pickup. She waved. "I'll see you tomorrow."

"Same time, same place!" Jasper called out. "Good work today, sunshine. Be sure you bring your A-game tomorrow too." His green eyes crinkled up in a grin as she shut the pickup door. Soon, he was leaving a thin trail of dust as he drove away.

Kessed walked to the ranch house, her body protesting from all the manual labor, even if it was only hauling out T-posts and using the fence stretcher, it wasn't exactly pulling shots at Starbucks. She stomped off the dust on her red boots and wiped them on the old doormat before she walked into the hall. Her stomach rumbled, and as she poured a glass of cool water and drank deeply, the empty ache in her belly only grew more demanding.

She searched the fridge, glaring at a half-eaten cup of instant noodles. The freezer was more promising, but thawing something would take precious time, and she was hungry now.

Glancing down at her dusty clothes, she vacillated between changing or just going out and to hell with her clothes.

Her impatient stomach won, and she dusted herself off as she walked to her hatchback while quickly winding her hair back up into a messy bun. Soon she was heading toward Ellensburg. As she drove down Main Street, she spotted Rodeo City Barbeque. The western storefront always made her roll her eyes, but the food was amazing! She would just order takeout then head back to the ranch. A shower sounded almost as heavenly as a Rodeo Reuben Sandwich. Almost. Food won, always.

Within ten minutes, she had her dinner and was walking to the car. As soon as she sat down, she pulled out her fries and took a bite. The crispy outside and salty flavor was almost better than sex. Almost. She noticed her small *hum,* as Jasper had referred to it, and her face flushed. She took another bite, guilt settling in her stomach along with the food as she remembered that Jasper wasn't eating. He was working.

Still.

She glanced from the paper sack to the door of the restaurant then back. "Damn it all," Kessed muttered and walked back in.

The waiter who had taken her previous order paused, glancing at her with some concern. "Was there a problem with your food?"

Kessed waved him off. "I need another order, for a friend," she answered.

The college kid nodded, blinking as if in disbelief.

Kessed almost made a sarcastic remark, but she was too tired.

Ten minutes later, she was driving back down Main Street and heading east toward Monson Ranch. Roy Monson was a regular at Starbucks, and she'd taken him coffee a few times, so she was familiar with the location. She rolled down the windows, letting the cooling air filter through the car as she took a gravel road, kicking up dust behind her.

The Monsons' place came into view, and Kessed drove around the house toward the various cattle barns that dotted the landscape. Jasper's dark green pickup was parked beside a John Deere tractor, and Kessed pulled up behind it. She walked around the front of the barn then peeked into it, not wanting to disrupt Jasper but also not wanting one of Roy Monson's dogs to snag his dinner.

"Easy, that's a girl." Jasper's tone wasn't soft as much as it was confident. He'd taken his shirt off once again, only this time tucking it into the back of his Wrangler jeans, blocking the view of his tight ass.

He guided his hands into the back end of the cow, and Kessed scrunched her nose. So that probably wasn't the best part of his job. His shoulders tensed, and he tilted his head down as if seeing with his hands, rather than his eyes.

"Right there. Got it!"

Roy nodded his approval and took a step back, watching as Jasper started to lean away from the cow, pulling back till two hooves emerged within his grip.

"C'mon, girl, work now. You've pushed all afternoon, you've got one more in you," Jasper coached and then leaned back again, his shoulders rock-hard, his teeth biting his lower lip as he pulled back.

The cow lowed, and the calf broke free, sliding out rear end first. A moment later, the head emerged, and Jasper lowered the slimy calf onto the clean straw. He picked up a piece of the golden straw and tickled the calf's nose and solicited one sneeze, then another.

"Atta boy! Fill up those lungs. Whew, that was a big-ass bull in there," Roy commented as he stepped around the newborn. The cow had moved around and was beginning to lick her baby, and Jasper stepped back, removing the long latex gloves from his hands when his gaze met hers.

"Kess? What are you doing here?" He wrapped up the plastic gloves within themselves and set them to the side, walking toward her.

"Didn't want to interrupt. Nice work." Kessed placed her hands in her jeans' pockets, feeling slightly awkward.

"Hey, Kessed! What are you doing out here? Not that I'm complaining!" Roy called out, heading their way.

"I'm doing good deeds," Kessed answered, holding up a paper sack, the scent wafting from it as she shook it slightly.

"If that's not for me, lie." Jasper groaned.

"It's for you." Kessed chuckled then held it out.

"Yes—no. Hold that thought. I don't want to—Roy, where's that damn hose?" Jasper glanced at his blood- and slime-smeared body and then back to the rancher.

"Where it usually is, boy." Roy arched a brow then pointed to the side of the barn. "Have at it."

Jasper jogged off to the side and started the water.

"And here I thought you were here for me. You're killing me, sweetheart. It's always the young bucks who get the fillies." Roy pounded his heart teasingly.

"Aw, Roy, you know I only have eyes for you," Kessed teased.

"Liar. Plus, I have Ethel. She keeps me busy enough. I don't need more than one woman in my life." Roy chuckled, shaking his head and causing his gray eyebrows to touch his owl-framed glasses.

"How's Ethel doing?" Kessed asked, her tone sobering.

"Better. We had a good report from the cardiologist. As long as she takes it easy, and I don't piss her off too much, she'll be around a long time to keep my sorry hide in gear."

"That's good to know."

"I'm back, I'm clean, and, woman, I'm starving. What did you bring me? Thank you, by the way." Jasper took the bag and opened it. He immediately grabbed a fry and devoured it.

"I'll have you know that this was a sacrifice for me. I still haven't eaten mine." Kessed turned toward her car, about to pick up her own bag when she heard a chuckle that turned into a full-blown laugh.

"Roy?" She turned, curious.

"Oh, it's nothing, darling. Don't worry about me." He held his hand in front of his mouth and took a step back. "I'm going to go check on number six-seventy-five." He motioned to the cow. "Thanks again, Jasper. Enjoy your dinner." He snickered at the end and then walked off, his small frame shaking with mirth.

"What am I missing?" Kessed narrowed her eyes at Jasper, who was chewing slowly, an overly blank expression on his face.

He shrugged, and Kessed waited.

Jasper placed the sandwich back in the bag and took a fry. "It's nothing, just Roy being an *ass!*" He almost shouted the last part, and Roy broke into another fit of giggles. "Let's get your bag." He started toward her car. "So, what did you order?" he asked offhandedly.

*A little too offhandedly.* She might have missed it had she not been looking for something suspicious.

"Reuben. Same as yours." She paused, regarding him.

"Great choice," Jasper replied with a wide grin.

"Really?" she asked with heavy sarcasm.

"Really!" Jasper held his hands up. "Thank you for thinking of me. I was starving!" He walked toward her car and opened the door before reaching in then handing her the sack. "You should eat too. Those dainty little hands of yours got more work than they're used to. Did you break a nail, sweetheart?" he teased, holding up her bag just out of her reach.

"If you were really thankful, you'd hand me my dinner." She crossed her arms and waited.

"Damn." He lowered the sack, and she grabbed it with a triumphant grin.

She leaned against her car as she unwrapped the sandwich, Thousand Island dressing dripping off the French roll. "Where have you been all my life?"

"Dramatic much?"

"And no, I didn't break a nail. I don't grow them very long anyway, so it's practically impossible." She took a bite.

"My apologies." Jasper picked up another fry.

Then it hit her.

"You don't like Reubens, do you?" She waited, watching as his chewing stopped then restarted slowly.

"I never said that," he replied innocently.

"Take a bite." Kessed bit a big hunk of her own, waiting, daring him.

Jasper swallowed his fry and lifted the sandwich. He took a big bite—

"I hope you have Benadryl on hand." Roy marched by, a wide grin still on his face.

Jasper's eyes closed, and his face flushed to an odd shade of red.
"You're allergic?" Kessed grabbed the bag from him, taking away the
sandwich. "Shit! Do you go anaphylactic? I'm allergic to bees, so I have an
EpiPen!" She dropped the bags, tossed the sandwich, and threw open the
car door, ignoring Jasper's protests. She took the EpiPen from her glove
compartment and pulled off the end.

"Damn it, woman! I'm not going to die on you!" Jasper held Kessed's
arms, forcing her to keep still.

"Better than reality TV," Roy commented as he leaned against the
outside of the barn, watching unashamedly.

"Doesn't Ethel need you?" Jasper replied.

"Nope."

One of Roy's dogs was finishing off the thrown sandwich, and Roy
walked over, patting its head encouragingly. "At least someone will
appreciate it, Kessed!"

"My throat doesn't close up. I'm allergic to the seeds in the rye bread.
I'm assuming you got this from Rodeo Barbeque, right? They don't use rye
bread, but they add the caraway seeds to the Thousand Island dressing. I
just can't have a lot of it. A little doesn't bother me much." Jasper slowly
released her then took a step back.

Kessed narrowed her eyes but placed the cap back on the EpiPen. "So,
we don't need to go to the hospital?"

"No."

"Why didn't you just tell me, you dumbass!" Kessed slugged his bare
arm, glaring.

"I didn't want to sound ungrateful! You were kind in bringing me
anything. It's not your fault I'm allergic to something so random as
caraway seeds!"

"Then why did you take a bite? If you knew—"

"Because I didn't want you to feel bad." Jasper sighed. "I can take the
few hives I'll get from it."

Kessed's shoulders slumped. "You're such an idiot."

"Why, thank you," Jasper replied with an exasperated tone as he bent
to pick up the bag with the remaining fries.

"Ethel always puts caraway seeds in her marinara sauce. Last year,
we had a few rough nights with the heifers dropping calves, and Ethel
brought out a few plates of spaghetti. We didn't know either, darlin'. But
I will say that all concern about the cows went out the window when this
guy here started growing lumps all over his body. Thankfully, we always
have Benadryl on hand. Took care of it right quick."

"Do you need Benadryl now?" Kessed asked, guarded.

Jasper rubbed the back of his neck, sending an accusing glare to Roy. "Probably wouldn't hurt. I have some in the pickup." With a long sigh, he took another fry and strode over to the truck, and Kessed watched as he the pills and washed them down with a bottle of water.

"Happy now?" He opened his mouth like a little kid showing his obedience.

"Better." Kessed slumped against her car. "I'm heading home." She walked around to the driver side.

"You have a hard-ass boss who will be all over your case if you're not up and at 'em by dawn," Jasper teased, meeting her by her door.

"More like an annoying coworker," Kessed corrected, her lips lifting into a grin.

"I'm telling you what to do, ergo, boss." He gave a wicked smile.

"I can take you out with little seeds. I win." She pushed at his very bare, very alluring chest, noticing, not for the first time, the way his clavicle pointed downward, tempting her gaze lower—and she snapped it up, meeting his green eyes.

"You don't play fair." Jasper narrowed his eyes, but there was a heat in them that made her want to both lean in and run away.

"Never will," she murmured, then before she did something really stupid like kiss him again, she ducked into the car and locked the door.

Kessed was in over her head, and she didn't even know how she'd gotten there.

As she drove home, her thoughts lingered on the day and on Jasper. He was annoying, and irritating, and stupid as hell to eat that sandwich, but in the strangest way possible, it added to his charm. And that charm of his was working its way under her skin, terrifying and enticing her all at once.

As she took a shower and washed away all the dirt crusting her skin, she decided that she was probably just too tired.

The sun was too hot.

A thousand excuses, a thousand reasons.

Surely, tomorrow would be different.

At least a little bit, right?

# CHAPTER SEVEN

Jasper pulled up to the ranch house, his eyes still feeling as if he'd washed them with sand. Damn Benadryl always did that to him, but at least he'd been saved from the hives. If he had to deal with the loopy, sleepy feeling Benadryl always left behind, at least he wouldn't be itchy as well.

Damn, he'd kill for a cup of coffee.

He'd slept in later than usual and forgotten to pour a cup before he dashed out the door. After pestering Kessed about being up early, he wasn't about to arrive late at the ranch.

He put the truck in park and killed the engine. Before he could walk to the door, it opened and Kessed gave a small wave. "Rough night?" she asked by way of greeting.

"Benadryl kicks my ass." He leaned against the doorjamb, regarding her.

Dark espresso hair was braided to the side, showing caramel highlights that accentuated her olive skin. Her face glowed, and if she wore any makeup, it wasn't obvious. Her eyebrows arched in question as he realized belatedly she'd said something.

"Missed that. What?" he asked, closing his eyes then opening them slowly.

She tilted her head. "You're not planning on operating heavy machinery today, are you?"

"Just my truck and your coffeemaker. I didn't grab my mug before I headed out the door."

Kessed opened the door wider, stepping aside to let him pass by. "And you warned me about being on time."

"I blame the Benadryl."

"Sure, sure," she patronized from behind him.

Jasper smiled all the way to the kitchen and pulled down an old RDO tractor mug then poured a cup of coffee. He took a deep sip, closing his eyes and wishing he could take the stuff by IV.

"Should I leave you two alone?" Kessed teased, and his eyes opened to glare at her.

"As if you have any room to talk," he replied.

"Whatever. What are we doing today? Fences are done, so what's next?"

Jasper took another sip. "The cattle are coming tomorrow, so we need to get the hay delivered and make sure the pasture gates are open so that all the different divisions of the range have access to water. When the steers arrive, we'll need to cold brand them and then set them out to free-range. From there, our work will be minimal."

Kessed nodded then set down her mug. "I think we can handle that."

"Let's hope so. We don't have much of a choice. I have to duck out early today too. I have several appointments I need to manage before the cattle arrive." He took a deep breath and stretched, rolling around his neck for good measure.

"Sore?" Kessed asked.

He shrugged. "Not any more than expected. I thought my shoulders would be screaming at me from the damned posthole pounder. But I'm not too bad. You?"

"I'm walking," she said by way of an answer. "Let's just say I'm sore in some places I didn't know had muscles."

Jasper chuckled. "Been there." He drained the rest of his cup and set it in the sink. "You ready?"

"As I'll ever be. What's first?" Kessed set her cup with his, and he followed her to the door.

"Let's get in the pickup and make sure all the gates are open. Hay will be delivered in about two hours, giving us plenty of time." He headed to the passenger side door and opened it.

"Thanks." Kessed gave him a curious glance but didn't remark further and got in.

He shut the door and walked around, biting back a grin. Soon they were driving down the now-familiar dirt road and toward the main gate to the pasture. Within two hours, they had gotten in and out of the truck at least twenty times. The gates had all been closed, but now they were swung wide open so that the steers could free-range all over the canyon, within the fence. The creek that ran along the north side would be more than enough water for the fifty head of cattle coming tomorrow, and now they all would have access to it.

The wind had kicked up, and the dust had been merciless. Jasper's eyes were no longer feeling like they had been washed by sand, but literally had sand in them now.

But to her credit, Kessed hadn't complained, though her hair was more of a brown than black tone by now.

They rounded the bend, and Jasper saw a gate they had missed. "Damn, I thought we were finished."

"No more dirt!" Kessed finally complained.

Jasper chuckled. "Done with it, princess?"

She glared.

"I'll tell you what. I'll drop you off at the house and then do a final check to make sure we didn't miss anything. Sound good? The hay truck should be there soon, and I want him to make sure he puts it under the covered shed."

"Sign me up."

"Was that sarcasm?" Jasper glanced to her.

"No," she replied with heavy sarcasm.

"Your sarcasm isn't sexy," he teased as he put the metal post-pounder in the back of the pickup.

"Hate to break it to you, but I'm not trying to be sexy for you."

"Sure, sure," he goaded her. He heard her loud sigh as he turned the truck toward the house.

"Not every girl falls for the country charm, Wranglers, and boots."

"You forgot abs of steel and a killer smile." He beamed at her meaningfully.

"You're impossible."

"So, you admit it. I have the killer abs and smile. It's okay. I saw you looking yesterday." He winked.

"We are not having this conversation."

"We kinda are." He nodded once and shrugged.

"Against my will."

"Eh, you'll get over it."

"Laken is my friend... Laken is my friend... Laken is my best, best, best— hell, she owes me so much for this."

Jasper turned his face to the window, hiding his grin before clearing his throat. "You're fine. Stop complaining."

"You're so kind," Kessed replied with heavy sarcasm.

"That's me. Always thinking of other—"

"Of course."

"Hey, can I finish?" Jasper speared her with a patient gaze.

Kessed nodded, then extended a hand magnanimously.

*Smart ass.* "Any hay-buck worth his salt should figure out that he has to put the hay under that shelter, but you never know." He pointed at a metal-roofed, twenty-foot-tall, lean-to building.

"Fine. I think I can handle that."

"Good. I'd be kinda embarrassed for you if you couldn't... just being honest."

"Can I go now?" She glanced to the house and back meaningfully.

"Already missing me?"

"Yeah, that's it."

Jasper pulled the truck into the drive and hit the brakes just before Kessed bolted out the door and strutted to the front porch. Jasper again watched the sultry way her hips swayed. And damn if she didn't look amazing in those red boots. He threw the truck in gear and headed back down the road. As much as his body was protesting, he appreciated the hard labor. It was the perfect distraction, the perfect outlet for the tension that crackled whenever he was around Kessed. His body responded far too enthusiastically, and he needed to channel that excess into something safer, something that wouldn't irrevocably destroy whatever tentative truce they'd developed.

Time. He needed time.

Thankfully, that's exactly what he had—at least today.

Less than an hour later, Jasper was following the same road back to the house, his body aching, sweaty, and sun-kissed. His stomach was rumbling with an empty hunger, and his jeans were the same color as the dirt he'd just driven over. An empty drop-deck trailer was driving away from the ranch, and Kessed was standing near the haystack, studying it.

The stack was arranged in a series of one-ton bales, stacked three high and four wide. At about fifty tons, it would carry Cyler through the winter with his new herd. Kessed turned as he arrived, and he couldn't help the flip in his stomach as she smiled. He hadn't mentioned the kiss yesterday; he'd been tempted to at least a hundred times, but something warned him to keep his mouth shut. Call it intuition, call it fear to push his luck—either way, he kept his thoughts to himself. But he'd be a liar if he didn't hope, or at least wonder, if maybe she was softening a little toward him.

*A kiss means something, doesn't it?*

He parked the truck and killed the engine. "How goes it?" he asked as he stepped out into the sunshine.

"Well, I've never seen a tractor trailer move that fast." Kessed gave a slightly concerned grin. "But he slammed those bales over like they were on fire."

Jasper chuckled. "Yeah, they usually move like a bat outta hell. Those guys are pretty crazy but good at what they do."

"Anyway, they already knew where to put it, and boom! It's done. All the gates open?" she asked, tucking a loose strand of hair behind her ear.

"Yup." He nodded. "I'm thinking we should break for lunch and then stop by the feed supply to pick up a few salt licks. We should be done for the day after that."

Kessed hitched a shoulder. "I'm game. There's food involved, so you can almost always count on my participation."

"I'll remember that."

"Not exactly what I meant."

"It's kinda what you said, sweetheart," Jasper teased then opened the cab door for Kessed.

"I see disappointment in your future," she replied as she stepped into the truck.

"So far, I've been pleasantly surprised," he challenged, shutting her door before she had a chance to use that razor-sharp wit of hers.

She was gunning for him when he got in the truck. "Overconfidence always lands you on your ass, just sayin'."

Jasper chuckled then started down the drive. About a mile away from Ellensburg, his phone vibrated. He slid it from his pocket and handed it to Kessed.

"Answer this for me? Just in case it's an emergency."

Kessed's gaze flickered from the phone, to him, then she took the device. "Hello. Jasper's Vet Service." She gave a wry grin as he held back an eye-roll at her antics.

"I see. Hold on." Kessed's amusement faded, and she held the phone down. "The guy says it's an emergency, something about a cow's stomach?"

Jasper slowed the truck and pulled over then took the phone from Kessed.

"This is Jasper." He listened closely and quickly figured out his suspicion was correct. One of the Van Pelts' dairy cows had a twisted stomach. It wasn't difficult to fix, but it was time sensitive, and the cow was suffering.

"I'll be right over." Jasper handed the cell back to Kessed, checked his mirror, and turned the truck around. He headed away from Ellensburg and farther north toward the dairy.

"So, no lunch?" Kessed guessed.

"Not yet. Sorry about that. Typical LDA, but I need to get her fixed up before she gets worse. It's pretty painful."

"In English?" Kessed's tone was dry.

"Twisted stomach. You know how cows have four stomachs?"

"No, actually, I didn't know that," Kessed replied.

"Now you do. Well, the larger of the stomachs can move a bit, especially if the cow hasn't been eating properly. When that happens, it creates a twist in the gut, and gas gets trapped, and digestion halts completely. It's one of the easier maladies to diagnose and not too difficult to fix. It's just an inconvenience for the cow and the farmer."

Kessed nodded silently. "Sounds fun."

"Sure." Jasper gave her a sarcastic grin.

He took a left and pulled into the large Van Pelt Dairy. He was more than familiar with the layout. Vince had shown him his first day. The Van Pelts were one of the largest clients in their practice.

"You can stay in here or come along. It's up to you, but I shouldn't be more than a half hour, I'd guess." Jasper hopped out of the truck then opened the quad cab and took out a small leather bag.

As he strode to the barn, he heard the pickup door shut and held back a grin. How true to form. Kessed hated to be left out.

"Is there something I can do to help?" she asked as she jogged to catch up.

"Says the girl who didn't know cows had four stomachs," he jibed.

"I'm a quick learner," Kessed retorted.

"Hi." Jasper lifted a hand in greeting at the herdsman.

Manuel was a stout brick of a man. He wasn't tall by any standard, but Jasper wouldn't want to piss him off. He could manhandle the bulls and shove around the cows. Few people knew how much strength that took. "You're quick, Vet. The *vaca* is over *aqui*."

Jasper followed Manuel as he strode to a stall in the hospital of the barn.

"You think it's twisted?" Manuel asked in his thick Latino accent.

"One way to find out," Jasper replied, then knelt. "Manuel, this is Kessed. Kessed, Manuel."

"*Hola.*" Manuel extended his hand, and Jasper almost winced in sympathy for Kessed.

"Hey." Kessed took his hand, and Jasper hoped that Manuel moderated his strength. The last time he'd shaken Manuel's hand, he'd almost fallen to his knees. Not a proud moment, but there'd been mutual respect since.

Kessed didn't wince, so Jasper sighed in relief and took out his stethoscope. He put the ends in his ears and leaned forward, setting the speaker end on the cow's stomach and flicking his fingers against her distended abdomen.

Sure enough, it pinged, making an echoing sound.

"LDA for sure. I think though..." He listened a little more, moving around the stethoscope and flicking his finger again and again, trying to determine just where everything was situated.

"What's up?" Manuel knelt beside Jasper, evaluating the cow.

"Let's roll her. I think it's a softer twist, so if we just give it the chance, it will move back into place. Then we can do a quick suture, tie it off, and give her a dose of fluids. You have something on hand to get into her stomach right away? We don't want a repeat."

"Sure, sure." Manuel walked away, giving Jasper a moment to shave and sterilize the site of the toggle.

"What are you doing?" Kessed asked, keeping her distance.

"Can you hand me my bag there? Actually, just reach in and grab the kit that says toggle."

A few seconds later, Kessed handed him a sterile package.

"Thanks. Basically, I'm going to roll the cow to get the rumen to float back into the right position in her belly then tack it into place."

"Oh," Kessed remarked. "I'm thinking it's harder than you're making it sound."

"All set." Manuel set down a bag of fluids and nodded to Jasper.

"Great. Let's get her rolled."

Working with Manuel, they rolled the cow onto her back at a ninety-degree angle, waiting for the stomach to float back into place. With quick movements, Jasper used the toggle to pierce through the skin of the cow, tacking the rumen into place. "I think we're good." He double-checked his work and stepped back as the cow slowly rose from her awkward angle.

"I'll finish up with the fluids if you need to go." Manuel shook Jasper's hand.

Out of anticipation, Jasper winced. "Sure thing. Let me know if she doesn't improve," he added.

"Speed-dial, man." Manuel grinned and walked toward the cow.

"Ready?" Jasper turned to Kessed, studying her expression at her exposure to his world.

"All in a day's work," she teased as she followed him to the truck.

"Saving the world, one cow at a time."

"You're the Superman of the bovine culture."

"I have a cape that's colored like a dairy cow." He chuckled at their random line of conversation.

"I'd pay money to see you in that." Kessed raised her eyebrows, clearly amused. "But first, let's eat."

"It's always food for you, isn't it?" Jasper asked, starting up the pickup and heading away from the barn.

"Always. And the sooner you learn that, the sooner we can be friends."

"Friends," Jasper repeated, testing the word, regarding her reaction from the corner of his eye. It was loaded.

"Friends," Kessed affirmed, but she glanced away, turning her head to gaze out the window.

He opened his mouth to protest, to push the issue...

But paused.

Time. He'd give her just a little more time. Because her words said one thing.

Her actions said another.

And actions always spoke louder than words.

She might say friends.

But he was still wearing her kiss.

# CHAPTER EIGHT

Kessed glanced at her phone, picking up with a smile as the familiar ring sounded.

"To what do I owe the pleasure?" she answered, waiting to hear Laken's voice.

"Hey you! Just checking in. Anything on fire? Any insurance claims we need to make?" Laken joked.

"Funny."

"No, but really, how is everything going? I feel super guilty about giving you and Jasper all this stuff to take care of."

"We're fine. You just need to relax and enjoy the time with Cyler. And no, I don't want any details." Kessed's eyes widened.

"So, it's going well?" Laken asked, her tone hopeful.

"I haven't killed him yet, so we're good. You won't have to bail me out of jail."

"Noted." Laken paused, and Kessed narrowed her eyes.

She could almost hear the gears turning in her best friend's brain. "What is it?" she asked hesitantly.

"Well, if you're not killing each other, does that mean that maybe—"

"No. Maybe. No. Just no."

"I heard a maybe." Laken pounced like a cougar on a jackrabbit.

"I slipped," Kessed covered.

"Liar face!"

"Shit, you're worse when I can't just threaten you."

"The phone makes me feel invincible. That, and I'm a thousand miles away. If you hang up, I'll just call back and—"

"I'll silence my phone?"

"You'll know... I'll keep calling, and calling..." Laken replied in a creepy tone.

"Weird. Crossing the weirdness line." Kessed glanced out the window at the darkening sky.

"Spill!" Laken encouraged.

Kessed groaned. "There's nothing to spill!"

"No way, not buying it. The last time you said *maybe* was when we were in high school, and you were talking about my stupid-ass brother and—"

"I was there, remember?"

"Then you know that I'm not going to let this go," Laken threatened.

"Fine! I kissed him," Kessed admitted, closing her eyes and resting her head against the bedframe, waiting for the realization to hit her friend then come back and give her whiplash from the assault of questions sure to follow.

But there was nothing. Silence.

Kessed opened her eyes then narrowed them. "Laken?"

"I was waiting for more..." her friend encouraged.

"That's it! I kissed him. We've worked well together, and he feeds me French fries and doesn't give me those fat judgment eyes when I order as much as he does."

"Marry him."

"Rein it in, Laken."

"Sorry, got carried away with the whole food revelation." Laken sighed. "So, what's the problem? I feel like you think there's a problem. Does he not like you? Because I'm pretty sure he does. Cyler said he couldn't keep his eyes off you at the wedding, which must have been pretty obvious because Cyler couldn't keep his eyes off me."

Kessed grinned, truly happy for her friend. "Why do I feel like we're passing notes in junior high again? Yes, he *likes* me." As Kessed emphasized the word, a wave of insecurity washed over her.

"Then what's the problem, and if you say my brother, I might puke."

"Dramatic much?" Kessed sighed then bit her lip. "Maybe?"

"You're killing me! Seriously. You are killing me."

Kessed suppressed a grin. "It's not so much Sterling as... the thought of it, you know? I mean, he's what I've wanted for so long."

"But maybe he's not what you need." Laken cut to the heart of it. "Have you ever considered that?"

Kessed glanced to the window at the setting sun. "You might be right. And before you go into your victory dance, I said *might*."

"Close enough!" Laken singsonged on the other line.

"Why are we friends? You're so annoying!"

"You love me!"

"Barely."

"Whatever. So, what are you doing to do?" Laken asked with eager anticipation.

Kessed turned her gaze back to the ceiling. "Not sure. Just take it one day at a time. Slow. Take it slow."

"You're so boring."

"Better boring than knocked up."

Laken giggled. "I guess that's right... but you know there's preventative ways—"

"Turn off the nurse-mode. I don't need *the talk.*"

"If you need resources, or feel alone—"

"We're so done with this conversation," Kessed interrupted, grinning at Laken's laughter on the other line.

"Slow is good. Be friends, learn about him. When do you see him next?"

"Tomorrow. We're getting your cows delivered, remember?"

"Honestly, no. That's Cyler's department, and I'm staying out of it."

"Lucky you."

Laken sighed dreamily. "I am."

"And with that, I'm going to let you go and—"

"Get lucky?" Laken finished.

"Wasn't going there, but thanks!" Kessed replied sarcastically. "Thanks for calling though. I kinda miss you."

"I almost miss you—if I had a chance. Cyler's been—"

"Bye!" Kessed hung up the phone before Laken could go into detail. It wasn't that she was a prude as much as she didn't want the specifics. She could guess, and that was enough. And Laken wandered into over-share territory a little too easily.

As she set her phone to the side and sighed, she thought about the conversation. Laken had a way of cutting directly to the heart of the problem. It was both helpful and irritating all at once. *Why is it that the heart of the problem usually wasn't what I want it to be, but something that can seem so small but feel so huge?* Kessed twisted her lips, thinking about Jasper.

Honestly, she didn't know where to go from there, but taking it slow— whatever that looked like—sounded safe. Safe was good. Safe wasn't getting heartbroken; safe meant she could keep her options open.

Even as she said the words in her head, she winced. It sounded fickle— disloyal—but it was the truth. Who wanted a broken heart? Not her. But she didn't want to hurt Jasper either, and what if it didn't work out?

What if she accidently led him on?

What if he didn't like her after all?

So much uncertainty, no wonder she was still single!

She sighed deeply and closed her eyes, resting on the feather pillow and forcing her body to relax. It had been a long day, but the sun hadn't set fully, and she felt like a kid going to bed when it was still light out.

Even if it was getting close to nine thirty. The perks of living north meant more sunlight in fall. Kessed let her mind wander, thankful she was at least ready for bed, and before she knew it, her alarm sounded.

Disoriented, she reached over and fumbled for her phone, growing more irritated by the moment when it wasn't in its usual spot. Groaning, she reluctantly opened her eyes and patted around on the bed, searching. Her hand came in contact with the cool screen, and she switched the alarm off then froze.

Alarm.

Morning.

How in the hell was it morning? She didn't even remember going to bed. Her mind slowly clicked into gear even as she sunk back into the pillow. But oddly enough, she wasn't overly tired.

*Benefits of going to bed embarrassingly early.*

Soon she was finished up readying for the day and padded to the kitchen for coffee. Cows. Today they dealt with the cows.

*Joy.*

After pouring a bowl of cereal, she waited for the inevitable knock on the door signaling Jasper's arrival. But this time, she was anticipating it more. After talking with Laken, her perspective had altered. It had colored everything differently, and as such, had Kessed a bit on edge.

"Hello?" Jasper's voice called, and Kessed jumped, missing the sound of his pickup due to her deep thoughts.

"In here!" she called out, smoothing a strand of hair behind her ear. *Damn, it is irritating to care all of a sudden.*

"Morning," Jasper mumbled softly, nodding once and turning to the coffeemaker, as was their usual routine.

"Sleep well?" Kessed asked, hiding behind her mug.

Jasper shrugged. "Yup."

"A man of few words," she teased, feeling a bit more at ease.

"You should try it. Especially in the morning," he shot back, arching a dark brow challengingly.

"Someone needs coffee."

"Someone needs to talk less in the morning. Silence is golden." He whispered the last words as if to emphasize his point.

"What?" Kessed asked with more volume than was necessary, just to piss him off.

*So much for caring. Again, probably why I am still single. Aw, to hell with it.* She inwardly sighed.

Jasper winced, set his coffee cup down, and strode over to where she sat, grinning. Her cheerfulness faded as he reached forward and placed his warm palm over her mouth then grinned. "Much better."

Kessed licked his hand, just to spite him.

"Not going to work." He sighed as if unimpressed by her attempt.

So Kessed tried to bite.

"Easy now." Jasper chuckled and removed his hand then patted her on the head.

"Not your pet," Kessed grumbled.

Jasper lifted his mug in salute. "No comment."

"Why do I feel like I've been insulted?" Kessed asked, lifting her mug again to sip her black coffee.

Jasper shrugged, took the final swig of his coffee, and set the cup down. "Ready?"

"As I'll ever be. When are the cows getting here anyway?" Kessed asked, standing.

Jasper chuckled. "So, technically, they are cows, but cow usually implies it's a female. These are steers. Gelded bulls. Just saying."

"Whatever. Boy cows."

"Steers."

"Steers. When are the *steers* getting here?"

Jasper wiped his hand down his face. His lips pursed as if restraining his amusement. "This morning around ten. So, let's get to the feed store, get some of those salt licks, arrange for grain to be delivered, and we're good to go."

"Lead the way." Kessed held out her hand toward the door.

It didn't take much time to pick up the salt licks and arrange for the grain delivery, and they'd made it back home long before necessary.

Jasper drove around the ranch, pausing in each pasture segment and setting a large cube of salt and minerals in the dirt.

The sky had started to take on a dark gray color as the wind picked up, and clouds converged around Rattlesnake Ridge. Being built on a semi-arid desert, Ellensburg didn't get much rain, but with all the hills around, when there was precipitation, it was almost guaranteed to be a gully-washer, and flash floods ran rampant.

As they drove back, Jasper put the truck in park. "Damn it."

"What?" Kessed turned to look where his gaze was focused.

"Wind must have shut the gate. Maybe I didn't lock it?" He tilted his head slightly then glanced around. There were several gates closed.

"We gotta get those open." Jasper moved to get out of the pickup but paused as he glanced in the rearview mirror. "Later apparently."

He nodded to the back, and Kessed turned. By the ranch house, a cloud of dust filtered through the air, signaling the arrival of the bull wagons, as Jasper had called them.

"Well, first things first?" Kessed said by way of a reply.

"Let's get those steers taken care of."

# CHAPTER NINE

Jasper studied the two trailers as they drew closer to the ranch. Disgusted with himself, he knew that the gates had closed because he'd been distracted yesterday, thinking about Kessed and not paying adequate attention to securing them against the fence.

Kessed waited next to him, a constant distraction of the best and worst variety. Her hair wasn't in its messy bun but braided down her back in a long, espresso-colored plait. Little strands of hair framed her face and teased the surely soft skin of her cheek as the breeze whirled around them. Impending rain scented the air and, based on the clouds, a fall thunderstorm was fixing to start up soon.

Jogging to the barn, he quickly whistled to Margaret, knowing she'd perk up at the sound. Sure enough, the mare's ears were facing front, her brown eyes alert and eager.

"You want to round up some cattle today, huh, girl?" Jasper asked as he strode purposefully toward the tack room. In short work, he had Margaret saddled, bridled, and chomping at her bit, ready to go. In one smooth motion, he swung up into the saddle and encouraged her to head toward the sound of semitrucks crushing gravel beneath their heavy tires.

Of their own volition, his eyes searched out Kessed, watching as she pushed her braid behind her back and met his gaze, arching a brow as if impressed.

He could only wish.

Though, as he moved Margaret toward the main gate, he had to admit that there was a subtle change in Kessed, but what exactly, he couldn't put his finger on.

She blushed slightly and turned away, not meeting his gaze when he turned his back to regard her.

Margaret stomped impatiently, and Jasper patted her neck, crooning softly.

When the trucks came to a stop, he rode around toward Kessed. "Can you open the gates full wide?" He motioned to the metal doors.

"Yup." Kessed gave a salute and strode off.

Jasper rode toward the cab of the first truck then waited for the driver to step down.

"You Cyler?" The gray-bearded man asked, his baseball cap shielding his face from the sun.

"Nope, but I'm his ranch hand. Need me to sign?" Jasper reached out and took the clipboard from the man before signing his name.

"That gate?" the driver asked, nodding in Kessed's direction.

"Yup."

"I'll let Mark know." He gestured to the other truck and walked away.

Margaret sniffed the air, her ears perked toward the bull wagon, the scent of cow manure and sweat permeating the air around them. He clicked his tongue twice and gently kicked the mare's flanks, and she immediately obeyed, walking forward toward the back of the trailer.

"You want me to turn around and back up?" the driver asked, striding toward Jasper.

"There's plenty of room to turn, so that might be easiest." Jasper glanced around the wide expanse of gravel between the barn and house. With only one horse, it would be much easier to herd the cattle into the pasture if it were much closer.

"Give me five minutes," the driver answered then hopped into the cab. He put the semi into gear.

Soon the trailers were beeping as the first one backed up to the gate. After stopping, the driver walked around to Jasper.

"You ready?"

Jasper glanced at Kessed. "Climb up on the fence, so you're not in the way in case they get a little wild." He'd noted that the steers were restlessly pawing at the trailer's floor, the metal sound ominous. Surely, they sensed the storm brewing as well.

As soon as Kessed was out of the way, he nodded to the driver. "Let's go."

The driver unhinged the back of the gate, and like a flood, the cattle piled out. Margaret whinnied at the rush, and Jasper moved to the side, flanking the trailer, keeping the cows moving toward the targeted opening. Once in a while, a steer would straggle, and he'd have to whip Margaret around to keep the line moving, but all in all, it was a painless process. As the cattle filtered through the gate, they dispersed, some sniffing a salt lick, others migrating toward the open field, their noses taking them in the direction of water.

The first truck pulled away, and the second pulled into its place. Much like the first time, the cattle eagerly exited the trailer and weren't unnecessarily stubborn about entering the gate. Margret was quick to respond to any outliers and arched her neck high, clearly enjoying the movement and excitement.

After the second truck finished, they drove off without a backward glance, probably on their way to the next load.

Jasper rode over to where Kessed sat on the fence, looking more natural at the country scene than he'd have expected a few days ago. "Easy." He shrugged, downplaying it a bit.

"Just another day in paradise," Kessed asserted, grinning. "What now, cowboy?" Her gaze took in Margaret, her eyes softening as she reached out and petted her velvet muzzle.

"Now we go and secure those damn gates and get out of the rain," Jasper answered.

Kessed glanced up, frowning. "What rain?"

As if nature decided to answer, a fat raindrop landed on her upturned cheek.

"That rain," Jasper teased, earning a glare.

"Fantastic," Kessed remarked dryly.

"I'll put Margaret away, and then we'll take the pickup. It will be faster. Give me a few minutes." Jasper didn't wait for Kessed's response but turned the horse around toward the barn. After taking off her saddle and bridle, he did a quick curry of her coat and tossed a few molasses oats in a bucket. Margaret's appreciative sniff was all the thanks he received. He jogged across the gravel as the rain starting to come down in earnest. He slid into the truck where Kessed waited, her hair slightly damp from the onslaught.

"Let's get this over with." Jasper put the truck in gear and headed down the road. Thankfully, there were probably only a few gates closed, but that didn't mean he'd escape getting soaked to the bone. He only hoped the heavens waited to completely open till he was finished.

As he pulled up beside the first gate, the sky let loose and poured down rain like an open firehose. "Well, damn," Jasper muttered, his windshield wipers failing to keep up with the onslaught.

"Have fun with that," Kessed teased.

Jasper sighed then reached behind the cab, pulling out his Stetson hat.

"If that hat fits…" Kessed teased as he put it on.

"Hey, this hat is going to make it so I can see where I'm going."

Kessed averted her eyes to the windshield. "I wasn't complaining."

That pulled him up short. "Oh." Maybe he needed to wear the hat more often!

Kessed spoke up. "I guess we could wait it out? I mean, usually cloudbursts don't last too long."

Jasper shook his head and placed his hand on the door handle. "Maybe, but I'm expecting the thunder and lightning to start any moment, and I really don't want to be out here when they do." He swung open the door and then closed it quickly behind him, the rain pelting his hat. Before he made it halfway to the closed gate, his jeans and T-shirt were soaked through. He walked the gate open, then fastened it into position so that if the wind kicked up, it wouldn't blow closed. Jogging back to the truck, he heard the low rumble of thunder.

"One down," he remarked, driving ahead as he waited for the lightning.

"And we have to do this now?" Kessed asked, her eyes like a warm touch as she gazed at him.

Jasper nodded. "Yeah, these gates lead to the stream. They'll need access."

"That's right. Well, fun?" Kessed chuckled, reaching over and touching his shirt. "At least you're not going to get any wetter."

His skin tingled where she had gently touched him, but he kept his expression impassive. "Nope. Nothing like a rain shower," he joked back.

He pulled up to the next gate and took off his hat.

"Don't you need that?" Kessed asked, but he ignored her as he stripped off his soaking shirt.

No reason to wear it; his skin would dry faster than the fabric. He'd need his boots and jeans when stepping across the barbed wire to get to the gate, but the shirt was expendable.

"You're taking the shower thing literally." Kessed blinked.

"Almost. Don't worry. I won't scandalize you… yet," he flirted and put his hat back on, running out into the rain and taking care of the gate.

When he returned, Kessed was biting back a grin.

"What?" he asked suspiciously.

"Nothing," she sobered, but her lips still twitched slightly.

"I thought we'd been over this. Nothing is never *nothing.* Spill."

He navigated to the final gate.

Kessed sighed then bit her lip again, distracting him from the flash of lightning that blazed across the sky.

"Whoa," Kessed remarked.

Jasper counted in his head. *One one thousand, two one thousand, three one thousand, four*—The thunder rumbled, letting him know the storm was moving dangerously close. The Rattlesnake Hills were often hit by lightning, and he didn't want to be out in the open when the storm was over them. He was also growing concerned about the flash flood possibility.

"Damn, this one has two very near each other. I don't want to be out here any longer than absolutely necessary with this lightning starting up. Do you think you can open the first one, and I'll get the second? I'm sorry about the rain...." Truck hit a rut, sending water splashing.

"Last I checked, I won't melt." Kessed regarded the downpour with resignation. "Let's get this finished."

"Thanks," Jasper added, pulling up the truck as close as possible to Kessed's gate. "There will be a pin to hook the gate to the fence. Just attach them, and you're good to go."

Jasper watched as Kessed nodded then ran out into the rain. He followed, keeping an eye on the distance, watching for lightning.

Sure enough, it struck the hill about two miles south. Relief washed over him when the smoke was immediately extinguished from the heavy rain. Heaven only knew how many brush fires they'd had over the course of the years. The rain was a huge blessing.

Dry lightning was far more dangerous.

He ran to the final gate, stomping through the normally dry streambed, noticing its visibly increasing gush as it wound down from the hills. He reached the gate and slid the pin into place so that the gate remained open. He caught sight of Kessed heading back to the truck, but she paused.

He studied her and then jumped when the thunder rumbled above them, signaling danger.

Jasper took off toward Kessed before noticing her reason for pausing. Flash floods were truly created in a flash, and this was a prime example. Not more than five minutes ago, she'd hopped the small stream without issue. But the stream was now a twisting torrent. Shallow, but swift.

"I'll help you." Jasper took her arm, holding her against his body as they moved forward. He'd have to navigate it as well just to get back to the truck. The wind picked up, pelting the rain against his face, and he glanced to Kessed, her hands wiping the water out of her eyes just so that she could see. In one swift movement, he took off his hat and set it on her head, hoping that it would shield her face from the whipping rain. Easing down, he jumped the eighteen-inch drop to the creek bed and turned. He grasped Kessed's waist and guided her down. They needed to cross the creek now before it grew worse. Wrapping his arm around her waist, he led them into the ankle-deep water, thankful for the boots they each wore. His knees strained to remain upright in the swift current, and he moved them steadily across the three-foot bed, dodging stray branches, tumbleweeds, and other debris. The muddy water grew deeper till it almost spilled over Kessed's boots, but it shallowed quickly as they made it to the other side.

Lightning flashed across the expanse of sky above them, and instinctively Jasper wrapped his arms around Kessed, shielding her body with his. As the thunder rumbled, he straightened. "Let's go!" he shouted above the wind and grumbling boom.

Kessed needed no encouragement, and she took off at a run for the pickup. Jasper opened the door for her, making sure she was in before slamming the door and rushing around to climb in himself. As he closed the door, he sighed heavily, the sound of the rain almost deafening as he threw the truck in gear and headed for the ranch house.

"Well, that was exciting," Kessed remarked after a moment, turning to him. Her braid was dripping water down her shoulder, her pale blue T-shirt leaving nothing to the imagination as it outlined her black lacy bra.

Jasper turned back to the road, swallowing. Damn, she looked good in the rain.

"Just another day in paradise," he replied, using her previous words.

Kessed's laughter warmed the pickup like he'd turned the heater up full-blast, and he no longer felt the chill of the rain, just a warm smoldering heat in his chest that threatened to build.

"So, I've heard of flash floods, I've seen the aftermath, but I've never seen it actually happen. That was insane," she remarked with a grave tone.

"You don't screw with mother nature. She can be a bitch," Jasper said honestly.

"Yeah," Kessed agreed. "What about the steers?"

Jasper bit back a grin at how she'd finally used the right word for the cattle. "This doesn't bother them at all. They won't like the thunder, but it's not going to faze them much." He pulled up to the house, expecting Kessed to hop out.

"Are you coming in?" she asked, and damn it all, if he didn't want to read into that simple question.

"I'm pretty soaked, I better get on home—"

"You're a mess. And knowing you, you'll get some call on the way and go and save some sick cow or horse or—bird."

"Bird?" Jasper chuckled. Bird was a stretch.

"You know what I mean. Come in. Dry off. I'll order pizza. We deserve it after herding cattle, risking our lives, and getting soaked. Don't you think?" She crossed her arms, challenging him.

Little did she know it wouldn't take much to convince him of anything where she was concerned.

But for her benefit—or maybe his ego—he twisted his lips, pretending to consider. "Only if you order pepperoni," he added after a few moments.

"Demanding much?" Kessed replied, but her face broke into a smile that had him immediately grinning back.

"Yes. Always."

"Noted," she replied with humor in her tone.

The thunder rumbled again as Jasper turned off the engine, and they made a run for the house. Kessed's giggle peppered the air as they stumbled into the foyer, dripping on the tile floor.

Kessed plucked first at her shirt then her pants as if surveying the damage. "I feel like a drowned rat."

"You kinda look like one," Jasper flirted, taking his hat off her head and setting it aside.

"Thanks, by the way. That actually helped."

He gave a sideways grin as he took off his boots. "So, you're saying thanks for the hat, not that I saved you from the rising creek."

Kessed sighed. "Thanks for both."

"You're welcome," Jasper replied with a wicked grin.

"Why must you take every opportunity to irritate me?" Kessed groaned as she pulled off her boots as well.

"It's fun."

"Glad I can be your entertainment." She set her boots to the side and peeled off her shirt.

Jasper froze then forced himself to keep his eyes off her delicate curves and the way they tapered down to her dark, soaked denim.

"I hate wet clothes." She walked toward the laundry room and tossed the shirt in the sink. "I'll start the shower. You can use the guest bath, and I'll use the master," Kessed tossed over her shoulder with a small shrug while Jasper's gaze was glued to the that ever-present sway of her hips... and the way her lacy black bra would be so easy to remove... and belatedly, the words slowly echoed through his mind sending his thoughts spiraling into a different direction down that same road.

As he heard the water start, he shook his head, pulling himself together. Damn. He was acting like a horny teenager, not a twenty-seven-year-old man! Grumbling against his own cursed lack of self-control, he strode toward the bathroom, forcing himself to meet Kessed's gaze rather than all the other deliciously exposed skin she was revealing.

"The hot water takes forever, but at least I got you started." She gently touched his shoulder as she passed, and his body reacted as if the touch had been much further south.

He closed his eyes and waited till he heard the door to the master bedroom click shut and then glared at the shower as steam started to pour out. What he really needed was a cold shower, icy enough to cool his fevered body. But the siren call for warmth was too strong, and he quickly stripped the rest of his wet clothes off and leaned into the warm water.

His mind replayed the sight of Kessed's exposed skin, studying the mental picture, memorizing it. The soft curve of her neck was only the beginning of the more defined curves just below. He already knew what it was like to hold her waist in his hands, to feel the shape of her hips within his palms when he helped her down after crossing the creek. It was an easy jump to imagine what that same sensation would be if she were naked.

He started to switch the water to cold when there was a knock on the door.

"Hey, I'm grabbing your clothes. Is that okay?" Kessed asked, waiting.

"Yeah." Though after the fact, he wondered just what he was going to wear. He peered out of the shower as Kessed walked in wearing a towel. She leaned down to pick up his waterlogged jeans.

"I'm going to start the washer so it doesn't take forever." She shrugged then paused, her gaze sharpening before she blushed and averted her eyes. Jasper figured that the frosted glass wasn't exactly giving him a whole lot of privacy—especially when certain parts of his body were being rather insistent.

Kessed bit her lip, took the jeans, and disappeared through the door without another word.

Jasper sighed. Well… if she'd had any questions about his attraction to her, they had just been answered. He closed his eyes once more and tried to figure out if there was any way he could stop laying his cards on the table when it came to Kessed. First, the wedding… then, the fry fiasco—though she had kissed him—then, the big shower reveal. He chuckled at his own expense. Fate wasn't fair, and time and time again he'd been far more direct than he was honestly comfortable with.

But it was what it was.

The door clicked, and Jasper stilled. He waited but heard nothing else and was about to disregard the sound when a shape took form on the other side of the frosted glass. The door rolled open, and Kessed stepped in, joining him.

Her brown eyes were uncertain, and he opened his mouth but was immediately silenced by her hand covering his lips. The chill of her fingers was a stark contrast to the warmth of the shower, and it was electric, jolting his already alert sense.

"Not a word."

Amazed and willing to obey, he trained his gaze on her soulful brown eyes. Her hand slid downward, leaving a trail of need in her wake and his body tightened to an almost painful degree. Her gaze followed the motion of her fingers. First she swept along his collarbone, tracing the outline of his shoulder. His body rejoiced at the sensation of her fingers on his bare skin. When she stepped closer, a hand caressed around his neck and pulled slightly, inviting him to meet her half way as she leaned in to meet his lips. As if he needed any encouragement. He'd been dreaming of her since the wedding, every luscious inch of her.

Without hesitation, he reached around and circled her waist with his hands, fulfilling his own fantasy as his fingers claimed her soft skin, pulling her close enough to remove all distance between them as he savored the reality of her lips on his.

The hot water pelted his back, and he shivered slightly. Turning them, he guided her into some of the warm spray without breaking the kiss. Immediately, her body relaxed against him, as if the hot water caused her to melt.

Kessed traced his lips with her tongue, and his body shuddered in reply, demanding far more than just a kiss, more than a touch.

Her hands left the back of his neck and trailed down his shoulders, mapping his geography with each delicate touch. As she traveled lower, she rounded his ass and pulled him tighter. It was heaven, every thing he imagined and more erotic than he could have dreamed.

He bit back a groan of desire.

But he didn't want to move too quickly. Lord only knew how fast it could be over if he didn't moderate himself.

And he wanted this to last, wanted it to be as powerful and intoxicating for her as it was for him.

Kessed's hips moved against him, begging silently, and he pressed into her leg, a low growl escaping his lips. Painfully hard, his body begged for release with each tight strain against his self-control.

Her lips fused with his, and he lifted her up, his body practically weeping with pent-up desire as she wrapped her legs around his waist. He pressed her back against the shower wall, and she slid down just enough to align their bodies. He kissed down the line of her jaw, burying his face in the crook of her neck as he slowly slid inside, nearly blacking out from the pleasure.

Kessed's soft moan almost destroyed whatever self-control remained, but Jasper clenched his teeth and took a deep breath, meeting her lips once more before he started to move.

Her hands knotted through his hair, tugging as he stroked her deep within, his passion building, yet reason threw a wrench into the mix, pulling him up short.

"Kessed—" he started, meeting her gaze.

"I'm on the pill. Shh, kiss me." She pulled his neck, angling her head to fuse her lips with his own, and any other thoughts scattered. Her body arched into him, tightening as her panting breath echoed his own. She leaned back from his kiss, but pressed her forehead against his as she whimpered, wrapping her legs even tighter against his waist, demanding.

As her nails dug into his shoulders, she shattered against him, around him, surrounding him with her release. Her pleasure pulled the trigger on his own, and he groaned against her shoulder, shuddering with the powerful sensations rocketing through him. His heart pounded fiercely, and slowly he became aware of Kessed's heartbeat as well, pounding against his chest, beat for beat, as he slowly took a deep breath and met her gaze.

"Hi." Her tone was slightly surprised, but her face held the most beautiful glow of rose-colored desire.

Though he chuckled at her anticlimactic response after the intense passion they'd just shared, a swell of pride, of possession, swept through him as he regarded her swollen lips from his kiss, her flushed face from his body joining hers.

"Hi," he replied, grinning as he slowly, gently, let her down.

Her legs untwined from around his waist and her feet landed on the shower tile.

Jasper grinned. "We should get caught in the rain more often."

Kessed swatted his arm, her own smile teasing those perfectly pink lips. "I guess I'm in luck that it doesn't rain here often," she challenged.

"Time to move to Seattle," he teased back.

Her face flushed a delicate pink color that highlighted her olive-toned skin. Her braid trailed her delicate back, and he reached out to grasp the woven locks, feeling each bump with his fingers.

"Beautiful," Jasper murmured, reaching up to trail his fingers along her jaw, pausing at her still-swollen lips.

Her gaze was uncertain, yet it slowly melted into a warm smile. "You're not so bad yourself." Kessed mirrored his movements, reaching up to stroke his face.

Belatedly, he wished he'd shaved earlier since his stubble was surely rough against her palm, and earlier, against her face.

A delicate shiver shook her body, and Jasper stepped aside, pulling her fully into the warm water. He ran his hands over her shoulders, pooling the water and then letting it cascade down her arms in a fuller, heated stream.

"I didn't realize I was so cold," Kessed remarked as she drew her braid over her shoulder and removed the band securing the end.

As she started to unravel it, Jasper stilled her. Her gaze shot to his, but she lowered her hands. He felt her eyes on him, intent, as he slowly unwound the plait, the act startlingly intimate, amazingly erotic. As he finished, she arched her back to place her head under the water, giving him a glorious view and reigniting the deep heat simmering just below the surface.

Restraining himself, he made the decision to let her lead. Kessed was a woman who knew her own mind—most of the time.

As she finished rinsing her tresses, she met his surely hungry gaze with a slight grin. "I think I'm good. Are you finished?"

He could think of a million responses to that question, none of which had to do with the act of cleaning himself, but he simply nodded. She switched off the water and opened the door. After handing him a towel, she quickly wrapped herself up once more, blocking the delicious view of her body and sending a pang of disappointment through Jasper.

Her stomach growled, and he couldn't suppress the chuckle as her face flushed at the sound. "Not a word."

"Where have I heard that before?" he teased, winking at her. "Let's get you fed. Fair warning"—he took a step closer to her, placing a lingering kiss on her soft lips—"I'm nowhere near finished with you yet." Jasper grinned at her shocked—then amused—expression as it flashed across her deep chocolate eyes.

"Is that right?" she challenged, her tone flirtatious in a way that sent blood to his already-excited southern regions.

"You can bet on it," he replied simply and dropped his towel, walking out into the hall.

He could feel her eyes on his back, and he hoped that he had at least a fraction of the effect on her that she had on him.

In short work, he located his phone in the laundry room. Thankfully, Kessed had removed it from his wet jeans before tossing them in the washer.

He quickly dialed up Domino's and ordered three pizzas and breadsticks. Then, on a whim, he ordered one more pizza just in case.

"You better order pineapple on one!" Kessed called out, and he chuckled as he completed the order, double-checking that the pineapple would be on two of the pizzas. He found his wallet and used a card for the order, immediately disappointed that the pizza would be delivered in less than a half hour. Not a lot, but perhaps *enough* time....

He set his phone back down and walked—still blissfully naked—into the hall toward the guest room where he assumed Kessed was staying.

"Pineapple ordered." He leaned against the door jam, utterly at ease.

"I think you'd better let me answer the door when the pizza is delivered." Kessed arched a brow as she regarded him. She was already wearing a sports bra and boyshorts underwear.

"Wouldn't want to give some poor guy an inferiority complex," Jasper flirted, watching her roll her eyes with amusement.

"Yeah, that's the reason," she replied, though her gaze lingered lower, filling him with a satisfied pride. "How long do I have to wait?" Kessed asked, meeting his stare.

Jasper tilted his head, his mind going in several directions with her question, but he answered the one he thought was most likely implied. "Thirty minutes, give or take."

Kessed nodded, a small smile teasing her lips. "That's good to know, but it wasn't exactly the question I was asking." She looked up at him through her lashes.

His body caught on even faster than his mind, and with a knowing grin, he scooped her up, laughing at her weak protests, and tossed her onto the bed gently, covering her almost-naked body with his. He kissed her soundly, noticing how her lips were spread wide from a lingering smile, and it resonated deep within him. Her hands tangled once again in his hair, and he gave himself over to the deeply pleasurable sensation.

Part of his brain registered his phone ringing, but he disregarded it immediately; rather, he deepened his kiss, responding in kind when Kessed pressed into him.

Another, different ring sounded, and Kessed pulled her lips back just enough to speak. "Ignore it."

Willingly obeying, he captured her lips in answer and ran his hand down the curve of her hip, reaching up to cup the swell of her breast.

Her perfect shape filled his hand, her breath coming in short gasps.

Then the ranch phone rang.

82 *Kristin Vayden*

"Damn it all to hell, if that's Laken, I'm going to kill her." Kessed panted, but Jasper could see her focus was lost, and he stroked her once for good measure, before kissing her nose sweetly. "Determined much?" he asked.

"You have no idea. She's the worst," Kessed replied, sighed, then rose as Jasper moved from her, his body acutely missing her warm frame beneath his.

Kessed picked up her cell phone and, as if on cue, it rang again.

"Impatient much?" Kessed said by way of greeting.

Jasper watched Kessed as she listened to her friend. "No, I wasn't running. I'm fine. What do you need?"

Jasper chuckled at the implication that Kessed was out of breath from exercising.

She glared.

He grinned deeper.

"I'm fine. What do you want?" she repeated.

Silence. Jasper traced the outline of her body with his gaze, hungry.

"No, I'm not being mean. You're interr—avoiding the question."

Kessed's face blushed slightly, and Jasper grew curious.

"I'm not saying anything. Tell me why you called a million times," Kessed answered after a brief pause.

She listened again, nodded, then replied, "Yes, they are all here. Tell Cyler he owes me huge. Jasper had to save me from the flashflooding and a runaway cow."

Jasper raised an eyebrow at her lie.

She stuck her tongue out in return.

"So no cow, but I got soaking wet, and we're—"

Kessed paused once more then answered. Her gaze slid to his for a moment before skittering back to the door. "Yes." She bit her lip. "There are many definitions of the word slow, Laken."

He heard Laken's laughter through the phone, along with what sounded like cheering. Apparently, Laken had connected some dots.

"Are you done now?" Kessed asked, her tone impatient.

After a moment, Kessed glanced at Jasper. "Cyler wants to talk with you for a bit."

"Sure." He shrugged, standing from the bed and taking Kessed's phone, but not before he stole a quick kiss, earning a weak smack on the shoulder.

"Hello?" he answered, grinning unabashedly.

"Hey! So, everything's good? You got the cattle all settled in? Any problems?" Cyler's baritone asked from the other end.

"All good to go. No issues. Got caught in a thunderstorm, but a little rain won't hurt anything."

Kessed snorted, and he turned to wink at her.

"Sounds like it was more than just a little rain," Cyler replied.

"We had some pretty decent flashflooding, but that will only give you more water for the herd," Jasper answered.

"Good, good. Wait." Cyler paused, and Jasper could hear Laken's voice in the distance. "Laken wants to talk with you."

"Okay." Jasper flickered his gaze to Kessed, who narrowed her eyes in suspicion.

"Hi, Laken. What's up?" Jasper asked.

Kessed groaned and lay down on the bed dramatically.

Jasper chuckled at her theatrics.

Laken answered, "It's like this. You hurt her, you will pay."

Jasper smirked at the way Laken championed her friend. "Yes, ma'am."

"And for the love of all that's holy, don't put up with her stubborn streak. Boss her around. Don't be afraid. She's all bark, no bite. I've only had to bail her out of jail once," Laken finished, and he heard Cyler's laughter on the other side.

Jasper mouthed to Kessed. *"Jail?"*

Kessed simply gave him a wide, innocent expression.

"Understood," he replied, biting back a grin.

"Good. We're done interrupting. Carry on..." Laken's words faded into a giggle.

"Yes, ma'am," Jasper replied enthusiastically.

"I like you," Laken added. "See you in a few days."

"Later." Jasper ended the call then turned to Kessed. "You want to tell me what that was all about?"

Kessed met his gaze then glanced away. "Nope."

He laughed, his face aching from all the smiling he'd done recently.

"So... about that pizza?" Kessed asked, a half smile on her face.

"Should be here any minute," Jasper replied, eyeing the beautiful woman on the bed and cursing the short time before they'd be interrupted again.

Kessed rose from the bed and pulled a pair of sweats from the drawer. She slid them over her long legs then quickly swiped a sweatshirt from the chair and sent a mischievous grin in his direction.

"I'd offer you clothes, but honestly, I don't want to." She smirked as the doorbell rang.

"I'm perfectly comfortable as I am," Jasper replied as she strode from the room.

"I see that," Kessed tossed over her shoulder.

A minute later, the scent of pizza preceded Kessed's arrival back. She set the cardboard boxes on the bed and opened them one by one.

"I love that they give paper plates. It's like they know it's a crime to order pizza and then have to do dishes."

"Mind readers," Jasper added seriously, earning a glare.

"So, pepperoni?" Kessed asked just as Jasper took a large bite.

He nodded.

"I'm all about the pineapple. In fact, if I could have just the sauce and pineapple, I'd be happy. But I do like the cheese," she answered, taking a bite and closing her eyes, the familiar soft moan escaping.

Jasper grinned, thrilled to channel that pleasurable sound in a way where they could both enjoy it.

"So good," Kessed replied, devouring her slice. "And I love that you ordered four pizzas and breadsticks. You're learning."

"I figured two for you, two for me, and if we get hungry, we still have bread sticks," he answered, watching her enjoy her food.

"Carbs. My true love." Kessed spoke around a mouthful.

"Sexy."

She moved her hands in a circular motion, holding the slice of pizza. "This is a judgment-free space."

He lifted his hands in defense. "Noted."

"You're distracting me." Kessed took a small pillow and chucked it at him. "For your... distracting parts."

Jasper blinked then chuckled, making a show of placing the pillow over his *distracting parts,* as she'd said. "Better?"

"Not really. I have a really photographic memory." Kessed arched a brow.

"You're impossible."

"Not entirely."

"Sure, sure. When do Laken and Cyler get home?" Jasper asked. He had ulterior motives for asking, but he also couldn't quite remember the exact date.

"They'll be home Sunday night, so three days," Kessed answered.

He nodded, taking a bite of pizza. "And when do you work this weekend?"

"I'm on for the next three days. I'm up for a position to manage the store. I'll find out about it this weekend." Her gaze lowered, and he suspected a hint of insecurity below the surface.

*Is she worried? Does she need the higher-paying job?*

"You're already bossy. I think it would be an easy, natural step for you," Jasper teased, hoping to lighten her expression.

It worked. Kessed tossed a piece of pineapple at him.

He picked it up and ate it.

"It's mostly just… progress, you know? I don't want to just stay static. I want to grow, be more than only a barista. It was fine when I was in college, but now that I'm graduated, it's—I want more." She met his gaze, and he read the sincerity deep within.

"That's a perfectly natural step. What did you major in?"

Kessed shrugged. "Business with a minor in marketing."

Jasper regarded her. "So, if you could do anything career-wise, what would it be?"

Kessed's brow furrowed, making a tiny valley as she thought. "This might not make sense, but I love talking with business owners and targeting places where they want to expand, grow and market, and develop a plan to reach those goals. But in Ellensburg, there's not a big call for that. I'd have to move to Seattle, and honestly, I don't want to go there. My grandparents live there, and I love to visit—it's where I grew up—but I don't want to make that my home. I love it here… thus, the job at Starbucks." She shrugged as if trying to diminish her words and their poignant truth.

Jasper leaned down, resting his elbows on his knees. "So you grew up with your grandparents?"

"Yeah, my parents died when I was a little over a year—car accident. I don't even remember them. My grandparents are amazing, but a little… overbearing? That sounds bad. But they just have definite ideas that they want me to aspire to, and those ideas aren't my dreams."

"Like?" Jasper inquired.

Kessed twisted her lips. "They'd love for me to work for a huge corporation in Seattle—and there's nothing wrong with that—but the idea of being here, out in the middle of nowhere it's… distasteful to them. They don't see the rugged beauty, the wide-open spaces, the way people are kind, helpful, not out to step on you to get ahead. I'm not saying that all people in Seattle are that way, or that there aren't people in Ellensburg that aren't that way. I'm just saying that it's a slower pace, a different life, and it's the life I love. I chose Central Washington University for those very reasons, hoping my assumptions were right, and I totally fell in love."

Jasper listened, watching how her brown eyes sparkled when she talked about the land, about the heart of the town. It was beautiful, a deep insight into her soul that he wasn't expecting but was thankful for, nonetheless. "I know exactly how you feel."

"Have you always lived here? I thought you just moved back…." Kessed asked, picking up another piece of pizza.

"It's a long story, and part of it isn't mine to share." He frowned, remembering.

"So, what's your part then?" Kessed inquired.

Jasper shrugged. "Family. I left after high school, got my education through the University of Washington, and then helped a friend start a practice in Colville. We did well, but family comes first, and my sister needed me. So, you do what you gotta do, and honestly, it worked out for the best. Vince needed someone to help out, and when I arrived, he let me know that he'd wanted to retire. It was the perfect setup. My buddy in Colville understood, and that's about it."

"Sounds like things worked out well," Kessed remarked.

"Yeah, I'm pretty pleased." Jasper smiled in spite of himself, allowing his gaze to lower over her sweatshirt, imagining the skin beneath.

Kessed shook her head in amusement. "Pizza first."

"So, in your life, food is first," Jasper reminded her from the day before.

"If that's a problem, we might have to reevaluate this." Kessed pointed between the two of them.

"I didn't say it was a problem." Jasper laughed. "Just making sure I have things straight."

"Good."

The rain continued to pelt the window, and Jasper glanced outside. "Well, at least we won't have to worry about the water supply for a while."

"Yay." Kessed lifted a fist to cheer in a mocking way.

"Sarcasm?" Jasper tilted his head.

"Always." Kessed glanced up with a grin. "So, tell me about your parents."

Jasper leaned back, resting his hands behind his body, thinking. "Well, my parents divorced when I was about ten. That would make Harper about four. My mom didn't stick around, but my dad did. He raised us and never remarried. He was a former marine, but took up hay-farming when my mom left him. He wanted us to have roots. He was in a tractor accident when I was eighteen. Our mom didn't even come to the funeral."

"Damn. That's harsh. I'm sorry." Kessed frowned. "I'm sorry about your dad."

"It was a while ago, but it still hurts. Especially for Harper. He was her idol."

Kessed reached out and placed her hand on his knee. "I can't imagine, but I'm sure she's thankful for you. Does she live by you?"

"Yeah, one bedroom down from mine." Jasper winked. "Harper doesn't do the alone thing." He shook his head.

"Ah, got it. Well, at least you have each other." Kessed took her hand back, smoothing her hair behind her ear.

"Yeah, she's one of my best friends. And almost a bigger pain in the ass than you," he teased.

"Hey!" She picked up another pillow and tossed it at him.

Jasper dodged it, then on a whim, took the pillow covering him and chucked it at her.

Kessed squealed as she ducked, but Jasper took the pizza boxes and tossed them to the ground, thankful that they hadn't spilled the last of their contents as he moved forward. Kessed shrunk away playfully till her back came in contact with the headboard, her grin widening even as her eyes opened fully, feigning fear.

"Trapped," Jasper remarked, closing the distance. With a smile, he ducked his head and bit the edge of her sweatshirt, tugging at the fabric with his teeth.

Kessed giggled then slowly lifted the bottom of the sweatshirt, and he released his hold, watching as she removed it and tossed it to the floor.

"Much better," Jasper murmured before taking her lips with his, savoring the touch, enjoying the slow and pleasurable process of removing one layer after another.

Doing his best to strip her bare of everything and opening the way to what he wanted more than anything.

Her heart.

# CHAPTER TEN

Kessed watched as Jasper drove away, bittersweet feelings swirling around her. It had been an amazing afternoon that had carried into the night, and now that morning had come, it was like the magic had ended and real life had come knocking.

And she really didn't want to face the truth.

That maybe it wasn't just *a* great night... maybe it was the start of many. And while she hoped for that, she was skeptical, too skeptical. She had meant to take it slow, and well... that had gone to hell in a handbasket. Yet, as she smiled and bit her lip, she wouldn't change anything.

Damn, it was all so confusing!

She was thankful to have work to occupy her mind. In just a few short hours, she'd be behind the familiar counter and distracted fully, but that left the question: When would she see him again? Should she call? Should she wait? She huffed out a sigh in indecision.

She'd find out soon enough. With reluctant steps, she strode back to the bedroom and swept her wayward hair from her eyes. As she readied herself for the shower, she couldn't resist the smile that teased her lips at the memory of yesterday's shower.

As the steam started to fill the bathroom, she replayed each moment. Part of her was still scandalized at her behavior. She wasn't one who slept around, but there was something so honest about Jasper it dissolved her resistance and was clearly her kryptonite. It also scared the hell out of her, because... what if that honesty wasn't authentic? While everything about him pointed that it was indeed an elemental part of his character, she still didn't know how to trust that, to trust him.

It wasn't something she could control. *He* wasn't something she could control, and that didn't sit right. *If I can't control it, then I can get hurt.* And pain really sucked.

As she washed her hair, her thoughts drifted to Sterling. But not in the usual way; rather, she regarded him differently—maybe honestly—for the first time in forever.

Old dreams died hard, but sometimes the new dreams were stronger than the old. And that certainly seemed the case with Jasper.

Kessed finished with her shower, checked the time, and soon was out the door with her familiar green apron. She twisted her hair up into a bun on her way to the car, and kicked up dust as she sped down the dirt road.

Starbucks was already open, but her shift didn't start for another fifteen minutes, which gave her the perfect amount of time to sip some coffee and steal a scone.

Or two.

"Cade!" Kessed waved to the barista behind the counter.

"Hey." He saluted quickly and went back to steaming some milk.

"Slammed?" Kessed asked, nodding toward the drive-through window.

"Every morning," Cade replied. His blond hair hung over his eyes, blocking them from view. He was a good kid, a freshman at Central, and adorably in love with his high school sweetheart who was finishing up her senior year at Ellensburg High.

"Regan be in tonight?" Kessed asked, even though she knew the answer.

"Yup! Homecoming is next week, and we're going over plans," Cade relayed over his shoulder as he finished up the two orders.

"Sweet. I'm taking two scones, so ring me up for one."

"On it." Cade paused, frowning slightly. "You on a diet?"

"Boo!" Kessed glared at him. "I ate two pizzas last night, and I'm still full." *Even after all that extra exercise,* she thought.

"That sounds more like you. I'll ring you up after this rush finishes up. Is Devon coming in later?"

"Should be." Kessed bit her lip as she poured herself a venti cup of Pike Place.

Devon was the current manager, the one who was moving to a different location, leaving the position open—the position Kessed wanted.

"Help a guy out and drink your coffee quickly. I could use a hand," Cade spoke just before hitting his headset to take the next order.

"Can't clock in early." Kessed raised a hand in surrender, and after Cade glared in reply, she took her two blueberry scones and took a seat.

The bitter flavor of the Pike brew was the perfect answer to the sweet tartness of the blueberry, and she sighed in appreciation.

"Clock's ticking," Cade singsonged.

She lifted her cup, taking an exaggeratedly slow sip.

He chuckled and took the next order.

Too soon, her time was up, and Kessed was tossing away her trash and walking behind the counter, waiting to take the next person's order.

The morning bled into the afternoon, the time passing quickly with all the customers who demanded coffee. As the end of her shift approached, Devon arrived, causing Kessed's chest to tighten with anticipation.

"Hey." Devon lifted a hand in hello but didn't single her out, simply started to restock the cold case and make necessary notes.

Each time Kessed would try to inquire, they'd have an influx of customers, and she'd be occupied, and the last thing she wanted to do was slack off on her job, not when she was hoping to get promoted.

Five minutes before her shift ended, the door swung open again, only this time she met the green eyes of Jasper. A slow smile spread across her face and started a tingling heat throughout her body.

He nodded to her then got in line. His gaze was warm on her skin. Even though she was listening to the customer several ahead of him in line, she could feel it.

It was deliciously distracting.

When it was finally Jasper's turn, he met her gaze with a wink, and a flush spread through her face. "Hey," she spoke, downplaying her reaction.

"Good afternoon." He grinned, one side of his lips lifting higher than the other, giving him a slightly lopsided expression. It was flirtatious and devastating all at once.

Damn, she was in trouble.

"What can I get you?"

"From the menu?" he asked.

"Please tell me you didn't just say that."

"It was the best I could come up with."

"It sucked."

"I'll work on it."

"Do that. So, coffee?" Kessed raised an eyebrow.

"Coffee. Lots of it." Jasper rubbed the back of his neck. "I'm a little sleep-deprived."

Kessed tilted her head. "Some of us are tougher than others. What kind of coffee, cowboy?"

"Pike Place."

"Boring," Kessed quipped, grinning.

"What do you order?" Jasper challenged, holding out his phone to scan his card.

"Pike Place."

"So, the same thing?" Jasper replied dryly.

"Yeah, but I drink mine with scones. It's better that way." She turned around to fill his cup.

"When do you get done with your shift?" Jasper asked.

She placed the lid on the cup and turned. "Almost done."

"Hungry?" he asked, leaning on the counter slightly.

Kessed eyed him. "What do you think?"

Jasper answered with a chuckle. "That maybe that was a stupid question?"

"Ding, ding, ding! We have a winner. Your door prize is that you get to buy me McDonald's." Kessed took off her apron and cast a furtive glance to Devon, checking to see if maybe he was waiting to talk with her.

No such luck.

With an inward growl of frustration, she clocked out then walked around the counter to meet Jasper.

At least she'd be on shift tomorrow as well. Hopefully, she'd find out more information then.

Or maybe she'd just ask rather than wait. She hesitated, glancing back to Devon, and then sighed. She could be patient. Maybe it would pay off. She wasn't sure how, but it seemed like the right thing to do.

Damn it all.

"Ready?" Jasper inquired, tilting his head slightly as she approached.

Kessed's lips spread into a grin, her frustrations melting away. "Eh, I guess." She shrugged indifferently, earning a glare from Jasper.

"Playing hard to get?" He teased, opening the door for her.

"Yup."

She walked out into the warm fall air then jumped when Jasper whispered in her ear. "Secret's out. You kinda like me. But I'll play along if you want me to." His hand squeezed her waist, and she squealed from the tickle. Reaching out, she smacked his shoulder. "Maybe, maybe not."

"Honey, if last night was you being indifferent, then I can't wait to see what happens when you're all in." He gave her a wink and walked around to the passenger side door of his pickup. He opened it and waited.

Kessed lowered her gaze, caught off guard and slightly embarrassed by his remark. She fumbled for a response.

"Wow, I think I just made you speechless. This is a first. I'm taking note."

"Are you going to shut up and feed me, or are you going to stand there and pat yourself on the back all night?" Kessed asserted, regaining control of her wits. She didn't wait for a response and shut the door, crossing her arms in challenge as she tapped her foot.

Jasper shook his head, an amused expression on his face, and walked around the back of the truck to his side.

"I'm assuming you're planning on taking me to work in the morning if I'm leaving my car here?" Kessed teased, not expecting him to agree.

"Is it that obvious?" Jasper gave her a sheepish grin.

Kessed couldn't stop the grin that spread across her face. "At least you know what you're getting into."

Jasper chuckled, the sound deep and rich. "Yup. So, same thing?" he asked as they made the short trek from Starbucks to McDonald's.

"You can't improve on perfection."

Jasper met her gaze for a moment then glanced away. "Truer words were never spoken."

And Kessed wondered if he was talking about the food...

Or her.

"So, have you heard about the promotion yet?" Jasper asked after he placed their order.

Kessed twisted her lips. "Nope."

"Sorry I brought it up." His brow furrowed as he pulled forward. "You worried?"

She waited as Jasper paid for the food and handed the paper sacks over to her. Silently, she kicked herself for not paying him back for the earlier lunch. She'd have to do that soon. She opened a bag and snuck a fry as they pulled away.

As they were driving down Main Street, Jasper repeated the question.

"Yeah, I'm nervous. I mean, who wants to stay in the same position forever? Life is about growing, moving forward. The next step for me is to make manager, and if I can't, then... then maybe I need to look at a different job. And honestly, that freaks the hell out of me," Kessed answered then took another fry—eating her feelings.

"But if you do something you love, then it's not settling to stay where you're happy," Jasper added softly in his low timber that vibrated through the truck.

"I *do* love coffee." Kessed arched a brow at him, a smile teasing her lips.

"You do a service to mankind." Jasper nodded, then turned his attention back to the road. "But it's also normal to want to grow. The only person who can tell the difference if you're growing or just being afraid to change is you." Jasper turned down a dirt road that led toward the wind farm up on the hill.

"I'm not afraid to change," Kessed muttered, snapping a crispy fry in half before eating one end.

"I didn't say you were. I said you were the only one who could determine that." Jasper put the truck in park and sent her a pointed glance before opening the door.

Kessed grumbled slightly but grabbed the bags and followed him outside. "What are we doing here?"

Jasper put the tailgate down and sat down, patting the metal beside him. "Have a seat."

"Bossy much?"

"You like it," he responded.

"No, I don't," Kessed replied but hopped on to the back of the truck.

The breeze softly teased her skin, cooling it against the afternoon heat. The white wind machines turned lazily in the wind, silently making their circular motion.

"It's calming, isn't it?" Jasper asked.

Kessed glanced to him. "Yeah, actually. It's kinda strange how something so big can be so quiet."

"Or how something so small can be so loud." He nudged her side, and she arched a brow in reply.

"You didn't complain…"

Jasper's grin widened as he glanced to the sagebrush-covered ground. "Not exactly what I was referring to, but nice to know your mind went there. And for the record, I don't have any complaints." His green eyes met hers, his expression amused.

"What were you talking about then?" Kessed asked, taking out another fry.

"It's not important. More or less teasing you. It's fun to get a reaction."

"I react plenty." She shook her head.

"Yeah, you do, it's fun. I really like that about you. You keep life from being boring."

"Heaven forbid life would get boring. Seriously, though, I can see how that might be an issue for some people. I tend to make my own adventure, danger, drama… I can go on forever." Kessed shook her head. "I don't really try to, but yet it happens."

"No," Jasper replied sarcastically.

"Ass."

He chuckled. "It's a good thing. Low-key, kinda boring people like me need people like you."

"Opposites attract and all?" Kessed questioned.

"Yup. I figure that's about right."

Kessed nodded then listened to the grasshoppers make their music. A jackrabbit ran across the brush, his long ears appearing almost comical against the smaller frame of his body.

A now-familiar ringtone echoed in the dry silence, and Kessed watched as Jasper answered his cell.

"Honey, calm down." Jasper's back stiffened, his tone gentle yet firm. Kessed listened closer.

"No, no. I'm sure it's fine. I'll be right there just in case." Jasper nodded, turned to Kessed, then glanced away. "Fifteen minutes, maybe thirty—" He waited while someone interrupted on the other line. "Harper, it's fine. Lady will be fine, and you're doing a good job. I'll see you in a bit."

He nodded once then ended the call, sighing. Tilting his head, he twisted his lips as he regarded Kessed. "So, what do you have planned the rest of the evening?"

"Why?" Kessed asked, her tone suspicious.

Jasper slid off the back of the tailgate and grabbed his bag of food. "Harper's horse, Lady, is in labor—she thinks. The horse is special. She's Harper's security blanket, if you will. Lady was there when..." Jasper rubbed the back of his neck and paused. "...when it all went to hell last year. Harper's freaking out, and I need to go and check out the horse. She's at home, and honestly—I'm not ready to say goodbye to you just yet." He shrugged his shoulders, spearing her with his green gaze.

Kessed took a breath, a slow smile spreading across her face. "Well, when you put it that way..." She slipped off the truck.

"I was hoping you'd say that." Jasper gave a half grin, showing off his dimple as he reached out and tugged on her hand, pulling her close.

His lips met hers, and all the memories from the night before acted like sparks that reignited the flame that had simply been smoldering under the surface, but all too quickly, he released her from the kiss, trailing his fingertips down her cheek. "If I don't get going now, I'm not going to go at all," Jasper admitted, kissing the top of her head.

"Let's go save a horse."

"And maybe later, ride a cowboy?" Jasper teased as he walked to the cab.

Kessed groaned. "So cliché. I don't even have words."

"Admit it, you totally remember that song."

"Against my will," Kessed replied dryly as she hopped into the cab and secured her seatbelt.

"It's a classic."

"No. Johnny Cash, 'Ring of Fire.' That's a classic."

"Good song too."

"Kenny Chesney, 'There Goes My Life.'" Kessed sighed. "Love that one."

"'Cowboys Like Us' by George Strait," Jasper added, pulling out onto the road. He started humming the tune then sang the words.

Kessed giggled at the way he furrowed his brows as he sang. His low baritone was sexy, alluring and surprisingly on tune as he continued. She listened, watching as he leaned into the song as he sang, the sound of his diesel engine humming in the background. Who would have ever thought?

But that was the beauty of it.

Sometimes a girl found herself in the last place she'd expect.

*And strangely enough, that very place is the one that feels like home.*

A green-eyed cowboy vet singing George Strait—that's what home looked like.

And she couldn't love it more.

# CHAPTER ELEVEN

Jasper hummed softly as he turned left onto the dirt road that wound around to his house. It wasn't much if taken at face value, but to him, and especially to Harper, it was the most beautiful place on earth.

Home.

A place that was safe.

Somewhere to belong.

"Anything by Garth Brooks," Kessed spoke up, a grin pulling at her full lips, reminding him of just how soft they'd been pressed against his.

"The thunder rolls..." he sang deeply.

"And the lightning strikes," Kessed finished in an out-of-tune alto voice.

He bit back a small chuckle, enjoying her enthusiasm.

"This is it." Jasper nodded toward the old white farmhouse. Its navy-blue shutters were faded to more of a gray, and the white paint was peeling at the peaks. The front porch sagged slightly from over fifty years of settling, but the old tire swing was still hanging from the sycamore tree out front.

"It's like every picture of an old farmhouse I've ever seen." Kessed blinked, a slow smile bringing his attention to her lips once more. "It's perfect. This is where you grew up?"

Jasper nodded once, pulling up in front and killing the engine. "Yup. Wind blows like a banshee out here. Nothing to block it, but it's home."

Kessed met his gaze, a slight furrow in her brow. "A little wind never hurt anyone. After all, this is Ellensburg."

"Indeed, it is," Jasper agreed and opened the truck door. He glanced toward the weathered barn, and sure enough, Harper was already headed in their direction. Her lips in a full grin, he tried to take it at face value but knew that the past haunted her—even if she didn't want to admit it. She'd been through hell, and she wasn't healed up from the burn. Pain like that took time to heal. And there just hadn't been enough time.

Yet.

"Hey, Harper, let me introduce you to Kessed." Jasper held out a hand to Kessed, his body relaxing the moment her skin touched his.

"Hi." Harper nodded once, her smile deepening as she glanced from him, down to his hand clasping Kessed's, then back to his eyes.

Damn, he hoped she kept her mouth shut. She understood too much, and her knowing expression reminded him of that fact.

"Nice to put a face with the name." Harper winked in Jasper's direction.

*Shit. She was going to be irritating.*

"Same to you, I've heard a lot about you. And I understand that you're the one to thank for my boots?" Kessed held out her hand and shook Harper's.

"I have impeccable taste in gear." Harper hitched a shoulder, drawing attention to the way her blonde tresses faded to deep purple, then black, almost matching the Indian feather earrings she always wore. She'd always complained that being a natural blonde was boring, so she'd taken to adding vibrant color whenever the mood struck. She'd stayed with purple for a while, and Jasper couldn't help but wonder just what that meant. Distracting himself, he met his sister's gaze.

"If you're done patting yourself on the back, can you fill me in on Lady?" Jasper asked, eager to steer the conversation into safer territory where Harper wouldn't interrogate Kessed or implicate him in some odd way. Lord only knew what she would say next. He'd always been close with his sister and hadn't kept the secret that he was falling hard for the petite brunette beside him. But he wanted to be the one to tell the story, not have Kessed hear it from his little sister.

*Something about little sisters never changes.*

Harper spoke up. "She's contracting, but it's taken a while, and I haven't seen any progress. She's waxing up, but I can't tell if that's a sure sign or not." Her eyes shuttered as she continued. "I can't have anything happen to Lady, Jas."

Jasper understood all too well. Lady was more than just a barrel racer; she was the best sort of therapy for Harper, the only other constant in her life other than him.

"I won't let anything happen to that old nag you love." Jasper tried to lighten the mood, ruffling his sister's hair, messing up her smooth locks.

"Really?" Harper shoved his hand away, using her hands to comb through the tangles he'd made.

Kessed giggled, and Harper shot her a glare. "Just wait. I'm sure he'll be a pain in the ass eventually, once his true colors shine through," she replied with a joking tone.

Jasper rose to the occasion. "Believe me, I love messing up *her* hair." Jasper winked at Kessed as he tugged her hand toward the barn.

"I really hope you don't mean what that sounded like..." Harper whined. "I don't want to know."

Kessed kicked him as they walked to the barn, and he bit back a chuckle.

"Really?" she whispered angrily, but he could hear the underlying amusement in her manner.

"Eh, you liked it," Jasper grinned unrepentantly.

Kessed bit her lip, glancing to Harper, who was catching up behind them. "That's beside the point."

"Whatever you say," he replied and released Kessed's hand to slide the faded red barn door open.

Lady nickered softly, shuffling her feet as she turned just enough to see who was interrupting her.

"Hey, girl. It's okay..." Jasper spoke softly, his trained eyes taking in all the details of the heavily pregnant mare. Her belly was swollen with foal, making her back sway deeper, which was perfectly normal. Lady whinnied once again, then stomped her feet, clearly agitated.

"Shhh, it's okay, baby." Harper spoke in the same soft tone as Jasper, passing him by and unlatching the stall. She stroked the white star on Lady's forehead, murmuring softly.

"Can I help?" Kessed asked softly from behind him.

Jasper turned to her and shook his head. "Not yet. But probably soon." At her nod, he turned back and walked into the large stall.

Jasper hummed quietly as he moved around Lady's hind end, patting her velvet fur softly so she would know not to kick.

Her stomach tensed up, and she nickered in response. His hands slowly stroked from her belly to her rump, feeling the muscles tighten.

"She's in labor all right," Jasper whispered to Harper. He lifted her tail to check her progress, and Lady swung her head back to nip at him.

"Easy, girl." He shot a glare to Harper. "She bites me, and I'm taking it out on you."

"You'd bite someone too if they were about to... do what you're about to do."

Jasper smirked. "Probably. Keep her calm." Jasper slid on a latex glove from his pocket and checked Lady's progress between contractions.

"Harper..." He felt around, counting silently once more just to be sure.

"Yeah?" His sister's voice was strained.

"She's not breech." Jasper slid his hand out then stepped away, turning the glove inside out and tossing it into the corner. "But we're still in first stage. She's stalling."

"So good news that the foal's not breech. That was my main concern." Harper closed her eyes, leaning against her horse's neck, and sighed softly. "You would freak me out by stalling."

"Stalling?" Kessed asked quietly. And Jasper turned to meet her gaze. "Mares can hold off birthing till they feel more comfortable. And I'm guessing that since Harper here has had her panties in a twist, Lady is responding to her stress and holding off on going into full labor." He turned to his sister and raised an eyebrow.

"I—I just need her to be all right." Harper's voice cracked on the last word, and Jasper turned to Kessed.

Her warm brown eyes searched his, and he wondered if she could sense the gravity behind Harper's words, if she could read what was really going on.

Lady wasn't just a horse; she was a lifeline.

Kessed's gaze shifted from him to Harper then back. She nodded slightly, as if piecing the story together.

"What time is it?" Harper asked, distracting him from Kessed's gaze.

Jasper pulled out his phone. "Little after six." He sighed. "Harper, might as well go inside for a while. Lady needs her space, and she'll probably wait to deliver till tonight when everything is more settled down. Horses are notorious for delaying till after ten at night to deliver. I doubt that Lady is any different."

His sister stroked Lady's nose tenderly, resting her head against the mare's when the horse sighed deeply, her body contracting once again.

"I'm not helping anything out here, am I?" Harper asked.

"As a general rule, you're not much of a help regardless, so don't take it personally," Jasper teased, striding over and placing a hand on his sister's shoulder. "Come in. I'll share what's left of my fries."

"I'd share mine, but I ate them all," Kessed added, and Jasper smirked at the unapologetic grin that spread across her face.

"Shocking."

"Don't tease me about food," Kessed warned, jokingly.

"I like her." Harper nodded to Kessed. "Girls need to eat."

"Amen," Kessed agreed.

"So, fries? What else do you have?" Harper stroked Lady's muzzle once more then followed them out of the stall.

"Depends on how much you annoy me," Jasper answered.

"If that were the case, I wouldn't even get one fry," Harper whined.

He shrugged. "True. I'm just feeling sorry for you."

"If pity buys me fries, I won't complain."

"I might like her more than I like you." Kessed nudged Jasper's side with her elbow, winking.

"That's usually the case." Jasper sighed dramatically. "But my charm gets better with time. Hers spirals fast."

"Hey, right here." Harper raised a hand. "Where's the food?"

"Easy. It's in the truck. Why don't you take Kessed inside, and I'll grab everything?"

"Fine, follow me, Kessed. By the way, love the name. I've never heard it before...."

Jasper grinned at his sister's intrigue and quickly jogged to the truck. He retrieved the now-cool paper sacks and hustled to the front door.

Kessed's voice met him as he stepped inside the farmhouse.

"Honestly, I don't know why my parents named me Kessed. It's not even our heritage. I think they were mostly impressed with the meaning. It's Hebrew and means unmerited grace."

"Huh, that's way better than mine." Harper arched a brow. "Fries!"

"Yeah, her name just means annoying." Jasper held the bags up. "And impatient."

"Liar. My name means I play the harp."

"Which you don't."

"I could if I wanted to," Harper retorted, jumping and grabbing a bag and making a run for it.

"I wouldn't do that!" Jasper called out. "Kessed gets mean when you mess with her food."

"Shit." Harper paused then tossed the bag to Kessed.

Jasper dangled the other bag and grinned. "This is way too much fun."

"You're such an ass." Harper strode over and held out her hand toward the remaining food. "Please?"

"Check it out. Little sister learned some big words."

"I know some other words I can educate you with," Harper threatened.

Kessed's husky laughter called to him, and as soon as he dropped his guard, Harper was walking away with a fry in her mouth and his burger in her other hand.

"Your fault." He pointed to Kessed.

"Making an honest man out of you. You did promise fries...." She arched a brow.

"Damn it all, I'm surrounded. Why did I bring you anyway?" Jasper collapsed onto the couch, shaking his head.

"I'm entertaining," Kessed responded, taking a seat beside him. "And because I take pity on you, here's my offering." She held out a single fry.

"It's cold," Jasper complained as he took it.

"Beggars can't be choosers."

"So, how did you guys meet?" Harper asked, sitting in the old armchair across from them.

Jasper stiffened, not sure how to answer the simple question.

Kessed's reply saved him from navigating the semiawkward interaction of Laken and Cyler's wedding. "He taught me how to use fence stretchers then gave me McDonald's. Laugh if you want, but it works for me." Kessed bit into a cold fry, her gaze sliding to his before lowering.

"And here I thought it was my abs and personality." Jasper nudged her elbow with his.

"Those help."

"Moving right along..." Harper cleared her throat. "So, you know Laken and Cyler?"

Kessed nodded. "Laken's my best friend. I know Cyler through her. He's a good guy, even if he did ask me to deal with his mess at the ranch. Hindsight, he must have been either desperate or crazy to involve me with that."

"Ah, I heard about that... more than once." Harper glanced to Jasper, a grin widening her lips. "Yeah, well, you got an education in ranch life."

"Sure did. I'm not exactly a cowgirl." Kessed tiled her head.

"But it seems like you did well enough. Jasper kept saying how hard you worked."

Kessed turned to him, brows raised. "Did he now?"

"Yeah." Harper shrugged. "And I can tell you, it takes a lot to impress him."

"Right here," Jasper added, using his sister's previous line. "And I'm not that hard to impress."

"Liar." Harper pointed to him, scooting to the edge of her chair and grinning. "Such a liar! Remember junior year, FFA? You were president of the club and everyone was scared shitless of you. You practically hazed the entire freshman class just to see if they were worthy of joining. It was the freaking FFA, Jasper. Not Mensa."

"It wasn't that bad." Jasper sighed.

"It was. I heard the horror stories. You can't stop someone from joining the FFA, especially around here," Harper all but yelled.

*Kristin Vayden*

"Fine. I'm a horrible mercenary who's impossible to please."

"Eh, he's not that difficult," Kessed argued, giving him a sidelong gaze that sent his body humming with electricity.

"And we're now changing the subject again." Harper stood, walking into the kitchen.

Jasper chuckled then reached over and grasped Kessed's hand. Her dark eyes met his as he wound his fingers around hers. He reveled in the simple contact and the intimacy it created.

"This is miserable. I hate waiting, and I'm already impatient," Harper complained from the kitchen. Her purple tips swung forward as she ducked her head inside the refrigerator.

"Don't eat your feelings," Jasper called out, teasing.

Kessed arched a brow.

"Kessed says eat your feelings," he amended.

"You're impossible." Kessed shook her head and stood up. "Why don't you show me around? It will kill some time, and I'm curious to see where you grew up."

Jasper rose from the couch. "There isn't much to see, except a lot of outdated wallpaper and a laundry list of things I need to repair. But it's home."

Kessed nodded. "And that's what matters."

"It's not so bad." Harper shrugged, shutting the refrigerator door, causing a picture to slide from the front and land on the ground.

Kessed eyed it.

"I've done worse." Harper picked it up and reset the magnet that held it to the fridge.

"As you can see, this is our kitchen." Jasper pointed to the open area. Mismatched appliances created an odd rainbow of color that ranged from the avocado-green oven to the almond-white fridge with wooden accents.

"It's warm, homey."

"You're stretching it a bit, but the warm part is right. About the only thing this oven does right is heat up the house," Jasper answered.

"It's not like you'd know how to use it if it did work," Harper chimed in.

Jasper turned to her. "As if you're better."

"I never said I was." Harper raised her hands in defense.

Jasper turned to Kessed. "The range works, and that's usually how we cook."

"When we cook, which isn't often."

"Are you giving the tour, or am I?" Jasper speared his sister with a glare.

"I'm adding detail," Harper asserted.

Jasper watched as Kessed brushed her fingers along the island's butcherblock. Its surface was cut to hell, but it was original to the house and well over a hundred years old. He glanced around at the floral tile, the faded curtains that framed the window over the stainless-steel sink, and the overly distressed wood floor and saw everything that needed to be fixed, updated, refinished. Yet, as he turned back to Kessed, her expression was soft, and he wondered if she saw the house differently.

Damn, he hoped so.

"Come outside. It's the best part." Harper headed to the Dutch door that opened onto the back patio, the floor creaking with each step she took.

Kessed followed behind.

Jasper pulled up the rear of the group and leaned against the door as the two girls walked out into the backyard. Wild grapevines climbed over the archway that led to the old and neglected garden area. The grass was shaggy but lush and green like a soft carpet. Just as he expected, Harper led Kessed over to the large oak tree and sat down in the bench swing that had hung there as long as he could remember.

"Isn't this fantastic? I love coming out here with my coffee and watching the sunset." Harper waited till Kessed took a seat then slowly pushed from the ground with her toes and set them to swinging back and forth.

"The wood is so soft." Kessed smoothed her fingers along the armrest.

Harper did the same. "Yeah, it's been here forever, but it's acacia, so it doesn't get weathered like other wood."

"I'll get you ladies something to drink while you relax!" Jasper called out, giving them both a smile before ducking back into the kitchen. He filled two glasses with water then pulled the well-used ice-cube tray from the freezer and plopped several into the glasses. The immediate cracking sound reminded him of summer, and he carried the refreshment outside.

"Here."

"Service with a smile," Kessed flirted.

Jasper saw Harper roll her eyes in response, and he was half-tempted to dump the ice-cold water over her head, just to get even. He restrained himself and handed it over instead.

"I know you were thinking about it." Harper eyed him suspiciously.

"Never," he answered, earning a glare from his sister.

The crickets sang, and the gentle breeze rustled the sycamore leaves as Jasper closed his eyes and simply listened as the wooden bench creaked with the girls' swinging.

It was evenings like these that made the best memories, the most peaceful ones. He opened his eyes and glanced to Kessed, a slow smile creeping across his face as he noted that she was doing the same thing, just listening, relaxing.

*How long has it been since she's taken a moment to just be?* She wasn't the type to simply be still, to not be a whirlwind of activity. It was part of her charm, part of her allure—yet, at the same time, everyone needed a break, a moment to just relax.

He was thankful she'd found it at his house. *That has to mean something, doesn't it?*

"It's so peaceful out here," Kessed commented, her tone soft.

"Yeah, it's pretty awesome." Harper's voice drew his attention. He noted how her brow furrowed, and he wondered if she was thinking about last year.

There were some things that time didn't heal very quickly.

Harper's brokenness was one of them.

Kessed's phone buzzed in her pocket, and she pulled it out, grinning as she swiped the screen. "I almost forgot. Cyler and Laken are back Sunday!" She tapped a few times on the screen and then groaned. "That was my reminder to feed Margaret."

"Margaret?" Harper asked.

"Cyler's pet horse," Kessed replied with a smirk.

Harper nodded. "Got it." She turned to Jasper. "You better take her home then. If Lady's waiting to drop her foal, then you might as well make yourself useful. Margaret's gotta eat." Harper beamed then stood from the swing, causing it to rock.

"And I was just getting comfortable," Kessed complained, yet she cast an amused grin in his direction as she stood as well, stretching her arms up and giving him a sexy view of her toned, olive-tinted stomach that made his own tighten with need.

"Take me home, cowboy. Better yet, take me to pick up my car. I have a feeling you're going to have a busy night." Kessed lightly punched him in the shoulder and walked toward the house.

Harper touched his chin, causing him to jerk. "Your jaw was hanging open, and I think I saw a little drool just there…" She touched his cheek. "Seriously, pull it together," Harper stage-whispered and jogged toward the back door, probably trying to keep one step ahead of him.

*Wise girl.*

Jasper rubbed his chin and followed the girls into the house and out to his pickup. "Kess, why don't you hop in, and I'm going to check on Lady one last time."

Kessed nodded, and as he walked away, he heard her say goodbye to Harper.

As he entered the barn, Lady nickered softly, her brown eyes curiously watching his approach. Her expression seemed to say, *"Nothing to see here."* And if that was what she was saying, she was correct. Jasper could detect no real change in her as he slowly walked around her backside, his hand stroking her chestnut-colored coat.

"You be good while I'm gone," he whispered softly, moving back around and pausing before her long nose. "We need you around here, girl."

Lady nudged his hand as if searching for a treat, and when she didn't find one, she blew impatiently on his hand.

"I mean it. Be good," Jasper reminded the ornery horse then left the barn, an uneasy feeling following him. He tried to put a finger on why he felt that way, yet he couldn't quite determine the source. Filing the sensation away for later, he strode to the pickup and tossed a wave to Harper. Soon they were kicking up dust and heading back to town..

"Harper is fun. I like her, and it's easy to see that you two have a good relationship." Kessed leaned back on the seat, resting her head and turning slightly to face him.

"Yup. She's worth her weight in gold and trouble," he answered. "She seems to like you well enough. That, in and of itself, is not an easy accomplishment." He reached over and grasped Kessed's hand, squeezing it softly.

"What's not to like?" Kessed asked, grinning.

"True," Jasper replied, yet his gut was tense, that sensation from the barn still lingering.

"What's wrong?" Kessed asked.

He shook his head. "I'm not sure. Just some weird feeling that I'm missing something with Lady. I—I'm not sure, and it's nagging the hell out of me."

Kessed nodded once. "Listen to your gut. I've learned it's usually spot on." She hesitated and then asked the question he'd been anticipating. "What's the story with Harper? I know that you've mentioned a few details that imply that she's had a rough past…" Kessed trailed off then sat up. "I know it's not my business, so you don't have to say anything. I was just curious. She seems happy, yet…" Kessed took a deep breath, pausing as if thinking about the next words. "She seems happy because she chooses to be, not because she really is… if that makes any sense."

Jasper sighed. "Well, that's a pretty accurate assessment for someone who just met her." He cast a glance to Kessed. "It's her story to tell, but I can give you a few details that will help you connect a few dots that are pretty much public knowledge." He bit his lip, the familiar hot rage and cold pain slicing through him as he thought about his baby sister.

About how he hadn't acted fast enough.

And what would have been different if he had known sooner.

But the past was the past, and he couldn't change it.

*No matter how I wish I could.*

He took a deep breath. "Harper was married right out of high school. She was head over heels for Brock Williams. He was a good enough guy, or so we thought. They'd met at community college over the summer, and the rest was history."

Jasper clenched his teeth, hating the bitter taste in his mouth left from that man's name.

"Brock's family owned a car dealership in Seattle, so Harper moved to the city. I was busy with my schooling anyway, and we kept in contact with the usual text or phone call, but not much. We were both busy."

He'd never outlive the guilt that weighed on him for not paying closer attention.

"I'll leave the particulars out, but last year I got a phone call from the Seattle Social Services. Harper was in the hospital. Her husband"— Jasper spat the word, clenching the steering wheel so hard the leather groaned—"was in custody, and the hospital was trying to locate next of kin to release her to upon discharge."

"Holy hell," Kessed murmured, and he cast her a glance, his body relaxing slightly in seeing the empathy and fear in her deep caramel eyes.

"Yeah, well, I dropped everything and was at that hospital as fast as possible. Kessed, I'm just being honest here, but it's only by the grace of God that I'm not in prison for killing that son of a bitch. Harper needed me, and that took priority. That and the bastard was already in jail." Jasper sniffed defiantly, a sneer crossing his lips.

"Was he convicted?" Kessed asked, her tone hesitant.

Jasper clenched the steering wheel once more, making a right-hand turn onto the road that led downtown. "His sentence was far lighter than I agree with, but the divorce was finalized almost immediately. What matters is that Harper is safe, here and she's healing…mostly."

He cast a glance to Kessed as she bit her lip, staring straight ahead. "I can't imagine. And, I… I can't imagine Harper not fighting back." Kessed turned to Jasper, confusion written across her face.

Jasper sighed, not blaming her. It was one of the first questions he had as well. His sister—brave, stubborn, and killer with a right hook—hadn't fought back till it was too late. "It usually starts small, Kess. And the abuser undermines the self-confidence, self-worth, and self-assurance of the other. And while they might not believe the lie at first, if you hear something enough, you start to wonder if maybe it's true, then you move to believing a little bit of it to be true, then you buy into the whole enchilada. It's usually a process—at least, that's how it went with Harper. When I finally got to her, she was a shell of the woman she had been, of the woman you see now. She believed she'd deserved what Brock had given her, of all the asinine things to believe." He released a breath, tired, weary, wishing he could change the past.

Kessed's shoulder sagged slightly. "I never understood it... but that makes sense in some weird, twisted, and depraved way."

Jasper eased the brake and put the truck in park just before where Kessed's car was parked. "There's one more thing, and"—he sighed—"it's part of why I'm kinda stressed about Lady delivering." He turned to face Kessed, watching her warm eyes sharpen as she waited.

"Harper was almost four months pregnant when Brock put her in the hospital. Technically, she had miscarried before the actual incident, so Brock wasn't implicated. But that didn't ease the trauma. And seeing her with Lady, I know that's what she's remembering." He lowered his gaze.

Kessed's hand reached over and grasped his. "Then you better get back, do what you do best, and take care of that horse."

A ghost of a smile tipped his lips. "I'll do my best."

"That's all anyone can ask," Kessed replied then opened the truck door and slid out onto the gravel.

Jasper followed suit, trailing a few steps behind her as he walked to her car door. "You work tomorrow too?"

"Yeah." She glanced over her shoulder and met his gaze. "You coming by for coffee?"

He grinned. "Can't go a day without it. And that's the truth." He chuckled. "It was a real pain in the ass to try and get coffee and avoid you at the same time."

Kessed spun and faced him. "Say what?"

Jasper rubbed the back of his neck. "I knew I'd struck out at the wedding. You made that crystal clear. I didn't want to look like I was stalking you, so I gave you space. But that was easier said than done. I can't tell you how many times I avoided going to Starbucks and went with McDonald's coffee instead. Not my favorite."

"You didn't." Kessed eyed him.

"Yes, ma'am," Jasper replied, chagrined at his confession.

Kessed regarded him as if taking his measure once more. "That's stupid, pathetic, and romantic all at once." She shook her head and closed the distance between them. She pulled his head down with her hand, meeting his lips.

His body surged with anticipation, even though he knew the kiss was both the beginning and end of the encounter; his body reacted as if it were simply foreplay. He nipped at her lips teasingly, savoring her unique flavor, the way her soft curves pressed into his chest. His hands circled her waist, holding her gently captive, deepening the exchange and wishing there was time for more. All too soon, he pulled away, resting his head against hers. "So, the pathetic and romantic stuff does it for you? I'll remember that."

Kessed's breath was slightly ragged, and she grinned. "What can I say? I'm a sucker for the underdog."

Jasper leaned back, glaring in a joking manner. "I'm anything but the underdog, sunshine."

"And we're back to square one." Kessed bit her lip. "I'll see you tomorrow." She slowly trailed her hand down from his neck and traced the curve of his biceps before squeezing his hand then releasing it.

Jasper watched as she walked to the door, his gaze dipping to watch her hips sway with the movement. "Tomorrow," he replied, then when she started up her car's engine, he headed toward his truck.

Back to work.

# CHAPTER TWELVE

Kessed drove to work the next day, frowning at her phone on the driver's seat. It wasn't as if she expected Jasper to call, but a text would have been nice.

Of course, she could have texted him, but, well... she didn't want to be that kind of girlfriend.

Holy hell.

She shook her head, amused. Yeah, well. After that one night, she better be his girlfriend. Not one for the Tinder type of all-nighter, she was usually a little slower mover.

Regardless, she didn't want to be the person who was needy, seeking attention. She was perfectly self-reliant.

Wasn't she?

She glared at her phone.

Maybe not as much as she wanted to be.

"Damn thing." Kessed groaned and pulled into the back parking lot behind Starbucks. Devon's truck was parked two spots away, and a tight anxiety wound her chest. Maybe today she'd find out if she'd gotten the job.

Her shift started during the middle of the afternoon rush, and she only caught a few fleeting glances at Devon, but he was busy handling the front counter. As her time started to wind down, she worked with Devon to close up, the lingering sunset filling the store with an orange glow.

"Kessed, when you're finished restocking the cups, can I speak with you a moment?" Devon called from the cold case.

Kessed nodded, her heart hammering in her chest. She glanced up, her eyes scanning the front of the store for any lagging customers. The doors would be locked in less than five minutes, and Jasper still hadn't shown up.

Just another reason to be all uptight.

*Gah!*

As she finished stacking the grande cups, Devon twisted the lock in the door and turned off the front lights, signaling their closure.

"Ready?" he asked, his bald head slightly shiny from the setting sunshine streaming through the window.

Kessed nodded, practicing a calm she didn't feel. "What's up?"

"Have a seat." Devon gestured to a small table. The chair scraped against the tiled floor as she pulled it out. When she sat, Devon took a deep breath.

*Oh. Shit. This can't be good.*

"As you know, the manager's position was available for this store, and your application was considered for the position."

He folded his hands on the table, and Kessed waited.

*Was.* That had to be a key word, a really bad one....

"And while you're more than qualified for the job, it was given to a manager from the Bellevue area who is relocating. His greater experience coupled with his longevity with the company made him a better candidate." Devon lowered his gaze. "I'm sorry, Kessed. I know this was important to you, and please know, if the decision had been up to me, you would have been hired without question." He raised his eyes, and Kessed noted the honesty in his pale blue irises.

"Thanks, Devon. I appreciate that." She exhaled, disappointed but not defeated. "I guess that's that." She moved to stand.

"Not quite." Devon spoke slowly, and Kessed had the sensation that the worse news was on the way.

"What?" Kessed asked, slowly sitting back down.

Devon glanced to his hands once more, his brow furrowing. "Corporate has asked we cut back on some hours. You're three-quarters time now, and we'll be cutting you back to half-time. You'll still get the full benefits—"

Kessed raised a hand, glancing away to pull together her emotions. "Why?" she asked after a moment.

"Efficiency. We've been slower than usual. It's probably just the fact that summer has ended, and fall is in full swing, but you know it's all about the numbers." Devon shrugged. "I wish I could do something, but I'm gone in just a few more days."

Kessed blew out her cheeks. "So, not the news I was hoping for... at all." She leaned back on the chair. "Damn, this sucks."

"Yeah, it does." Devon sniffed, turning his head away, his brow furrowing. "Friend of yours?" He nodded his chin toward the door.

Kessed turned, and a weak smile bent her lips as she saw Jasper lean against the window, cupping his hands to see in against the sun's glare. "Yeah."

"Go ahead. I'll finish up here. I'll email you the new schedule once everything is settled."

Kessed nodded. "Thanks, Devon." She shook his offered hand and waved to Jasper.

He grinned, but it seemed forced.

Her brow furrowed as she held up one finger, signaling that she'd be out in just a moment. He nodded in understanding and turned away from the window, his hands tucked into his tight jeans, giving her a prime view of his ass.

Devon cleared his throat.

Kessed sent him a glare then went to retrieve her purse. Soon, she was unlocking the front door and slipping out into the warm evening.

"Hey."

"Hey." Jasper pulled her into a tight hug, his chin resting on her head. His body was tense, and she leaned back, studying his face.

"Sorry I didn't make it sooner, today was… hell." He sighed and forced a smile that didn't reach his eyes.

"You too, huh?" Kessed arched a brow and started walking to the back lot where her car waited.

"What happened with you?" Jasper asked, taking her hand in his warm one.

"I didn't get the manager's position, and the cherry on top is that they are cutting my current hours." Kessed sighed, unlocking her car.

"Ouch." Jasper winced. "I'm sorry, Kess. How are you taking it?" He tugged on her arm gently and pulled her into a hug.

"I haven't decided yet," she muttered against his solid chest, inhaling the scent of dirt, cedar, and all man.

Jasper gave a short laugh. "Let me know when you figure it out."

"Yeah," Kessed replied weakly. "What about you?" She leaned back to study his face.

"It's a bit of a story." He gave a weak smile.

"I've got time… apparently, lots of it." She sighed. "Are you busy now?" Jasper shook his head. "No."

"Follow me back to the ranch. I'll toss a frozen pizza into the oven, and we can drink. Sound good?" Kessed wagged an eyebrow, grinning.

"Sounds amazing." Jasper kissed her forehead. "See you in a bit."

Kessed slid into the car and was pulling out of the lot and onto the road before Jasper had even made it to his truck in the front lot. When she arrived back at the ranch, a bittersweet ache filled her chest. This was the last night before Cyler and Laken came home, then it was back to her small, lonely apartment. There was something about the ranch, about being out in the wild that was oddly safe and homey to her. She'd miss it.

She quickly tossed her green apron into the laundry room and went to the kitchen. After preheating the oven, she pulled out several frozen pizzas and set them on the counter. It had been a while since she'd bought wine, but a quick glance in the fridge told her there was plenty of IPA.

Pizza and beer.

Life was looking up.

Jasper knocked once then let himself in, his boots making loud footsteps in the hall.

"You finally made it?" Kessed teased, handing him a cold Iron Horse IPA.

Jasper took the beer and gave her a stern glare. "I don't drive like the devil's on my tail."

"I don't either." Kessed shrugged, taking a swig of the smooth brew.

Jasper shook his head. "Sure, you don't." He glanced to the bottle. "Love these guys." He took a long drink.

"Buy local." Kessed wiggled her fingers, shrugging her shoulders a bit. The oven dinged, and she turned to the pizzas. "Hope you like pepperoni, and… wait for it… pepperoni," Kessed teased, setting the pizza onto the bare rack of the oven.

"Are you sure you don't have pepperoni? It's my favorite," Jasper joked from behind.

"Funny." Kessed closed the oven, then turned. "Have a seat. Spill. Is it Harper's horse?"

Her eyes studied the way Jasper tensed, then frowned, creating deep creases in his forehead, as if he'd done a lot of it recently. He took a deep breath, tapping the table a few times with this thumb before answering.

"We lost Lady."

Kessed froze midstep to the table. Jasper's tone was broken, lost, powerless… and immediately her thoughts ran to Harper.

"How's Harper?" she whispered, taking the last few steps to the table and finding a seat.

Jasper shook his head slowly, his gaze communicating what a hundred words would have lacked in meaning.

Kessed bit her lip, leaning across the table and grasping Jasper's hands, her fingers rubbing across his calluses till she laced her fingers through his. "What happened?"

He shook his head. "You know how I said that something felt off?" She nodded.

Jasper took a slow breath. "I checked everything beforehand, and the foal was in the perfect position, but the cord was wrapped around him. When Lady pushed, he ripped the cord out from inside her, and I"—he closed his eyes—"I couldn't stop the bleeding, and if I worked any harder on her, I'd have lost them both. The foal needed me to get it breathing since it ended up being a traumatic birth and—" Jasper set his head in his free hand, closing his eyes tightly as if reliving the whole nightmare. "Harper was crying. I could hear her sobbing as I'm trying to do everything in my power, and all I could think… I was too late… again. I couldn't do a damn thing to save Harper. I couldn't do a damn thing to save Lady." He sighed heavily, his shoulders tense as if bearing the weight of the world—his family. "And then she was gone. There's so many large blood vessels in the uterine wall during pregnancy, Lady bled out in a matter of minutes. She didn't suffer," Jasper whispered.

Kessed tightened her grip on his hand, waiting, just listening, feeling powerless herself to do anything but be present, share his pain.

"I keep telling myself that there was nothing I could have done. And in my head, I know that. But that doesn't keep me from wishing it weren't true, or thinking that maybe I could have seen some warning signs. This is the last thing that Harper needed." Jasper met her gaze with a direct one of his own, his pain echoing in her heart.

"Jasper, knowing it's not your fault and believing it's not your fault are two separate things. And I know it's new, and it's fresh, but… be careful. You're not a help to your sister if you're drowning in self-recrimination. Harsh, but true." Kessed held her breath, hoping she hadn't gone too far.

Jasper's green eyes cooled, then he blinked, breaking the gaze. "You're right. And I might need another reminder in a day or two. I'm man enough to admit that." He shrugged his burly shoulders, his powerful form a sharp contrast to the kind heart within.

Kessed blew out a tense breath, hesitating before asking the next question. "The baby?"

Jasper relaxed slightly, his ridged shoulders bowing ever so gently as a ghost of a smile teased his full lips. "Full of piss and vinegar, white as a ghost, and already has decided that Harper's his new mama." He gave his head a small shake. "It's the only saving grace in this hell of a mess."

Kessed nodded, releasing a pent up breath. "That's… that's good. Harper will need that little baby horse, and that horse will need her just as much."

"Yeah, he's in for a rough ride, but he's a pretty determined little cuss. Already kicked me twice." Jasper absentmindedly rubbed his shoulder.

"I like him already."

"You would." A little more of his grin came to life.

"Does he have a name?"

Jasper closed his eyes, a beleaguered expression on his face. Kessed thrilled to see his mood shift to a lighter tone. "This one is all Harper. She named the poor bastard Rake."

Kessed frowned. "Rake… like what you use to pick up leaves?" She scrunched up her nose.

Jasper shook his head, his grin widening. "No, it's from all her historical romance books. A rake is actually the bad boy in old-time London."

"Oh!" Kessed grinned. "Yes! I know now! Ah… I like it." She arched a brow.

"Why doesn't that surprise me?"

"Basically, it's like calling him charming, dangerous, and a ladies' man. Yup. Good work, Harper."

"Poor bastard."

"He's going to live up to the name, you watch."

"That's kinda what I'm afraid of."

"Hey!" Kessed released his hand and smacked him gently. "A horse with this kind of entrance into the world needs to make a mark. It's only fair."

Jasper grinned a crooked smile, shook his head slightly, and sighed. "You might be right. *Might.* We'll see how much trouble this little colt becomes."

"If he's already kicked you twice, and he's about a day old, I'd say the odds aren't in your favor."

Jasper took a long breath. "Yeah."

The oven timer dinged, and Kessed stood from her chair. "So, when do I get to meet this tall, dark, and handsome stranger?"

Jasper's tone was dry. "He's white, short, and anything but dangerous. His baby kicks are less than threatening."

Kessed shrugged then pulled out the drawer with the insulated mitts. The oven's heat blew hot across her face as she opened the door and pulled out the pizzas. The pepperoni was starting to get dark and crispy, just like she preferred.

"That smells so good." Jasper groaned from behind her. "I haven't eaten in…" He trailed off. "Damn, I can't even remember." The sound of his chair scraping the tile let her know he'd stood from the table.

"Forgetting to eat... something I've never done," Kessed voiced over her shoulder. The drawer below the counter held the knives, and she pulled out a pizza cutter and began to slice.

"Here's the plates." Jasper set the white dishes beside her, and she started loading them up.

"Praise God." Jasper stole a piece and took a bite.

Kessed grinned and handed him a plate. He smiled his thanks and walked over to the table once more.

A comfortable silence surrounded Kessed as they ate. It was nice, relaxing, to just simply be at rest.

Especially after the hell of the day they'd both experienced. As she took her seat once more, Kessed found her mind wandering to Harper. Torn between opening up the subject again and concern for Jasper's sister, she didn't know how to proceed.

"What's on your mind?" Jasper's enticing baritone surprised her, and she glanced up, meeting his inquiring gaze.

"What do you mean?" she asked, tilting her head.

"Your expression... it's asking a question." He circled his face with his finger and then picked up another slice of pizza. "And that question is..."

Kessed sighed impatiently. "Am I that transparent?"

Jasper nodded. "Yup."

"So frustrating," she grumbled. "Fine. I was wondering about Harper. I'm worried about her, and I didn't want to reopen the subject since we landed on kind of a high note and... yeah." Kessed picked up her piece of pizza and took a huge bite.

"Easy, killer." Jasper arched a dark brow. "And you're not reopening a conversation. This whole mess, it isn't over, and won't be for a while. It's a process, and it's healthy to end on a high note, as you put it, but it's not the only part of the ordeal. You can't just have one conversation make it all right. But I get what you're saying, and I'm glad you were being sensitive since it's so fresh for me. But Harper... she's hurting right now. She will be fine... with time. And this little colt is exactly the right medicine. Harper needs someone to look at, other than herself. She's not selfish, by any means, but it's easy to collapse on yourself after trauma, and this will force her to keep her eyes open, her hands out, and keep stretching herself. She shut down so much over the past year, a survival mode. Rake"—he winced when he said the name, and Kessed bit back a grin—"is going to be the best thing to ever happen to her. At least for now." Jasper took another bite and nodded once, as if stamping his approval on the subject.

"Can't argue with that logic," Kessed replied. "In other news, this pizza is pretty much my favorite frozen variety of all time, in the history of ever."

"You and food."

"A girl's got needs." She arched a brow.

Jasper's eyes shot to her, his green eyes smoldering before he glanced away.

"If you don't stop that I'm going to get turned on every time I eat pizza... not the best situation for me."

Kessed frowned then remembered that the other night they had ordered the same food as well. "No way. That's funny." She giggled. "I seriously didn't see the connection. Hey, we're being totally platonic here." She gestured between the two of them.

"For now," Jasper challenged, giving her a dangerous grin.

Kessed shrugged, even as her whole body warmed from the inside out with a radiant heat that smoldered deep. "For now."

Jasper tossed his final pizza crust on the plate and leaned back. "Seriously though, that was the best pizza, probably because I was so damn hungry, but I don't think I ever said thank you. So, thank you, Kessed. Dinner was amazing."

Kessed grinned. "Guys gotta eat too. C'mon. I'll wash. You dry. And then, if you're feeling energetic, you can help me finish up the last few things for Laken and Cyler tomorrow."

"Yay." Jasper gave a pathetic little fist-pump and stood.

"I'm going to need more enthusiasm if you're going to get laid tonight." Kessed waited, giving him a teasing grin.

"I can give you enthusiasm." Jasper placed his hand on his heart, his grin widening as his green eyes sparkled with a dangerous glow.

Kessed shook her head and giggled.

"So, they come home tomorrow? You know what? I don't think I even know where you live when you're not here. That's kinda lame of me."

"Super lame. You should be ashamed of yourself." Kessed flicked water from the faucet to Jasper's face.

He twisted his lips. "Thanks."

"You're welcome," she replied cheerily then stopped up the sink and added the dish soap, causing the white bubbles to fill the larger basin.

"Why are we not using the dishwasher?" Jasper asked, arching a brow as he handed her their two plates.

"Because it's stupid. We have two plates." She shook her head, scolding, then grinned. "So, the vet's not afraid to get dirty but gets all snobby about cleaning. Interesting."

Jasper sighed impatiently, and Kessed watched him from the corner of her eye as she dipped the plates in the hot water.

A slow grin widened his face and had her turning to look at him suspiciously.

"What's that grin for?"

"Nothing." He shrugged, moving to stand on the other side of her. He reached down and picked up a plate from the soapy water then rinsed it off. With slow strokes, he started to dry it. "You know, I was plenty clean in the shower the other night... you know, the one just down the hall...."

Kessed couldn't help but laugh at his challenging expression. "Fine. You win."

"That's right, baby. Talk dirty to me. Say it again," he whispered by her ear, earning another laugh.

"Seriously!" Kessed swatted at him, flinging a few bubbles onto his shirt.

"See? Clean." He pointed to the bubbles and shrugged.

"See? Pain in the ass." Kessed pushed his solid chest with her finger.

"Also true." Jasper shrugged as Kessed pulled out the last plate and rinsed it off.

He took it from her hand and wiped it dry then took both plates and set them in the cupboard.

"Was that so hard?" Kessed asked, popping her hip.

Jasper glanced over his shoulder then closed the cupboard door. "Insanely so."

"Then the next few things might kill you. We're talking full-on sweeping the front porch, checking on Margaret in the barn, and who knows what other torture," Kessed replied with dry sarcasm.

"I'll take care of the horse. You tackle the rest of it. Fair?" Jasper leaned back against the countertop.

"Not fair. Plus, Margaret likes me more. I give her special treats."

Jasper shook his head. "I do too." Jasper's cell buzzed from his pocket. With a frown, he pulled it out and unlocked the screen.

Kessed waited, watching as he quickly finger-tapped a reply.

"Harper's just checking in. She said not to worry if I didn't see her in the house. She's spending the night in the barn with Rake." He gave a sad smile then tucked his phone back in his tight pocket.

Kessed appreciated the view his jeans offered before forcing herself to focus. "In the barn?"

"Yeah, so she can feed Rake. He needs to eat every few hours for the next while. It's going to be a job, but Harper will be the best adoptive mama ever."

"Yeah, I'm sure she will be," Kessed added honestly. She took a deep breath. "Go, give Margaret an extra sugar cube and tell her it's from me. Really, don't even think about taking credit for it, because I'll cut you. That's the only horse that I've ever actually loved and so, yeah..." Kessed arched a brow.

"Yes, ma'am." Jasper held up his hands in surrender. "I wouldn't think of stealing your glory... or credit."

"I'll finish up in the house."

"Hey, you never answered my earlier question. Where do you actually... uh, live?" Jasper asked, his brow furrowed in confusion.

Kessed shrugged as she pulled the broom from its little nook beside the refrigerator. "I live in a small apartment in downtown Ellensburg. Not an exciting story, but it's home for now."

"Got it." Jasper pushed from the counter and walked toward her, causing her to pause. He grasped her hand, enveloping her chilly fingers in his warm ones.

She met his gaze, startled anew by the green hue of his eyes.

"Anywhere you live would feel like home, Kessed."

He leaned down and gently kissed her lips, sending a thousand delightful shivers down her back that bloomed in her belly. He lingered in the contact, then slowly drew away, leaving her stunned in silence as he walked to the back door and out to the barn.

A slow smile lifted her lips and she tightened her grip on the broom.

She had always thought of home as a place.

But maybe, just maybe... home was a person.

And Jasper just might be hers.

# CHAPTER THIRTEEN

Jasper walked out to the barn, his thoughts lingering on the woman back at the house that had him hogtied in every way. It freaked him the hell out, to be at the mercy of someone else, yet, the greater the risk the greater the reward, right?

The risk was worth taking, but *damn* it would suck if she wasn't falling as hard and as fast as he had already fallen. He wanted to think that Kessed had strong feelings for him, but a lingering doubt always persisted in his mind.

Sterling.

*What if I am just a replacement?* What if he was just available, and she would rather have someone than be alone? He didn't think Kessed would do such a thing, but she might not realize it either.

And what if Sterling ever decided to have an interest in her? Would he always be her number-one choice? Or had Jasper effectively stepped in fully? Even marginally?

The hard part was not knowing, at least not knowing for sure. But that was part of falling in love.

*Having faith in the person who is falling with me, hoping she is holding my heart as tightly as I'm holding hers.*

Margaret nickered as he slid the barn door open, the evening light spilling into the dim room.

"Hey there, love. You doing well?" He sauntered over to the stall.

Margaret arched her head over the gate and hung it down, waiting for him to give her a gentle pat.

Jasper obliged and softly stroked her muzzle then scratched her forelocks, earning a low rumble of appreciation. When he stepped back to get her flake of hay, Margaret shook her head, whinnying once again.

"Felt that good, huh?" Jasper teased then tossed the green hay into the pen.

Margaret went over to her dinner, sniffing and scattering the dry leaves of alfalfa with her warm breath before muzzling the flake and taking a bite.

"I'll be back with your treat." Jasper patted her solid shoulder and walked to the tack room. He pulled out the small box of sugar cubes, and just as he'd been told, took two from the box and walked back to the stall.

"You want your dessert first?" Jasper asked, holding out one cube in his flat palm.

Margaret's ears pricked at the words, and she lifted her head. Her soft brown eyes studied him then the white cube in his palm before gently lipping it up.

"I've got one more for you. This one is from Kessed. She wanted proper credit," he added with an amused tone. He pulled the second cube from his pocket and held it out.

Margaret ate it up without hesitation.

"Greedy thing." He ruffled her forelocks affectionately once more before she lowered her head and reevaluated her dinner of hay.

Jasper gave her one more pat on the shoulder, double-checked her water, then strode to the barn door. The wheels squeaked as he rolled it closed and stepped into the warm air.

The crickets had started their chirping. The scent of warm resin from the sagebrush and Russian olives hung thick in the air, the very smell of the end of summer. It was a beautiful evening, and part of him wished to linger in the warm peace of almost-silence, but Kessed waited just inside the ranch house.

And Kessed trumped everything else.

Soon, he was opening the back door. "Margaret is fed, happy, and you got credit for your sugar cube!" he called out, shutting the door behind him.

But there was no answer.

Curious, Jasper peeked in the kitchen then down the hall, but there was no sign of Kessed. He remembered her saying something about sweeping the porch, so he walked to the front door and opened it. She leaned against one of the beams supporting the porch, her hand holding her phone to her ear, listening.

"Are you sure?" Her voice broke, alarming Jasper.

He closed the distance and stood in front of her. Red flags of concern were raised as he took in her stricken expression and the way she didn't meet his gaze, simply focused unseeingly at ground just past him.

"I'll be there. Text me the time, address, everything. I'll meet you at the hospital. It's going to be okay, Laken."

But her voice sounded anything but certain of that fact.

Jasper's heart pounded, his body still tightly strung, still exhausted from the trauma from the night before.

What else?

Cyler?

*Dear Lord, let it not be Cyler.* He and Laken had just found each other....

"Okay, bye." Kessed ended the call, pulling his attention back to the present.

"Who?" Jasper asked, holding his breath.

Kessed swallowed, her beautiful face pinching in a painful frown. "Sterling."

A thousand emotions slammed into him: fear, concern, confusion, and competition. He waited, giving her time to collect her thoughts.

"He's alive. But his Humvee triggered an IED in Afghanistan. It actually happened almost two weeks ago, but they had a hard time getting ahold of Laken with her being gone. There were a few phone calls here, but nothing that set off any concerns, but now I understand that they couldn't talk to me. I'm not family," Kessed finished, her frown deepening. "He's stable, able to be discharged from the hospital, but they won't do that till he's under a family member's care."

Jasper let out the breath he was holding. "What injuries?" he asked, gently taking her hand.

Kessed woodenly returned his grip, but he could tell she wasn't fully aware. "He had a mild concussion, but the real damage was to his leg. Laken said they were able to save it, but he lost a lot of muscle mass on his calf. It's going to take long to heal."

"Not to mention the emotional trauma," Jasper added softly.

"Yeah, to say the least." She met his gaze for the first time. "I'm going to Seattle tonight, to Fort Lewis. He's at the military hospital there, and Laken is getting me access in her place since she's still out of the country. At least he won't be alone, you know? And then when Laken and Cyler get home, they'll arrange for him to come here and... I guess they'll figure out what to do from there." She took a deep breath, a slight hitch to the sound.

"Are you all right? This would shake anyone up, but you've known Sterling for a long time," Jasper asked, hating that he was weak enough to be searching for affirmation of his own hold on her heart, even in the midst of Sterling's injury.

"Yeah, it's a bit shocking. Sterling always had this aura about him, like he was bulletproof, you know? And he's not. I guess I just kinda thought that maybe he was."

Jasper nodded, even as his heart clenched. Did she hold such a high opinion of him? "I'm sorry." He pulled her in close, relaxing slightly as she melted against him, needing him.

Needing. Him.

Not Sterling.

He reminded himself of the truth.

"Do you want me to go with you to Seattle?" he asked, kissing her dark hair, inhaling the intoxicating scent of lilac and lemon.

She sighed. "Yes. But you can't anyway. Laken's going to have to pull some strings to get me in, and I don't think she could do the same for you. Plus, Harper needs you, Rake needs you, and I'm pretty sure you didn't get any sleep last night, so you probably need your rest." She mumbled into his shirt, almost pouting.

He chuckled, and she raised her face to glare at him. "What are you laughing at?"

"You. You sound like a wounded puppy. And sleep is overrated." He tucked her head under his chin, kissing her hair as she settled into his arms.

"You just wanted sex," Kessed mumbled against his shirt. "But that's okay. I did too. Raincheck?" she asked, her arms binding around him and holding tight.

"Any time." He laid his cheek on the top of her head. "Need help packing?" he asked, releasing her before he didn't have the strength or the will to do so anymore.

"It will only be a day, and thankfully, I have the next few days off."

"Silver lining." Jasper tapped her nose, earning a playful glare.

"Fine, whatever. I can pack in about five minutes, and everything here is pretty much squared away. I just need to fill up my car and then head over the pass."

"Is there anything you need me to do?" Jasper asked, following her into the house.

Kessed sighed. "Nope, I won't really know until Laken knows more information about Sterling. Their flight gets in tomorrow at eleven a.m. in SeaTac. It's actually only about thirty minutes from Fort Lewis, so they'll probably be there around twelve to one in the afternoon."

"You have my number if you need anything," Jasper added, watching as she flipped a small blue suitcase onto the bed and tossed a few random things in before darting into the bathroom and coming out with a small bag of makeup and a toothbrush.

"All set."

"When you get back, I need you to give lessons to Harper," Jasper said. "You've got to be the fastest packer I've ever seen. And Harper, well... let's just say she'd be begging me to unhook the kitchen sink and toss it in the back of the pickup, you know... just in case."

Kessed giggled, and the sound warmed his heart. Heaven only knew how much she needed some lighthearted joy in the middle of this. "I'll try, but my lessons come with no guarantees."

"I'll take my chances."

She zipped the suitcase, and Jasper picked it up off the bed before she had a chance to do it herself. With a shy smile, she let go of the handle and walked to the kitchen. He heard her keys jingle a moment before she ducked back into the hall with her little black purse slung over her shoulder. "I'm all set, I think. Oh! Can you just double-check the cows before Cyler gets home?"

"Was already going to."

"You're such a stud." Kessed winked then walked out the front door.

Jasper grinned and followed her to her small sedan. The hatch popped open, and he slid the suitcase in then shut it.

"I'm set. Wish me luck. At least I'm missing rush hour." She shrugged, her expression slightly hesitant.

Jasper was torn between wanting to kiss her senseless and hold her tightly just to give her some security, a safe space, to be her strength rather than support herself all alone.

He opted for both.

Tugging on her hand, he pulled her close, binding his arms around her and holding her near, secure and strong as he met her lips. His body ached for more, and he nipped at her lower lip then caressed her upper with his tongue, feeling her delicious surrender as she melted into him, meeting his kiss with the passion of her own. He lost himself in the soft press of her body, the sensual touch of her lips caressing his as his tongue darted out to savor the sweet flavor that was all Kessed. He wanted, needed, so much more... but rather than pull her in tighter, he slowly pushed her away.

Because love never thought of itself first.

It thought of the other.

And right now, he needed to let her go, even when it was the last thing he wanted to do.

Let her go, watch her drive away, and spend the night in the company of another man.

The man she'd loved for so long.

The fact that that very man was in a hospital bed didn't offer Jasper any comfort.

He only prayed that as he let her go, she'd come back still his.

Only his.

Assuming she'd been his to begin with....

# CHAPTER FOURTEEN

Snoqualmie Pass, the interchange, and the rest of the trip was nothing but a blur as Kessed pulled up to the front gate of the Fort Lewis Army Base in Tacoma. She picked up her phone and reread the last text from Laken, giving her the number to call when she arrived at the gate. She tapped send and waited. When the line was answered, she gave all her credentials and watched as one of the guards picked up a cell at the guard station just as she ended the call.

When it was her turn in line, she pulled out her ID and handed it over to the woman in uniform.

Her trained brown eyes scanned Kessed's ID with practiced care. "What's your business here?"

Kessed swallowed, anxious to just get to the hospital but not wanting to look agitated. The last thing she needed was to set off some warning flag by her stressed behavior. Not exactly helpful.

"Sterling Garlington is a patient at the hospital, and his sister has arranged for me to see him in her stead, since she's out of the country at the moment," Kessed replied, keeping her tone even.

The woman's eyes narrowed, as if studying the truth of the statement, then relaxed slightly. "You've been given clearance. Drive straight through the first two stoplights then turn left. You'll see the signs to the hospital."

"Thank you." Kessed nodded, taking back her ID. She rolled up her window and pulled slowly away from the guard booth, sighing in relief.

Sure enough, as she drove toward the middle of the base, the signs started to point her to the hospital. As she passed through several stoplights, she was startled at how large the base was from the inside. She'd always known about it, seen parts of it from the freeway, but it truly was a massive operation. Barracks lined the streets; the commissary sign illuminated the night sky. Soon she was pulling up to the hospital, her body tightening with stress as she parked.

Grabbing her purse, she slid from the car. As she walked toward the entrance, she pulled out her phone and shot off a quick text to Laken, letting her know she was there. Next, she sent off a quick text to Jasper, telling him the same. A small grin teased the corners of her lips. It was nice to know someone cared, someone who wasn't just her friend, but more.

As she walked through the automatic doors, the scent of hospital cleaner and sterile soap greeted her, sobering her outlook. The nurse at the reception area glanced up as Kessed approached.

"Can I help you?" the man asked, his dark blue scrubs a contrast with his pale skin and bright red hair.

"Yeah, I'm looking for a patient. Captain Sterling Garlington."

The nurse nodded then glanced down, searching on the computer. "Are you family?"

"His sister has made arrangements since she's out of the country at the moment."

"So, no. You're not family." He glanced up at her.

"No."

"I don't see any notes concerning your clearance to see the patient. And visiting hours are over—"

"Could you please call his doctor? Call his nurses' station. Something?" Kessed asked, leaning on the yellowing countertop.

He paused then nodded once. "I'll check."

"Thank you." Kessed offered a polite smile and waited, refusing to check her phone as it continued to buzz in her purse.

She listened as the nurse called, but she couldn't gather if she'd been given permission or not.

When he hung up the phone, she held her breath.

"You're clear. Go to the third floor, take a left, and go to the nurses' station. They'll direct you from there." He gave a curt nod and turned back to his work.

"Thank you." Kessed flashed him a grin, even though he wasn't looking, and turned to the elevator.

Soon she was striding toward the nursing station, her heart pounding in her ears as she greeted one of the staff with a smile. "I'm here for Captain Garlington."

The older of the three nodded, stepping from the desk. "I'll take you there." The nurse's bright white tennis shoes almost sparkled against the plastic wooden floor as Kessed followed behind. "You're the advocate for the family?"

"Yes," Kessed answered.

"He's been waiting for someone, so I'm glad you showed up." The nurse paused beside a dark door. "I'm guessing he's not asleep yet, but I'll check. Wait here."

She ducked inside, and Kessed waited, her knee bouncing with impatient anxiety.

"C'mon in, sweetheart," the nurse called, and Kessed slowly stepped into the dimly lit room. She swept away the curtain, and Kessed first noticed the thick bandages over his left leg, sticking out from the thin blue blanket. Monitors beeped, and her gaze lifted from his leg to the hospital gown that gave his skin a sallow color before meeting his gray eyes.

"Hey, Sterling." She spoke softly, attempting to smile but feeling every bit as fake as it surely looked.

"Hey." He nodded once, his full lips tipping into a slight grin. "It's about time one of you showed up," he teased, sitting up further in his bed.

"We figured making you wait was good for you. Makes you appreciate us more." Kessed smiled.

The nurse cleared her throat. "I'll be at the station if you need me." Then she walked out the door.

"So, saving the world finally kicked your ass, huh?" Kessed asked, walking over to an upholstered hospital chair and setting her purse down.

"You win some, you lose some."

"Clearly," Kessed retorted. "Laken said you sounded pretty good on the phone when she called earlier."

"For once, the tables were turned. You know, she was always complaining at how hard it was to get ahold of me, and I got a taste of my own medicine." He shrugged his broad shoulders.

"Serves you right."

"Probably. Doesn't mean I have to like it though. And I guess that if I can't have her, you'll do in a pinch." He leaned back, placing his hands behind his head. The movement accentuated his biceps and highlighted several healing gashes that dotted his skin.

"Compliments? From you? What drugs are you on?" She raised her hands in question.

"Good ones." Sterling chuckled. "So don't take any of my sweet side to heart. I'll be a jerk soon enough."

"Good. Wouldn't want you going all soft on us."

"No worries about that."

Kessed studied his face, noticing that he'd lost weight, his angular jaw more defined than normal. "We need to feed you better."

"What am I, your dog?" Sterling replied in a joking tone.

"I'd say a step below the dog."

"You know how to build a man up," Sterling replied. "But yeah, I know. The food here sucks."

"Says the man who thinks MREs actually taste good."

"Hey, you learn to love them."

"No, I don't think I would." Kessed shook her head, her thoughts drifting to Jasper and their mutual love of food.

Damn, she missed him.

"Kess, I'm fine. Don't be sad." Sterling misread her expression, but she didn't correct him.

"I know, but you're not as bulletproof as I thought."

"Kinda freaky, huh?"

"Yeah. Actually, it is. But I'm not going to give you a tongue-lashing, I'm saving the honors for Laken. And dude, your ass is going to get chewed… just saying. You know, after she hugs you and dotes on you and tries to fatten you up."

Sterling shook his head, a wry grin teasing his lips. "Yeah, she gave me phase one of *the talk* this morning. She was just getting warmed up too, I think Cyler saved my ass."

"Probably." Kessed took a seat on his hospital bed, placing her hand over his forearm on top of the Semper fi tattoo. "I'm glad you're okay, Sterling. You gave us all a heart attack."

"Sorry about that. Wasn't exactly planning on getting hurt…" He trailed off, arching a brow.

Kessed paused then asked the deeper questions. "So, your leg… what's the deal?"

The mischievous light in Sterling's eyes faded. His smile was forced as he shrugged. "It will be fine."

"Any other details that you can add to that?" Kessed asked, pulling her hand back as she regarded him.

Sterling sighed, rubbing his hand down his face. "About twenty percent of the calf muscle was destroyed. It doesn't sound like a huge amount, but it's enough that it will take me a while to get up to snuff, if you know what I mean."

Kessed nodded. "Well, at least you'll have a pretty awesome scar. Chicks dig scars," she added soberly.

Sterling started to laugh, his grin widening as his eyes relaxed into an amused expression. His white smile was powerful against his tan skin. Even in the watered-down hospital lighting, he was beautiful to watch.

"Thanks. At least there's a silver lining. Leave it to you to find it."

Kessed grinned, thankful she was able to at least make him smile for a moment. As she studied him, she felt a strange twinge, but rather than evaluate the origin, she simply stood from the bed and walked to the chair where her purse rested. "So, one more night, and we're busting you out of here."

"Praise God." Sterling groaned. "Seriously, I'm going stir-crazy."

Kessed arched a brow. "You? Never."

"Whatever. If you were stuck in here, you'd be climbing the walls. I know how you work, Kess. You'd be just as bad as me. Now, enough about me. Tell me about what's going on with you. I need some distraction, and your life is usually full of drama, so..." He waved a hand, waiting.

"My life is never filled with drama." Kessed replied with heavy sarcasm. "And I want to point out that this is coming from the guy in the hospital bed because he just played Captain America."

Sterling just folded his hands and waited.

"Gah, you're impossible."

He smiled sweetly.

"And annoying," she grumbled.

He grinned wide enough to show off his white teeth and deep smile lines along his lips.

"Fine! I'm—"

Her phone buzzed loudly from the chair and then buzzed again, signaling that it was a call rather than a text. She reached in and pulled it out then slid across to answer Laken's call.

"Yeah?"

She listened as her friend told her about an earlier flight they had caught. "We'll be in by seven thirty a.m. and should be there no later than nine. The nurse made it sound like they're already prepping the discharge papers, so we'll head out shortly after."

"Sounds great. I think Captain America is ready to get out of here."

"Are you really going to call me that?" Sterling asked, his tone irritated.

"Yes," Kessed answered.

"I second!" Laken shouted from the phone, and Kessed pulled it from her ear, grimacing.

"Thanks... I'm deaf."

"I wanted him to hear," Laken replied.

Kessed glanced at Sterling. "If he didn't, I'll be sure to pass it along."

"China heard you, sis!" Sterling called from the bed.

"He got the memo," Kessed added.

"Good. Are you staying there, or are you getting a hotel roo—" Laken asked, and the airport speaker sounded as she finished, drowning out her last word.

Kessed waited till the noise ended. "Not sure. I'll text you when I know."

"We're going to grab some coffee, and I'll text you when we're in the air."

"Yay, nothing like early-morning texts."

"You love them."

"Go," Kessed answered, a grin forming on her lips.

"Bye!" Laken ended the call.

"So, they are getting in earlier?" Sterling asked.

Kessed lowered her phone and started to scroll through her texts.

"Yeah," she mumbled distractedly as she read through Laken's few messages and then one from Jasper sent over an hour ago.

> *Thanks for letting me know you're there safe. Steers are good. Margaret got another sugar cube, and the ranch house is all set. See you soon but not nearly soon enough.*

Kessed bit her lip, her chest burning with a warm glow as she slipped her phone back in her purse.

"Anything else I need to know?" Sterling asked, his eyes slowly closing as he leaned back on the pillow.

"Tired?"

"Too damn tired for doing jack-shit all day."

"Your body is healing. That counts for something." Kessed picked up her purse and walked to his bed. "I think I'm going to get a hotel room. That way, you can sleep without my snoring." She winked as he opened his eyes slowly.

"Good plan." He nodded, closing his eyes once more.

"I'll see you in the morning."

"Yay." He lifted his hand in a little fist-pump.

Kessed smacked his hand. "See you soon."

She was almost to the door when Sterling called her name.

Turning, she waited.

"Kess, thank you. I know you dropped everything to get here and check on my sorry ass. It was really nice to see a familiar face."

His steel-gray eyes met hers, sending a fluttering to her belly. Silently, she nodded then all but ran down the hall.

*Damn.*

Her reaction shamed her, yet at the same time it was Sterling! It was utterly involuntary to react to his smile, his gaze... everything about him. Yet her heart whispered the truth that followed her long into the night.

*How do I move on to the future when my heart is stuck in the past?*

She didn't know.

And honestly, she was scared as hell to find out.

Thankfully she fell asleep around one a.m. in her small hotel room on the base. Her alarm chirped at six, but she awoke far too alert to have slept hard. Her thoughts lingered on Jasper as she changed into her other set of clothing and twisted her hair up into a bun.

Picking up her phone, she sent off a quick text.

*How's Rake?*

Her grin reflected in the phone's glossy screen as a tiny bubble immediately appeared.

*Living up to his name. He bit me yesterday. Sorry cuss. Of course, I was giving him a vaccination...*

Kessed giggled at the mental image his text created.

*Serves you right. Shots suck.*

The bubble appeared then disappeared. Her face squeezed into a slight frown just before her phone screen lit up.

"Hey," she answered, anticipating his deep baritone.

"Hey yourself. How are you, sunshine?" Jasper's voice was soothing, secure, and everything she needed after a night of confusion. Life always made more sense during the day.

"Better now."

"Listen to you, trying to sweeten me up. Seriously though, are you doing all right? How's Sterling?" Jasper asked, his tone sobering.

Kessed shrugged as she tossed her dirty clothes into her suitcase. "Annoying, like a caged tiger and ready to bust out of the hospital on his own in a wheelchair."

Jasper's deep rumble of a laugh echoed on the phone, warming her from the inside out. "Sounds about right. Poor guy probably has been seeing those four walls for longer than anyone could handle."

"Pretty much. Laken and Cyler got an earlier flight, so we'll all actually be at the ranch by midafternoon," Kessed added. "I didn't get the rundown from the nurse yesterday. Pretty sure they wouldn't release any medical information to me anyway, but it will be nice to know what kind of a road he has ahead." Kessed sighed, wondering how Sterling was going to adjust.

It was going to be hell.

"Yeah, they're pretty tight-lipped about disclosing information. It's a good thing though. Protects people in the long run. But I can understand that you'd be anxious to find out." Jasper's voice faded slightly, then he shouted something at Harper.

Kessed's brow furrowed. "How is she?"

You could almost hear a shrug on Jasper's side. "She's still processing. Crazy woman made me dig a hole the size of China with our dilapidated tractor, just to bury the damn horse," Jasper mumbled softly, probably so that Harper wouldn't overhear.

Giggling, Kessed spoke through her amusement. "You damn well should have buried that horse on your property. It was only right."

"You're worse than she is." Jasper let out an amused chuckle. "Well, not quite, but you're still right. As much as it was a pain in the ass to do, it was good for Harper to have that closure."

"Closure is important."

"Over a horse." Jasper sighed.

Kessed shook her head. "All this coming from a vet..." she taunted.

"You're on fire this morning. Sleep well?"

Kessed sobered then zipped up her suitcase with a pinched brow. "No, not really."

Jasper took a deep breath, the sound speaking louder than his words.

Curiosity.

Confusion.

Because from the start, she knew he'd always known her heart belonged to Sterling.

But that was before, and damn it all, they needed to have a serious conversation when she finally got home.

But it wasn't the time.

Not now.

And Jasper must have sensed the same, because he simply changed the subject. "So, when do I get to see you next?"

Kessed relaxed. "Probably this afternoon, if you're lucky."

"I'm a pretty lucky guy, just sayin'," Jasper answered.

"Then may the odds be ever in your favor," Kessed quoted, earning a laugh from Jasper.

"Thanks, I think." He sighed. "Well, get your cute ass in gear. Hurry home and drive safe. Do me a favor?"

Kessed nodded then answered, "Yeah?"

"Call me when you leave. Just so I know. I don't want to be one of those demanding and controlling asses, but well... even the best of us have our moments."

"Fine. I was going to anyway."

"Good girl."

"Not a pet."

"You're much higher maintenance."

"Hey!" Kessed placed her hand on her hip and glared at the bed.

Jasper's deep laugh echoed across the line. "I'm just messing with you. Take care, sunshine."

"Okay. See you." Kessed waited till he echoed the goodbye then ended the call. As she tossed her phone on the bed, her lingering smile faded as she glanced at the clock. Laken and Cyler would be landing soon, and she needed to head to the hospital to check on Sterling.

It was going to be a long, hard day.

She only hoped she kept her heart in line.

Jasper deserved better than a confused heart.

But she was afraid she didn't have anything else to offer. At least not yet. Damn, life was complicated.

# CHAPTER FIFTEEN

Jasper stared at his phone as it sat on the old dinner table. His brow furrowed and his lips twisted. He couldn't get a solid read on Kessed, but something felt off. He hoped to hell that it wasn't what he thought; yet deep in his gut, he knew the truth.

Conflicted.

If there was one word that could summarize Kessed's tone, that was it. And it was the last thing he wanted her to feel. He was all in, and it sucked to know that she wasn't there.

At least not yet.

And damn it all, it was even worse waiting to find out if she'd ever get there. But what other choice did he have? None, not unless he wanted to slink away and not take the risk. He'd damn well take that risk every day... but that didn't make it easy.

Or pleasant.

"You're trying to move the phone with your mind?" Harper asked, bumping a hip on the table and startling him from his concentration.

"What? No." Jasper shook his head and grabbed his phone. He slipped it into his pocket.

"What's with the deep frown face?" Harper asked, not letting go of the topic.

"Nothing."

"Liar."

"Nothing that I want to discuss with you right now."

"Ah, there's the truth I know and love," she replied sarcastically. "Spill. You don't have any appointments for the next hour, and I'm good at listening."

Jasper sighed, studying his sister. Her slight frame was a stark contrast to the hugely stubborn and kind heart that lived within, and from experience, he knew that if he walked away without spilling his guts, she'd nag him to death till he did. "Fine."

"Good boy." Harper winked.

"Not helping," Jasper groaned.

"Wasn't trying to. Spill." His sister pulled out one of the ancient chairs; the sound of it scraping along the wooden floor filled the dining room.

Jasper grabbed a chair as well, only he straddled it backward, leaning against the high back. "It's Kessed."

"Figures. It's always a girl."

"You're a girl," Jasper pointed out dryly.

"Which is why I can unabashedly call myself an expert."

"Great." Jasper twisted his lips.

"So…?" Harper asked, leaning forward slightly.

Jasper hesitated, then the words flowed like that flash flood he and Kessed had waded through. He finished with the heart of the matter. "Sterling is the guy she's always been in love with, and I'm scared as hell she'll remember that, meaning she'll walk away from me." He shrugged then rested his chin on his hands as he leaned against the front of the chair. "Let your wisdom pour forth."

Harper twisted her lips, her expression thoughtful. "Honestly, there's nothing you can do. But it's good that she is at least going to find out."

"Not helpful." Jasper sighed.

"No, really. It's better for her to figure this out now, and this is a perfect opportunity. Plus, how do you even know that this Sterling guy likes her?"

"How could he not?" Jasper flipped the question. "Granted, the man's had his head up his ass for years concerning Kessed, but he's going to start reevaluating everything, and Lord knows, the first thing he's going to see is her."

Harper sighed. "You may have a point. But that was before you guys were together, right? I mean, she is…" Harper paused, narrowing her eyes. "You're like, in a relationship, right? You had that discussion…"

Jasper's gaze dropped to the floor. He'd meant to, but it never seemed like the right time. Something had always come up. "Not exactly… yet."

"Damn it. Jasper!"

"I know!" he answered. "But it's a little late now. Besides, I think it's safe to say that even if we didn't officially communicate it, there's something there."

"Men." Harper groaned. "So, it's not the ideal situation, but it could be worse."

"Sure. The woman I love is playing nurse to the wounded warrior that she's been in love with for years. Yup. Nothing could go wrong in that scenario." Jasper closed his eyes and shook his head.

"Give her some credit. You just might be surprised. And until then, you need to let her figure this out. You don't want to pressure her and then learn later that she never really gave you her heart. But honestly, Jas, I don't think you have anything to worry about. Have a little faith in her."

Jasper took a deep breath and released it slowly. "I'm trying."

"Love is a bit irrational, huh?" his sister asked with a lopsided grin.

"Irrational as hell," he conceded.

Harper gave a small laugh then stood and walked over to her brother. She placed a warm hand on his shoulder, and Jasper relaxed at the contact. "One day at a time. Don't assume anything till you hear it from her. Okay? Many men have made themselves jackasses by jumping to conclusions. Don't be one of them. Good talk." His sister smacked his shoulder once then walked away, the sound of her cowboy boots tapping against the floor as she walked to the door. "I'll be out with Rake if you need me."

Jasper grinned at the mention of Rake's name—the damn horse. The chair groaned as he leaned back then stood, swinging his long leg over the seat as he twisted the chair back to front facing so he could tuck it neatly under the table. As much as he hated to admit it, Harper was right.

He was jumping to conclusions, making assumptions, and as a result, acting like an ass. Kessed deserved more than his suspicions. It was difficult as hell to do that, not just say he was going to do it. But actions spoke louder than words.

Odd how he'd always been the one to act rather than speak.

And he was flipping that coin.

His phone buzzed, and he welcomed the distraction. A farmer had texted, needing assistance with AI, artificial insemination, for his heifer herd. With a deep sigh, Jasper pulled his truck keys from his pocket and made the drive to Thorp to help out Jason with his Holsteins.

From that point on, each appointment bled into the other, causing the day to progress quickly. But it didn't stop him from glancing at his phone as he left one appointment to get to the next and wondering if Kessed had left for home yet, or if she had texted.

By four in the afternoon, his phone battery was dying, and he still hadn't heard from Kessed. By four fifteen, his cell shut itself off as he was heading to his last appointment, just down the road from the Elk

Heights Ranch. As he finished up with the vaccinations for the piglets, he tossed his worthless communication device into the passenger seat. After a moment of debating, he pulled out onto the highway and then took the ranch's drive. If Kessed, along with everyone else, hadn't arrived yet, he needed to check on Margaret and the cattle. It was the neighborly thing to do, but it would also satisfy his curiosity in wondering if they had made it back from Seattle. As he drove up to the house, no cars were parked in the drive, signaling that they still hadn't made it home. Jasper pulled into his usual place and killed the engine.

The crickets chirped in the shadows of the slowly setting sun as the dust settled from his truck. As he opened the barn door, Margaret nickered a welcome, causing him to grin. "Hey, ol' girl. You hungry?" he asked, petting her soft nose.

She huffed impatiently against his hand, earning a chuckle from Jasper. He walked around the stall and flaked off a portion of Timothy hay then tossed it into the stall to a very interested mare. She took a large mouthful and raised her neck, making eye contact as if conveying her gratitude.

"You're welcome, sweetheart. I know that girls gotta eat." He patted her shoulder as her head lowered to take another bite. His thoughts drifted back to Kessed as he heard the sound of tires crunching on the gravel outside. With one more pat to Margaret's shoulder, he strode to the barn's exit. After sliding the door shut, he walked out to the drive. Sure enough, the familiar blue sedan was parked beside his truck.

A smiling Kessed met his gaze as she slid from the driver's seat.

"Hey there." He grinned in welcome.

"Hey yourself." She shrugged, her own smile widening.

Jasper's shoulders relaxed; his lungs took in a full, deep breath as she met him halfway and wrapped her arms around him then pulled him into a big hug.

"Miss me?" he asked, keeping his tone light when the question felt heavy.

"A little," Kessed flirted, reaching up and kissing him on the cheek.

He'd be lying if he said he wasn't disappointed that the kiss wasn't of the more intimate variety, but he'd take what he could get.

And having her in his arms went a long way to soothe his concerned heart.

"I tried to call, but it went to voicemail." Kessed stepped back out of the hug.

"Yeah, my phone died, and I left my charger at the house." Jasper shrugged. "Where's everyone else?"

Kessed started back to her car. "They will be here in about thirty minutes. I left early. The doctor didn't want to release Sterling till he'd gone through some therapy. They took some time to teach Cyler and Laken the exercises as well, so they can help him out. I headed back, so I could check on things and clear out the guest room for Sterling. Basically, nothing that he can trip over on the way to the bathroom."

Jasper nodded, following her. "Need help?"

Kessed shrugged. "Honestly, I think I'm good, but if you know how to throw together some spaghetti or something else quick, that would be great. My cooking skills suck."

"Really? Is that the reason you have a soft spot in your heart for fast food? It just might be a deal-breaker for me," Jasper teased.

"I make up for it in different ways." She winked, his body responding to her implication with enthusiasm.

"Did I say deal-breaker? I meant deal-sealer," Jasper added, grinning.

"Yeah, yeah. Whatever." Kessed lifted her suitcase from the back of the car, and Jasper took it from her hands.

"I'm capable of making spaghetti as long as the right stuff is in the pantry. You go ahead and remove all the hazards from the poor guy's room." Jasper waited for her to unlock the house.

"Deal."

He glanced to the suitcase then frowned. "Wait, why are you bringing this?" Wasn't she going back to her apartment?

"Laken asked me to stay a few days longer, just till they get everything organized. She's a nurse, for pity's sake, but she's kinda wound tight since the patient is her brother. Cyler has to head back to his construction company tomorrow, so he's not going to be much help during the day. I don't work till Thursday, so I offered."

Jasper set the small suitcase down in the living room, forcing himself not to frown. "That was really kind of you."

"Thanks. Sterling can be a pain in the ass, and I don't see this sweetening up his disposition."

"Probably not." Jasper grinned, relaxing slightly. "I'll leave this here and start everything in the kitchen. If you need help, give me a shout."

"We've got this." Kessed activated her biceps, winking.

"You should really flex when you're trying to show off," Jasper called over his shoulder as he walked to the kitchen.

"Ass."

Jasper chuckled the rest of the way to the kitchen then focused on the task at hand. There wasn't much in the pantry but a few cans of tomato sauce and two boxes of angel-hair pasta. It wasn't going to be gourmet, but it would have to do. In short work, he had the noodles boiling and another pot holding the tomato sauce as he tossed in some Italian seasoning and salt.

"Smells good." Kessed's voice came from the doorway.

Jasper gave her quick grin. "Not just a pretty face, you know."

"Who said you had a pretty face?" Kessed teased back.

"Ouch."

Kessed's giggle called to him, made his body burn. He wanted nothing more than to back her against the kitchen wall and press into her, kissing away every shred of doubt in her heart, branding her with his body.

He met her gaze, her deep brown eyes sobering as he stepped toward her, needing her to be closer, then the squeal of the front door opening interrupted his progress.

"We're here!" Cyler called out.

Jasper closed his eyes, his body demanding he ignore his old friend. But a moment later, he heard Laken's voice and the sound of wheels tracking over hardwood floors.

"Kessed?" Laken called.

Kessed's eyes were apologetic as she took a deep breath and broke their gaze. "In here!"

"Jasper?" Cyler called out a moment before walking into the kitchen. "Hey! You've been such a lifesaver." Cyler pulled Jasper into a one-arm hug as he thumped him on the back, making a hollow sound as Jasper returned the gesture.

"Nothing to it," Jasper replied, releasing his friend as a genuine smile lifted his lips.

Cyler's blue eyes were sincere; the hard edge that had always made his gaze harsh was completely gone, and Jasper was thankful to see his friend at peace. It had been a long, hard road with his father, Jack. But that was water under the bridge, thankfully.

"I doubt it was nothing," Laken replied, wheeling Sterling into the kitchen.

Jasper's attention focused on the man, the possible rival for Kessed's heart. First, he noticed the way Sterling's smile didn't reach his eyes. It was forced, but who could blame him? Rather than feeling jealousy and tension, Jasper immediately empathized with the guy. He'd seen Harper put on a brave face far too many times to not recognize it in someone else, even if that person was putting a lot of effort into making it believable.

Sterling's gaze met his, something almost imperceptible passing between them before he extended his hand.

Jasper reached down to grasp it. "Nice to see you again." He gave Sterling's hand a firm shake. The man might be in a wheelchair, but his powerful handshake said he was anything but weak.

"I smell food," Laken commented, breaking through Jasper's observation of Sterling.

"Yeah, Kessed put me to work. I'm not promising much, but at least it will be better than nothing."

"She's good at being bossy," Laken commented, casting an amused grin to Kessed, who simply tilted her head and arched a brow.

"You're one to talk," Sterling added.

"Nothing wrong with his mouth," Laken teased.

Jasper smiled in response to the way Laken and her brother acted so similar to the way he interacted with his own sister. Sibling interaction was universal, as far as he knew. He walked to the stove and lifted the pasta spoon and checked the noodles. They were a little overdone, but there wasn't anything he could do to change that, so he turned off the heat and glanced to the adjacent sink. "Comin' through." He spoke before hauling the big pot over to the sink and sliding the lid just off-center enough to drain the water. The steam threatened to scald his forearm, so he adjusted his grip to remove the last of the water.

"Kess, can you grab the plates?" he called over his shoulder as he set the pot back on the stove.

"Yup."

"That's my line."

He caught her grin from the corner of his eye as he turned off the heat to the sauce. "Come and get it while it's hot."

Kessed set the plates beside the stove and backed up.

Jasper touched the edge of her elbow, lowering his head to speak in her ear. "Did you actually just move away from food?"

She tilted her head slightly, giving him a wry grin. "Don't expect it to happen often. I just figure that since it's their house…"

"Ah, manners. That's why I didn't recognize it."

"Hey!" Kessed punched him in the arm, and he ducked just a little, feigning pain.

"Knock it off, you two," Laken interrupted Jasper's flirting, and he watched as her gaze bounced from him to Kessed and then back, her grin widening.

"It's her fault." Jasper shrugged, crossing his arms.

"What?" Kessed smacked his shoulder again.

"Abuse." He shook his head slowly, as if feeling sorry for her.

Kessed sputtered, earning a muffled giggle from Laken.

"I knew I liked you," Laken replied, filling her plate with pasta and pouring on the sauce. "You cook, and you don't take her smartass sass. Well done."

Jasper bowed slightly, earning another glare from Kessed.

"She's right. You do need someone to put you in your place," Cyler commented as he filled his plate next.

"Who asked you?" Kessed asked.

"No one. My house. My rules."

Laken gave him a curious glance.

"Uh, I mean, our house, our rules."

"There ya go," Laken replied, grinning.

"Is there anyone on my side?" Kessed threw a hand in the air dramatically.

"Yeah, usually I go for the underdog, but in this case..." Sterling replied from the doorway, his face stretched into apologetic grin. "Sorry, sport. You're on your own."

"You know—"

"Shh, just walk away." Jasper tapped her nose and handed her a plate. Kessed snapped her teeth at his finger.

"Easy, killer." He grinned as he backed away. "Sterling, you hungry, man?"

"I've got him covered." Laken gave Jasper a quick smile as she handed her brother a plate and pushed his chair into the room.

"I can wheel myself, thank you. I'm only in this thing for a few more days," he grumbled, sighing as if itching to get up and run.

"I know you can, but let me do something. It makes me feel better. Shocking, I know... but deal with it," Laken said.

Jasper didn't miss how Sterling's gaze bounced between Kessed and himself.

Soon they were all gathered around the table, passing napkins as the noise level continued to rise.

Jasper leaned back, watching the interaction between Laken and Cyler, grinning to himself when Cyler's hand would reached below the table and Laken's face would flush bright scarlet. He'd averted his eyes and watched Kessed do the same, meeting his gaze with a knowing one of her own. Sterling's expression was the only one that wasn't open, but guarded, from pain or from trauma, Jasper couldn't begin to know.

"So you said you only had the wheelchair for a few more days?" Jasper engaged Sterling in conversation between bites of pasta.

"Yeah." Sterling shrugged, his beefy shoulders a firm reminder that the man was anything but frail. "The doc says it's easier for me to keep in line, not overdo it. Damn bone was exposed, so I'm on a freaking horse-dose of antibiotics, and they don't want me to reinjure myself." He shook his head and took another bite.

"It's good you're listening to the doctor."

"He doesn't have a choice," Laken chimed in.

Sterling gave her a patient grin. "You're going to be all sunshine and rainbows, aren't you?"

"As always."

Cyler choked on a bite.

"Not funny."

Cyler held up his hands in surrender. "Not intentional. I swear."

Kessed giggled behind her hand.

"Not helping," Jasper whispered under his breath, teasing her.

"Not usually the helpful one in this group."

"That's the truth," Sterling added, casting a wink to Kessed.

And Jasper felt his heart sink when Kessed blushed and averted her gaze. *Damn it.*

Sterling hadn't glanced away from Kessed but was watching her with what appeared to be more than passing interest.

"Jasper, can you show me what you guys did while we were gone? I want to make sure I'm up to speed on the repairs and anything else that needs work." Cyler's voice cut into his attention on Sterling.

He cleared his throat. It would be a good idea to get some fresh air, distance himself from wanting to be an ass and jumping to conclusions. "I'm about done. You ready?"

Cyler nodded. He stood and walked to the sink. He quickly rinsed his plate and set it in the dishwasher. He waited while Jasper did the same and then followed him to the door.

"Men who do dishes… nothing sexier!" Laken called out as they walked into the hall.

"That's not what you said last night!" Cyler yelled back, and Jasper could only imagine the way Laken's face blushed.

They walked into the evening air, and the tension in Jasper's shoulders released like a weight had been lifted. "How are you doing?" he asked Cyler, keeping the focus off himself.

"Better now. It was freaking awesome… till we got the news about Sterling. But he's here and on the mend, so I'm sure Laken will finally relax."

"I imagine she was wound pretty tight."

"Yeah, to say the least," Cyler answered. "So, what did you all do?"

Jasper gave him the rundown, pointing out the several directions they had gone with the fence repairs. The steers lowed in the distance, kicking up dust as they migrated to the creek for a drink.

"Sounds like you guys were busy. I knew there was a laundry list of things that needed to be done, but you went above and beyond. Thanks, man. I appreciate it." Cyler held out his hand, and Jasper shook it.

"On another topic… I didn't miss the little spark between you and Kessed. Is something going on?" Cyler asked, grinning as they strode to the barn.

Jasper rubbed the back of his neck. This was going to be difficult to navigate. After all, Sterling was Cyler's brother-in-law.

"Nothing's official." *Damn it all.* "But yeah, I think I'm wearing her down," he added noncommittedly.

"Hmm, I think you're being a little conservative on that assessment," Cyler replied. "Is she still hung up on Sterling?"

*Don't hold back any punches,* Jasper thought. "I don't know." He paused, not sure if he could continue.

"But…" Cyler encouraged as he slid the barn door open.

"But I sure as hell hope she isn't," Jasper answered honestly. "The woman's got me all tied up in knots." He shook his head, following his friend into the barn.

"Hey, girl. Miss me?" Cyler called to Margaret.

The mare stomped the ground impatiently till Cyler pulled out a sugar cube from his pocket and fed her.

"I missed you too." He turned to Jasper. "It will all get sorted out. Don't worry about it. I know that's easier said than done, but give her some time."

"That seems to be the common advice." Jasper kicked his boot into the dirt.

Cyler raised an eyebrow.

"I think Harper said that I needed to not be an ass and make assumptions. I'm translating that to patience."

"Ah, yeah. She always was a bright girl."

"Yeah, don't tell her that. It will go straight to her head," Jasper teased.

"Noted. How is she?" Cyler sobered, facing his friend.

"Healing." Jasper went into the tale about Lady, and now Rake, earning a chuckle when he explained the name of the colt. "Kessed appreciated the name, too."

Cyler headed out of the barn then turned to slide the door shut. "It's been a big week for all of us, it seems. Let the dust settle, and it will work out, Jasper." He laid a heavy hand on his friend's shoulder. "Head home. I'll hold down the fort here. Sound good?"

Jasper nodded, casting a glance to the house then back.

"I'll tell her you said goodbye, give her a chance to miss you a bit more." Cyler winked, and Jasper shook his head.

"Fine. This backfires... I'm kicking your ass."

"Deal." Cyler nodded once, walking to the house as Jasper walked to his truck.

After sliding into his pickup, he turned over the engine. His gaze wandered to the ranch house, watching the lights come on in several windows, and a deep longing settled over him.

Why did it feel like he was walking away from the very thing he wanted to walk toward?

But maybe Cyler was right. So, with a swift motion, he threw the truck into gear and drove away before he changed his mind.

But damn it all, a sense of foreboding followed him all the way home.

Time could only tell.

And time was the very thing he feared most.

# CHAPTER SIXTEEN

Kessed blinked awake, hearing the soft sound of the television from the family room. Fumbling, she checked her phone, blinking at the bright screen and squinting till she read the time.

Two o'clock.

*Who in their freaking mind is up at two in the morning?*

With a slight groan, she rose from her warm bed and padded out into the hall, the blue glow from the TV illuminating her path. As she rounded the corner, she saw Sterling leaning back in his wheelchair. His upper body was bare, showing off the several tattoos across his arms and chest, drawing her eye to the solid curve of his muscled abs, his tight chest, and arms that had a few bandages still attached. Even in her foggy state of mind, he was beautiful to behold, and a deep longing surged through her, reminding her of the reasons she'd wanted him for so long.

"Hey," she called out softly, distracting herself from the confusing emotions.

Sterling didn't even flinch but continued to flip through the channels. "I was wondering how long you'd just stand there and stare." He gave her a quick grin and turned back to the TV.

Kessed avoided the implication. "Can't sleep?"

"Nope. I'm all jacked up from the jetlag, meds, and everything else. Besides, what in the hell have I done to make myself tired? I've literally sat or laid down all day." He sighed heavily.

"You're healing. It takes energy," Kessed replied, crossing over to him and taking a seat on the arm of the couch.

"Thanks, Dr. Phil. Anything else?" Sterling asked then turned back to the TV.

"Nope. But if you're not really invested in channel surfing as a sport, I can always put on a movie," Kessed offered.

"Make yourself useful then." Sterling handed her the remote.

"I feel all sorts of special," she commented, waving it in the air. "I hold the controls."

"Don't let it go to your head." Sterling chuckled, his full lips widening to a grin that accentuated his lone dimple.

Kessed walked to the screen and pulled out a drawer with older movies. "I'll try. So, what will it be? *The Notebook? A Walk to Remember?* Oh! *Moulin Rouge!*"

"I hate you."

Kessed laughed quietly and pulled out *Ferris Bueller's Day Off.* "How about this one?" She held up the case.

"It'll do," Sterling commented.

Kessed quickly started the movie and took a seat on the couch beside Sterling's wheelchair.

A few minutes into the film, Sterling shifted, and Kessed glanced to him, watching as he frowned.

"What's up?" she asked.

"So... you and Jasper?" Sterling questioned.

Kessed swallowed. *How do I answer? I mean, it isn't as if they had made anything official, but it felt official....*

"If you have to pause when answering, then I'm thinking it's a no." Sterling grinned widely.

"It's not a no. It's a—"

"Kess, if it's not a quick yes, then it's a maybe, at most. And a *maybe* sure as hell isn't anything deep," Sterling added, glancing to the movie and chuckling at something on the screen.

Kessed sighed. "It's complicated."

"No, it shouldn't be." Sterling turned back to her. "Either way, I'm glad. It kinda freaked me out to see you with him. I thought there was a lot more going on." He shrugged.

Kessed opened her mouth, but Sterling interrupted.

"I'm not saying that there's nothing going on between you two, I'm just saying that nothing's set in stone, and"—he leaned forward and speared her with his gray gaze as the music from the movie played softly in the background—"I've pushed you away a long time, Kessed. And I think it's about time I pulled you closer." He shook his head and frowned slightly, taking a deep breath as his gaze lowered to his leg. A frown pinched his brow. "Shit like this"—he pointed to his leg—"makes you reevaluate life, and as much as I've loved being a marine, I don't have a lasting legacy aside from leaving half my calf muscle somewhere in the dirt back there." He sighed. "I want more than that, and... I want to explore what it would look like if you were part of it." He took a deep breath, watching her intently.

Kessed blinked, pulling together her jumbled thoughts and the millions of directions they pulled her heart.

"Don't say anything now. It's late, it's been a long day, and a longer week... at least for me. Just... think about it." Sterling reached out, trailed a warm finger down her cheek and then placed his hands back on the wheels. "I'm heading back to bed. See you in the morning." He whipped around and started rolling back toward his room. "Unless you want to join me?" he teased over his shoulder.

Kessed shook her head, the fog of confusion lifting as she arched a brow. "Yeah, no."

"My door's always open." He disappeared through his room's door.

Kessed turned back to the movie.

*What. In. The. Hell?*

Her heart kept flipping through the pages of her life, going between the pictures of Jasper and the pictures of Sterling, confusing her further. She pinched her nose and took a deep breath through her mouth. Rationally, she considered her situation. Who is to say that Sterling would even remember the conversation in the morning? Or that he wasn't on some killer pain meds clouding his mind? Why should she take his words at full weight and run? There was no reason! Maybe all this... whatever it was... wasn't what it seemed.

Sterling was in a vulnerable place; she needed to remember that.

And Jasper... she grinned just thinking his name. How could she even think about walking away from whatever it was that they had? Just thinking about it made her heart ache. But if that were the case, why hadn't she corrected Sterling?

So many questions.

Not enough answers.

And damn it all, the day had only begun.

Kessed groaned softly, leaning her head back on the couch. Not enough coffee in the world to deal with this.

Especially at 2:00.

Rather, 2:15.

With a deep sigh, she stood. After grabbing the remote, she turned off the TV and walked back to her bedroom. Her sheets were still slightly warm as she snuggled into the bed, but her body was anything but relaxed, and her mind was spinning.

What if Sterling had been thinking clearly? What if he'd actually meant what he'd just said? Would she be willing to end everything with Jasper on that risk? No. Of course not.

It wouldn't be wise. It wouldn't be fair.

But that didn't stop it from being tempting.

It was like looking at the two parts of her life and trying to figure out which was more important. Her past, and everything that it represented for her future? Or her present and the new hope it had given for what lay ahead? It was impossible to compare the two; they were both important.

Her mind continued to spin till beeping awoke her from the small amount of restless sleep she'd been able to snag. Groaning, she fumbled with her phone till she silenced the alarm and leaned back into her pillow, closing her eyes.

After a few moments of self-talk, trying to motivate herself to get up, she swung her legs over the bed and sighed. Soon she was dressed in her jean shorts and T-shirt, sporting her usual messy bun. The scent of coffee wafted through the hall as she headed to the bathroom and then beckoned her to the kitchen once she brushed her teeth.

The pot was half full and still steaming when she grabbed a mug. As she scanned the countertop, she found a note.

*Good morning beautiful.*
*I love you, and I'll miss you every moment of today.*
*Cyler.*

Kessed grinned wildly for her friend and the love she'd clearly found with her new husband.

She filled her mug with coffee and moved to the back door. Her red boots were on the mat where she last left them, and the sight of them brought a grin to her lips.

*Jasper.*

She slipped them on, once again appreciating the way they hugged her feet, and walked out into the morning air. The sunlight was streaming over the canyon, and the lawn was wet with the fresh dew, making the green sparkle. She took a long drink of her coffee and strode to the barn as the sound of the cattle lowing in the distance enveloped her. She slid the wood door open and called out to Margaret.

"Morning!" As she approached the mare's stall, she noticed that the horse had already been fed, probably by Cyler. "I guess you don't need me anymore." Kessed patted her neck.

Margaret huffed.

"But I'm sure you'd still appreciate your treat." Kessed walked to the tack room and took out a sugar cube, which Margaret happily accepted. "There. Now your day is all set."

The greedy horse sniffed her hand to check for more.

"Nope, eat your vegetables." Kessed nodded to the pile of hay, and Margaret sighed heavily but lowered her head.

"Good girl." Kessed gave a short laugh and walked back out into the yard, keeping the barn door open to let in some light and fresh air.

As she glanced to the house, she hesitated to head back to the kitchen. The events from the night before still hung heavily with her, and she wasn't sure if she was ready to face it all yet. She turned her attention to Rattlesnake Hills, the large expanse of Elk Heights Ridge, and the slopes below. It was beautiful country and she'd miss seeing the view each morning.

*Who knew I am a country girl at heart?*

"Hey." Laken's voice startled her, and Kessed jumped slightly before giving her friend a chagrined smile.

"Hey."

"Jumpy this morning." Laken closed the distance and took a sip of her own coffee.

"Just enjoying all this beauty." Kessed dodged the question.

"It's pretty amazing, huh? I fell in love with this place almost as fast as I fell in love with Cyler." She spoke softly.

"Did you see your note?" Kessed asked, arching a brow.

"Yup. I already miss him. Stupid working and having to make money," she grumbled good-naturedly.

"Yeah, life's hard," Kessed replied with heavy sarcasm.

"He'll be home by noon. He's just there for the morning."

"Nice," Kessed answered, turning her attention back to the view. "How are you holding up with the whole Sterling thing?"

Laken paused. "Better, now that I can actually be with him. I was going a little—a lot—crazy. I'm glad you're here though. Moral support and all."

Kessed gave a little fist-pump. "Moral support is my jam."

"And here I thought it was sarcasm?" Laken teased. "I'm going to start breakfast. I'm sure Sterling will be up soon. You hungry?"

"You cooking?" Kessed eyed her friend cautiously.

"Hey, Cyler has taught me a few things." Laken placed her hands on her hips.

"Did you learn them? There's a distinction between being taught and actually mastering the skill—"

"Are you hungry or not?" Laken asked, arching a brow as she tilted her head.

"Kinda," Kessed answered non-committedly as she followed her friend into the house.

"You can go and get something at McDonald's if I screw it up, okay? You're not going to starve."

"There's always a chance."

Laken blew out an exasperated breath. "Some things never change."

"Why improve on perfection?" Kessed questioned as they walked into the kitchen.

"Look who decided to show up?" Sterling asked from the table, his large hands wrapped around a coffee mug with the Seattle Space Needle pictured.

"We've been up for a long time. We just wanted to give you time to sleep," Laken spoke over her shoulder as she walked to the stove.

"She's cooking?" Sterling stage-whispered to Kessed.

Kessed nodded.

"You know, I'm not really—"

Laken pointed at him with a spatula. "Do not finish that sentence."

He closed his lips and shared a glance with Kessed.

"Look who's learned to listen? I'm so proud of you," Kessed teased, her nerves tight as she waited to see if Sterling remembered the early-morning conversation.

"I listen well. Sometimes so well that I actually hear those wheels turning. It's an effort, isn't it?" Sterling replied to Kessed's barb.

"Guys, knock it off." Laken glared as she cracked eggs into a bowl.

Sterling waved Kessed closer.

As she bent over, the scent of his soap mixed with shaving cream called to her. "You, me, McDonald's... thirty minutes."

Kessed swallowed hard. "We're in this together," she answered lightly, though her heart felt anything but.

"What are you two conspiring?" Laken asked without turning around as she placed the eggs in the skillet.

"Nothing," Sterling answered but winked at Kessed.

"Liar."

"Still not telling," Sterling replied.

"I'm not going to burn the eggs," Laken almost whined.

"We'll see. I need proof," Kessed teased her friend, relaxing slightly. She took a seat across from Sterling and avoided eye contact. Her phone buzzed in her pocket, and she slipped it out.
*Jasper.*

> *Morning.*

Kessed lips pulled into a smile. Leave it to him to let a simple word mean so much. He could have said it many other ways.
*I'm thinking of you.*
*You're on my mind.*
*I just wanted you to know.*
Yet he'd put it into one word. So like him.
Kessed replied.

> *Morning to you too.*

She set her phone on the table, watching as the little bubble popped up.

> *Full day today, but can I see you tomorrow?*

Kessed replied.

> *If you're lucky.*

She could almost hear his laugh.

> *I was born lucky.*

She sent off a quick text.

> *Then I guess I see you tomorrow. Go save some animal lives today.*

Jasper's reply was quick.

> *I need a theme song. You should work on that.*
> *See you soon, but not soon enough.*

Kessed smiled wide.

> *Look at you, being all sappy. I'm not complaining. And we'll see about the theme*

*song... I gotta go. Laken's cooking, and that translates as a fire hazard.*

Jasper replied with a fire emoji.

Pain in the ass.

"Now, if you're done grinning like an idiot, I have some pretty amazing eggs for you." Laken set the skillet down on the table on top of a hot pad.

"I'm impressed, but reserving judgment until I taste them," Kessed replied then glanced to Sterling, grinning, but her smile faded as she watched his expression.

A mix of calculation and curiosity filtered through his gray eyes. "Tell Jasper hi for me." He spoke with an almost challenging tone.

Kessed nodded once. "You bet."

*Did he watch me as I texted back and forth with Jasper?* Apparently, and why was he still watching her with that same strange intensity? Well, that certainly implied that he was fully aware of the conversation last night.

Well, life hadn't gotten any less complicated; that was for sure.

Kessed needed something to do, so she rose from the table, walked to the cabinet, and pulled down several plates. Next, she grabbed out a few forks from the drawer and set them all on the table.

"Salt?" Sterling asked, a wary grin on his face, and Kessed was relieved that the previous expression was no longer there.

"Sure thing."

"I already salted them." Laken spoke up, and Kessed paused, her eyes widening as she glanced to Sterling.

"Okay."

Laken served the eggs onto three plates and handed each over.

Sterling lifted his fork with a bite of scrambled eggs and watched as Kessed did the same, both waiting for the other one to take the first taste.

Laken sighed heavily and took a big bite. "It's fine." She spoke around the mouthful.

Kessed followed suit and was surprised when the eggs tasted like... eggs. "Cyler is magic. Seriously, he taught you how to cook. The impossible has been accomplished." Kessed took another bite, watching as Sterling finally took one as well.

"Look who decided to strap on a pair and be brave?" Kessed harassed.

"I've lived with her cooking longer than you. There's a deep fear," Sterling replied after he swallowed. "But, Laken, these are actually really good. Nice work."

"Seriously, it's eggs. They are hard to mess up."

"Yet you consistently have done that," Sterling retorted.

"Fine. But I didn't, so... there." Laken took another bite and winced. She lifted a hand and spit out a piece of shell then aimed a glare at her friend and brother. "It still counts. Shell or no shell."

"Still a solid win, sis." Sterling nodded, but Kessed noted that he chewed a little slower, as if testing the bite before swallowing.

She did the same.

"So, what's on the agenda today?" Kessed asked, pushing her plate away and picking up her coffee cup.

"I've got a full day." Sterling stretched his back and then leaned forward, spearing her with his gaze.

Kessed's brows pinched.

"Yup. You've got your antibiotics, and I'm helping you do your exercises for rehab, not to mention today we're going to get you up to walk a little bit." Laken punctuated her words with her fork.

"I'm moral support." Kessed lifted her hand, grinning.

"That's not exactly what I meant, but nice to know you're taking over my life, sis." Sterling groaned.

"Happy to." Laken winked.

"Actually, I was talking about my personal schedule." He arched a brow to Kessed. "How long are you staying here?"

Kessed shared a glance with Laken, her tension growing. "A few days...."

"Enough for a solid start. Good."

"Start for..." Laken asked, her gaze darting between her friend and brother.

"Enough to start what I should have done years ago...." He crossed his built arms as he'd proverbially thrown the gauntlet on the breakfast table.

Well, at least it answered one question.

He'd known what he was saying last night.

He meant it.

And now Laken was a witness.

"Sterling, I... I'm not sure that's a great idea," Kessed started, but he raised his hand.

"Kessed, I'm not blind. I'm not the only one playing for keeps... but you should be fully aware that I'm laying my cards on the table, and if this Jasper guy wants to play, he's going to have to break out the big guns—because I'm all in."

Kessed watched as he wheeled away from the table and rolled down the hall.

"Well, that was interesting," Laken whispered, and Kessed met her bewildered gaze.

"Yeah."

"So..." Laken glanced to the table then back to Kessed. "What do you think?"

Kessed dropped her head in her hands. "I thought I knew, and now..."

Laken's palm rested on Kessed's head. "One day at a time. You'll figure it out."

"You make it sound so easy," Kessed grumbled.

Laken gave a short laugh. "Love is never easy... but it always works itself out. You'll see."

Kessed sighed. "How do you choose between two great things?" Kessed asked, turning her head to make eye contact with her friend.

"You don't. Mark my words... life will choose for you. Just walk the path."

Kessed sighed.

That was easier said than done.

# CHAPTER SEVENTEEN

Kessed all but avoided Sterling for the rest of the morning. As the afternoon approached, she was running out of excuses to be outside, or in the kitchen, or anywhere else.

Laken found her in the laundry room, folding the still-warm bath towels. "Kess, I gotta run to town. Can you make sure that Sterling doesn't do anything stupid?"

Kessed tilted her head. "No guarantees."

"Don't I know it." Laken shrugged. "Cyler will be home in about an hour or so, but I'm the only one authorized to pick up Sterling's meds. Plus, I want to get a few odds and ends that will make his rehab a bit easier."

"It's who you know," Kessed asserted. "He's lucky his sister's a nurse. You've got some connections."

"Yup. Basically." Laken picked up a few towels that were folded.

"When do you go back to HCEW?" Kessed asked, knowing her friend was passionate about her work with hospice care.

Laken's face broke into a grin. "Next week. It's been fun to take a break, but I really miss it."

"I'm sure they miss you," Kessed replied.

"I'll just be happy to put my scrubs back on," Laken spoke gently.

Kessed regarded her friend. Kindness radiated from her from the top of her blond head to her tanned bare feet. It took a special person to help grieving families say goodbye to loved ones, but Laken was a natural and had more compassion than anyone Kessed had ever known. "Those families are lucky to have you."

"Ha, sure. I'm all but invisible, but that's the point. Focus on the patient, on the family..." She shrugged. "I'm taking these to Sterling's bathroom and then heading out. Good luck."

"Thanks," Kessed replied with light cynicism.

And a little more fear.

When she heard the front door close, Kessed took a deep breath and walked to Sterling's room.

"Hey." She leaned against the door jam, watching as he lifted his gaze from his phone and gave her a heart-melting smile.

"Hey yourself. Keeping me company?" he asked, using his muscled arms to lift himself into an upright position on the bed.

"Not really. I'm here to make sure you stay in line." Kessed grinned, feeling slightly more at ease.

"Tough job."

"You have no idea," Kessed teased back.

"Pull up a seat. Tell me what I've missed these past few months." He waited.

Kessed sat on the edge of the bed, on the furthest corner from him.

"I'm not going to bite." Sterling mock-glared.

"Pain meds do weird things to people." Kessed's tone was wary. "Not taking chances."

"Why are you so scared of me?" Sterling leaned forward, his gaze intense as he regarded her.

"I'm not scared of you," Kessed answered immediately, though she fought the instinct to inch away.

"Yes, you are." Sterling's sandy-colored brows furrowed over his expressive eyes. "Why?"

Kessed took a shallow breath, not sure how to even articulate. "It's not that I'm scared. It's that I don't... I don't know how to take this sudden change of heart. And honestly, I think you're looking at me because I'm safe, known. Not because I'm me," she answered then turned her attention to her hands as she folded them on her lap.

"Makes sense. I can follow that. It's not true, but I can at least see your perspective." He shrugged and leaned back. "So, what's going on in your life?"

Kessed frowned as she glanced up, curious about the sudden change in topic, yet welcoming it. "I'm still at Starbucks, but I'm not exactly moving up. If anything, I'm being lowered on the totem pole."

"That sucks."

"Pretty much. Aside from that, I've..." She paused, a smile raising her lips. "I've learned how to use a fence stretcher and how to wade through a flash flood."

"All good life skills, but not ones I would have pegged you to know." Sterling chuckled. "I'm assuming you learned from Jasper?"

Kessed's smile faltered at hearing Sterling say his name. "Yeah. He's a... good teacher." She found her smile once more.

"Tell me about him." Sterling's eyes narrowed slightly, but not in a suspicious way, seemingly only curious.

Kessed glanced to her hands once more. "He's a vet and has a sister named Harper. You need to meet her. You'd like her. He totally gets my love for all things food and doesn't give me judgment eyes when I order more than he does. He knows everything about a ranch, and it's weird—almost instinctive for him. Second nature. He doesn't even need to think about it, but just runs with it like it's all he's ever done. Which is probably the truth. He doesn't let people push him around, but he'd totally give you the shirt off his back." Kessed smiled, remembering how she'd driven away like a banshee when he'd worked without his shirt for the first time.

"Seems like a good guy." Sterling interrupted her memory.

"He is." Kessed met his gaze.

"But he's not me." Sterling lifted his lips into an uneven grin. "Now describe me, Kessed."

Kessed swallowed, feeling her eyes widen at his request. "Well..." She took a breath. "You're a pain in the ass. Stubborn, dedicated, and loyal to a fault. You have this need to save everyone around you, even at the cost of yourself. You phone your sister, even when it's almost impossible, and aren't afraid of anything. Fearless... to the point of stupidity," Kessed finished, shooting him a quick grin.

"I like to think of it as badass, not stupidity," Sterling corrected. "But it's nice to hear that I've got some redeeming qualities too."

"You do," Kessed answered honestly.

"Why don't you go and get me a deck of cards? We can play... unless you've learned chess since I've been deployed?" Sterling switched gears again.

Kessed shook her head. "Nope. Cards it is."

As she left, her mind reflected on everything she'd just categorized of the two men. Why would Sterling ask those questions? What was his reason? It was baffling and didn't clarify anything... for her.

As she walked back into his room, she tossed the Corona-labeled cards onto the bed. "What are we playing?"

"Hearts," Sterling answered immediately.

Kessed began shuffling, wondering if the game had a double meaning. But she was probably just reading into it.

"The loser has to play Truth or Dare," Sterling stated, and Kessed glanced to him.

"Is that so? Says who?" she challenged.

"Unless you're not brave enough..."

Kessed narrowed her eyes. "Fine. Be prepared to lose."

"Nah, when it comes to hearts, I always win." He shook his finger at her. *So maybe there is some symbolism to the game he picked.*

"Deal." Kessed handed him the deck and repositioned herself to face him as they played. It was a harder game to win with just two people, but as long as she upped her strategy, it was totally doable. As she arranged her cards by suit, she squinted her eyes as Sterling gestured to her.

"Ladies first."

Kessed led with a high diamond, and soon they were going back and forth till Sterling played the three of hearts.

"Breaking hearts?" Kessed asked, holding onto her last diamond before she'd have had to do the same thing.

"You bet, except for yours. I'll just keep that one for myself." He arched a brow and waited.

"Don't hold anything back," Kessed replied, trying to joke while the stronger emotion was discomfort. *Damn, Sterling can be a force when he wants to be, and it appears he is pulling out all the stops.*

"Not in my nature," Sterling retorted, waiting for Kessed to take her next turn.

In less than a few minutes, the game ended as Kessed tossed down her last card and did a little victory dance.

"Damn, I hate it when you do that," Sterling teased as he leaned back on the bed. "So, hit me. I pick truth."

Kessed's smile faded as she glanced away, trying to hide her response. "Hmm..." A hundred questions filtered through her mind, but she chose a different direction than what she suspected Sterling wanted. "What are you most afraid of?"

Sterling blinked then pursed his full lips. "Not running."

"Really?" Kessed asked, finding herself curious. "But the doctor said you'd make a full recovery. It would just take time—"

"He said I'd walk. And after time, I'd redevelop the muscles in my leg so that I could move better. He never said I'd run. I mean, I'm sure I'll be able to jog a bit, but that's totally different than knowing I could hike for several days, up hills and over the Cascade Mountains…" He lowered his gaze. "It's being trapped by your own body."

Kessed reached over and placed a hand on his bandaged leg. "You'll get there. I don't see you backing down from a challenge just because it's going to take work."

Sterling flashed her a smile. "You're right."

"Next?" Kessed dealt the cards once more.

Sterling won the hand quickly, a smug and satisfied grin on his face. "What's your choice? Truth or dare? I bet you'll pick truth. You're going to take the chicken-shit route," he tested.

Kessed tossed her cards on the bed. He was right. She didn't trust his choice of dare.

"C'mon, Kess, don't be a coward." He arched a brow.

"Fine. Dare." Kessed immediately regretted her rash decision as a victorious grin lit up his face.

The front door opened, and Kessed stood from the bed, happy to dodge whatever Sterling's dare was going to be, and stepped back toward the door. "I'd better say hi to Cyler. Laken wanted me to pass along a message."

"Run away, Kessed. That's fine… but you owe me a dare, and you're not going to dodge it forever," Sterling warned as she walked out into the hall.

Sterling was right. She was running away… but she wasn't ready to face what he was forcing her to face.

She needed time.

The one thing Sterling wasn't about to give her.

Cyler met her in the hall with a welcoming smile. "Hey. Laken home yet?"

Kessed shook her head. "Not yet, but she should be back soon." She cast a furtive glance behind her, even though she knew Sterling wasn't walking on his own yet.

"Well, thanks for being here. I'm going to go and check on the fences that you and Jasper fixed up and check off a few other things on the list. Can you let Laken know where I'm at?" Cyler asked as he set his keys on the side table beside the front door.

"Sure thing."

"I'll take Margaret out. It will be good for her." He gave Kessed a parting pat on the shoulder and walked toward Sterling's room.

Kessed turned but didn't follow.

"Hey, man. You holding up?" Cyler leaned against the frame.

"Life could be worse," Sterling answered.

"Good work staying positive. You'll need it when your sister starts rehabbing your ass." Cyler gave him a wry grin, and Kessed found herself smiling at the mental picture.

Laken would give him hell just to make sure he recovered completely.

"Believe me, I'm fully aware. But since I've lived with her torture longer than you, and I've survived so far, I'm pretty sure she won't kill me."

Cyler chuckled. "I'll be back later. Text me if you need me to come save you from my wife."

Kessed's lips tipped into a smile at the obviously enamored way Cyler had said *wife*. It was sweet, and she was thankful her friend was so adored. Laken truly had an amazing capacity for love, and it looked like she had a perfect match in her husband.

Cyler gave a quick wave and headed out the back door.

As it clicked shut, Sterling called out, "You can run, but you can't hide, Kess!"

"Hungry?" Kessed popped her head into the room, doing her best to distract him.

His eyes narrowed. "You're stalling."

"McDonald's… or whatever Laken comes up with." Kessed offered him the options. "I can call her to find out how close she is to being home, and then I can make a run for it."

"Damn. You win round one. I want a Big Mac, fries—and if you get me anything but orange soda, I'll hunt you down when I can finally move on my own."

"Sure thing." Kessed grinned, not even attempting to hide her thrill at victory.

"But you're just postponing the inevitable," Sterling mentioned as she turned to walk away.

"I'm not afraid of a little dare," Kessed lied through her teeth.

"Yes, you are. But I won't push you… this time."

She walked away, texting Laken to find out when she'd be home. The door opened, answering Kessed's question.

"I'm back!" Laken walked into the house carrying a few sacks and one box resting on her hip.

"Need help?" Kessed placed her phone in her back pocket and reached out to take the purchases from her friend.

"Thanks. I got the meds, a few random snacks that will cheer up Sterling, and a few stretching bands for later when he can move."

"Sounds good. I actually just texted you. I'm going to make a run to town—"

"To get lunch, right?" Laken interrupted.

"Yeah. You want anything?"

"Nope. I'll swipe a protein shake and then start to work on Sterling. And I already saw Cyler. He was walking Margaret out of the barn and filled me in."

"Sounds good. I'll see you in a bit." Kessed picked up her keys and slid past her friend. She walked outside and to her car, exhaling the tension.

As she drove to town, she tried to focus on anything but Sterling or Jasper. The whole ordeal was consuming too much of her world, but as much as she tried, she couldn't keep the issue from her mind.

As she placed her order in the drive-through, she smiled at the memory of doing the same thing with Jasper.

And it struck her. When she thought of Jasper, she always smiled, always relaxed. It was natural, normal. Whenever she thought of Sterling... as much as there was such a history attached to him... she felt the tension rise.

She collected her food and headed back to the ranch, wondering if she had known the answer to the question of Sterling and Jasper all along.

Because with Sterling, it was a fight, a battle to win.

With Jasper, it was like finding out she was the winner all along.

And for the first time in days, her chest wasn't tight.

And that alone was her answer.

# CHAPTER EIGHTEEN

Jasper peeled off his latex glove and tossed it into the dumpster just outside the barn. "Looks like you're all set." He offered his bare hand to James, the rancher who'd needed his heifer's pregnancy checked.

"Happy for the good news." James nodded, taking Jasper's hand and giving it a firm shake. His gray hair peeked out from his John Deere cap, and his jeans were almost as dirty as Jasper's.

"Come spring, you'll have quite a few new additions."

"The grandkids will love that. They always adore the babies." James gave a gentle chuckle. "I'll see you later." He gave a quick wave and sauntered away.

Jasper took a deep breath and pulled out his phone. The heifer was his last appointment, but he'd felt a buzzing alert when he'd just finished up. Sure enough, he had an emergency call to a farm down the street.

Damn, he wished he had an assistant to nail down some kind of scheduling. His thoughts settled on Kessed as he took several long strides to his pickup. *Would she be interested in the position? Should I offer it? Or should I wait?* Only a few of the millions of questions that kept centering on that woman. He shook his head and turned the truck around. As he drove down the dirt road, he tried not to think about how Kessed hadn't texted, called, or communicated at all that day. Of course, he'd told her he'd be busy, which he had been—but that didn't stop the worry from spinning through his mind.

Thankfully, the emergency call wasn't too difficult, and he was able to head home not long after treating a cow with milk fever. It was that time of year, and there were always a few per week that needed the potassium and glucose pumped into their system.

As he made his way toward his ranch house, he mentally checked off what he was going to do tomorrow. He didn't fight the grin as he thought of seeing Kessed, but he also remembered the other important appointment would be to check on a barrel-racing horse for Harper.

Because Lady had been with foal, Harper hadn't been able to compete for nearly a year, and while it had been necessary to take the break, he knew she missed the thrill. It was in her blood, and as she raced around the barrels, he'd seen her eyes match the smile on her face. But with Lady gone, it would be years before Rake could be a barrel horse, and Harper needed one to get back into the sport.

He'd followed a few leads and had several prospects lined up to check on tomorrow. Most were local, but a few were in the lower valley. Barrel-racing horses were unique, and the ultimate choice needed to be made by Harper, but he wanted to do a preliminary check on a few of the possibilities. As a rule, quarter horses were a healthy breed, but it never hurt to be thorough.

He purposefully had scheduled an early half day tomorrow for appointments so that he'd have the last half to check on the racing horses before seeing Kessed. Though less than twenty-four hours away before they were together again, it felt longer, and he couldn't help the thought that in those few hours, she would be with Sterling.

As he pulled up to his house, he saw Harper walking Rake around the arena. The little thing followed her like a puppy; it was damn cute.

"Hey!" Jasper called out as he exited his pickup.

Harper waved. Turning, she petted Rake on his little white star and led him back to the barn.

Jasper went inside and started scrounging around for something to eat for dinner. If he'd have been close to town, he'd have stopped and picked something up, but his last appointment had been closer to home than town.

"If you're hungry, I have some taco meat left over."

"Perfect." Jasper grabbed the glass bowl from the fridge and heated the food up.

"So how was your day?" Harper asked, taking a seat at the table.

"Busy."

"Here too. I think I'm going to put a halter on Rake tomorrow. He doesn't need one, doesn't leave my side, but I want him to be used to it."

"Sounds like a plan." Jasper removed the warm leftovers from the microwave and took a seat, taking the Tabasco sauce and pouring it over his plate.

"Easy there."

"The hotter the better." Jasper took a bite.

"Did you hear from Kessed?" Harper asked.

Jasper choked on his bite.

"I'm not sure if that's a good or bad response." His sister handed him a napkin.

Jasper cleared his throat and took a sip of water. "This morning. She's still at the ranch helping out Laken and Cyler with Sterling."

Harper tilted her chin. "You never told me exactly what happened with Sterling. What's his injury?"

Jasper swallowed another forkful. "His calf muscle was severely damaged, and he suffered a few injuries from shrapnel."

"Can he walk?" she inquired.

"Not yet."

"Will he? Is he in therapy?"

"What is this, Twenty Questions? Why the sudden interest?" Jasper regarded his sister as he bent over his plate.

Harper shrugged. "It's just that… remember Meghan? She was in that car accident where her leg was pinned. She had to do all this therapy to get her mobility back. But what helped her the most was horse therapy. I was just wondering if maybe that would help Sterling."

Jasper considered her words. "I'm not sure. But it's worth mentioning. I remember Meghan, yeah…. It's actually a similar kind of injury." He thought over the details. "I'll text Cyler."

"I can help. Meghan's trainer is still around, and I've been volunteering here and there."

Jasper regarded his sister. "That's generous of you. How did I not know you were involved in this? Where have I been?" he asked, arching a brow with a grin.

"Busy with some girl." Harper winked.

Jasper sobered, but forced his smile. "True. I'll let them know. Mind if I give Cyler your number?"

"Nope. Go for it. I'm going to work a little more with Rake." She stood from the table.

"See ya."

Jasper finished dinner and washed his dishes, considering his sister's insight. She had a solid point, and it just might help out Sterling. No matter how much he saw the guy as a rival for Kessed's heart, he didn't wish him any more pain.

He'd seen enough.

Without a second thought, he shot off a text to Cyler, explaining. Then flipped back to Kessed's name, sending off another text.

*Sweet dreams.*

It might only be eight o'clock, but he was bone-tired, and his schedule would start before daybreak tomorrow.

Without pausing to think about it, he put his phone on silent and went to bed. Tomorrow would be here soon enough, and in the meantime, there was nothing left to do but wait.

And waiting went a hell of a lot faster when he was asleep.

Sure enough, morning came quickly, and as his alarm went off, his screen lit up with missed texts. He was both thrilled and disappointed.

Thrilled... because they were from Kessed.

Disappointed... because he missed the chance to talk with her.

He read through them. Mostly it was just an update on her day, but he loved every word.

He debated on texting back but didn't want to risk waking her up. He'd wait till later.

Soon he was navigating in the dark down his driveway to his early-morning appointment. He wasn't sure if he was thankful that farmers and ranchers got up with the sun, or if that was a negative aspect of the job. After a moment, he decided that he hadn't drunk enough coffee to come to any conclusions.

He passed downtown Ellensburg and pulled into the Starbucks drive-through. Though he knew Kessed wasn't scheduled to work, he still had a pang of disappointment when he picked up his coffee from a stranger. As he pulled out onto the main road that led to Yakima River Canyon, he sipped his steaming brew and mentally prepared for the day.

Which proved to be a wise choice.

Absolutely nothing went as planned. Every appointment took twice as long, and he had to work through lunch just to make up enough time to check out one of the barrel-racing horses on time.

The first was a sorrel quarter horse. He was a ten-year-old gelding who had been used for barrel racing, but more recently for herding cattle. As Jasper pulled into the rundown ranch in Selah, he saw several red flags that said this wasn't the horse for Harper. As a vet, he noticed the odd things that said an animal hadn't been given good care, even if the person tried hard to make it look otherwise.

Moldy hay was piled up on the side of the barn, a fire hazard if he'd ever seen one. The building itself listed heavily to the side. The fences were twisted barbwire around decrepit wooden posts, but what gave him the final clue was how the horse stood.

It was clear he'd been recently shod, but improperly, as his hooves had been cut back too far, leaving him tender-footed. The poor animal kept shifting his weight, no doubt to try to alleviate the pain.

If that weren't enough, the contact who was supposed to be selling the horse wasn't even home. Jasper made a note of the address to alert a rescue agency. While the animal wasn't malnourished or abused, it was still wise that someone be aware that the horse wasn't being properly cared for.

As he pulled out of the dirt drive, he placed a quick call to the next appointment to confirm. He completed the call then tossed his phone to the passenger side and debated internally if he should send a quick text to Kessed. Even though he'd see her in a few hours, it was incredible how much he missed her.

*Her smile... the way she giggles... her sarcasm... and the soft curve of her hips when she walks away, usually after giving me some sassy remark.* He forced his attention back to the issue at hand and checked the address for the next horse.

Soon he was pulling into an old ranch close to Thorp. The ever-present wind had caused the trees to grow lopsided, looking as if they were always being blown to the east. A gray-haired woman walked from the weathered barn as he approached. A wide grin split her face. *This is already more promising.*

"Hey there." The woman extended her work-gloved hand as Jasper walked away from his pickup. With a firm grip, she shook his hand and then stepped back toward the barn. "You're here to meet Spartan, right?" she asked.

"Sure am," Jasper answered as his eyes adjusted to the lower light of the building.

A magnificent neck arched above a stall door, nickering loudly as the horse pawed the ground.

"Spartan's a beauty and, frankly, he knows it. But he can do anything you ask, as long as he's fully aware that you're in charge. I'm Stella, by the way."

Jasper watched as she unhooked the gate and attached a lead rope to the horse's halter. As soon as the corral opened, Spartan moved out into the barn, testing the amount of lead Stella would offer. His knee action was high, lifting his feet more than necessary—obviously showing off. He was sixteen hands of storm-cloud-gray muscle.

"Proud cut?" Jasper asked, noting the high arch of Spartan's neck and the way his legs flexed with each step.

"Yeah. He's got a bit of a story," Stella started, gently pulling in the rope so that Spartan had less room to prance.

The horse jerked his head then reluctantly obeyed, quieting fully when Stella began to stroke his shoulder.

"We actually bought him at the Roundup about five years ago. He was one of the wild ones in the herds from Satus. You know what I'm talking about?" she asked.

"Yeah. Up on the Yakima Indian Reservation."

"Exactly. Each year, they herd up some of the stallions, needing to control the population so the herds don't over-graze and then starve. He was about five when we got him. As close as we figure, he's Kiger Mustang and quarter horse."

Jasper whistled lowly. "That's a solid mix."

"You ain't a kiddin'," Stella replied. "We named him Spartan since he was hellbent to have his own way. But after working with him for about a year, he started to pull a few aces from up his sleeve." She chuckled, moving to stroke his neck.

"He can turn on a dime and is smarter than is good for him. He's voice-command trained but likes to pretend he doesn't know what you're saying. But if you can earn his trust, he'd bring you through brush fire."

Jasper nodded and slowly closed the distance, giving Spartan a chance to notice and accept his presence. The horse arched his neck, snorting as he approached. Jasper held out his hand, letting the animal get a good whiff of his scent before carefully stroking his nose.

Spartan pressed his head against Jasper and nudged him.

"He likes you," Stella replied, chuckling softly.

"He knows I like animals. They can always tell."

"Emotional thermometers." Stella nodded. "They can read people better than people can read books."

Jasper nodded his agreement then slowly walked around the horse. Spartan's legs were sturdy, and he had a few dapples of white on his hindquarters. He had a few white scars, probably from his days bacheloring it out on the open range. Stallions were notoriously hard on one another when competing for mating rights to the herd. He assumed Spartan had taken his share of beatings before he was rounded up.

"So, he's about ten years?" he asked, coming around to stand beside Stella.

Spartan kept an eye on him.

"Give or take. My assumption is that he's a little younger, but we're not quite sure. You're the vet." Stella handed the question back to him.

"I can check his teeth, but really, it's not necessary. He looks good, strong."

"You want to ride him?" Stella asked.

Jasper took a breath, considering it. "No. He would be for my sister, and even if he was perfect for me, it's more about what horse is perfect for her. But I'd like to bring her back tomorrow to check him out, if you're available."

"I'm here. Just give me a heads-up." Stella nodded then started to lead Spartan back into his stall.

"Thanks. I appreciate it." Jasper waited till she was finished and held out his hand. "Till tomorrow."

As he walked back to his truck, he pulled out his phone and gave a quick call to Harper.

"Sup." His sister answered on the third ring.

"What are you doing tomorrow?" Jasper asked, turning the key in the ignition.

"Why?" Harper asked suspiciously.

"I have a surprise for you, but I need you to actually leave Rake alone for a few hours. Think you can do that?"

Harper hesitated. "Potentially…. I ask again, why?"

"Always suspicious."

"Still waiting…"

"I'd think the term *surprise* was enough of a hint that I wasn't going to explain myself further."

Harper sighed heavily onto the receiver. "Fine. What time?"

"Evening."

"Can we go in the morning?" Harper asked, her tone hopeful.

"Nope."

"So, you're not telling me, and I have to wait all day. Yay."

"You'd think that you'd have a little more gratitude, brat," Jasper teased.

"How can I be grateful when I don't know what I'm grateful for? Hmm?" Harper countered.

"Such an ass."

"Takes one to know one."

"Go do whatever you were doing, and I'll see you tonight." Jasper sighed.

"Deal. Bye." Harper ended the call, and Jasper swiped to call Kessed.

It rang though to voicemail, and he left a quick message. He opened up his messaging app and sent off a quick text as well.

*Heading your direction. See you soon!*

It would be a good twenty-minute drive to Elk Heights Ranch, and with each minute that passed, where there was no text back...

No call...

His tension mounted.

Jasper knew it was stupid and juvenile... but that didn't make it feel any different.

Because fear was a dangerous thing. All it took was a chance, a *what-if* to spin into a million possibilities that all hurt, all undermined the good.

This had to end tonight. No more fear, no more what-ifs. Tonight, he was going to lay it all on the line, pride be damned.

Kessed deserved to be free, to love him... or to love Sterling.

And he was going to give her the wings she needed.

Even if he cut his own in the process.

# CHAPTER NINETEEN

Kessed lifted another pillow and tossed it on the floor of the living room. "Damn thing."

"That narrows it down." Sterling leaned against the doorframe of his room. His dark brows were pinched with the effort it took to stand, but that didn't take away from the magnitude of his success or the way his very presence commanded attention.

"You're up?" Kessed asked, blinking as she tried to ignore the way his gray Under Armour sweats slung low on his cut hips, highlighting the $V$ that was proving impossible to disregard. "Have something against wearing shirts?" she asked, forcing her eyes away.

"Nope, but they do kinda rub against the last bandage." He shrugged and started to walk slowly into the living room.

Kessed frowned, leaning forward. "Do you need help?" She took a step toward him.

"Nope. Just moving slow."

"I did see a gray hair or two, just acting your age," Laken replied as she walked out of Sterling's room, a wide grin on her face.

"Yeah, we share genetics, so that means you will be having those soon too, sis. In fact, I bet you already have started finding them, and that's why you're coloring your hair."

"I won't go gray. I'll just go platinum-blond," Laken retorted.

"Sure," Sterling patronized.

Kessed watched as Sterling started to walk around the living room in a wide circle.

"Go slowly. Give your leg time to adjust to the shifting in weight," Laken instructed, observing her brother closely.

"Yeah, yeah." Sterling frowned as he stepped over the small area rug.

"Kessed, can you babysit him for a little while? I promised Cyler I'd meet him for dinner. We won't be gone long, but he called a little while ago from work and said he had some news to celebrate. I'm kinda waiting to hear what it is." Laken grinned.

"That's why I'm here." Kessed returned her friend's smile.

"I know, but it's still polite to ask."

"I swear... you are the politest person I know, Laken." She glanced to Sterling. "What's your excuse?"

"Don't care," Sterling answered.

"At least you're honest," Kessed teased.

"One of my many redeeming qualities."

"Yeah... sure." Laken nodded. "I'll be back soon." She pointed to her brother. "Be good. Please."

Sterling lifted his hand in a two-finger salute. "Yes, ma'am."

Laken narrowed her eyes at him but shrugged and walked away. Her keys clinked softly as she pulled them from the wall, and soon she was out the door.

"So, what were you looking for?" Sterling asked as Kessed lifted another pillow from the couch.

"My damn phone." Kessed all but growled.

Sterling shrugged, placing his hands in his sweatpants pockets.

Kessed noted the way he shifted his weight, apparently to keep the bulk of it on his good leg.

"Does it hurt?"

He shook his head. "Not enough that I can't ignore it. Where was the last place you saw your cell?" he asked, directing the conversation away from himself.

"That's the problem. I thought it was in the kitchen, but it's clearly not there, and the only other place I can think is that it fell between the couch cushions or something random like that." She blew out a frustrated breath and tossed another cushion to the floor.

When she didn't find her phone, she picked up the discarded cushions and pillows and arranged them quickly back on the couch. "Where's your phone? Can you call me or something?"

"So, it's not on silent?" Sterling asked, shifting his weight again as he placed a hand on the back of a chair, supporting some of his mass.

"Damn," Kessed muttered. "It's on silent. Seriously."

Sterling tilted his head as his gaze zeroed in on her. "Are you afraid of what Jasper will think when you don't answer your phone? Or a text?"

Kessed glanced to the floor. "Yes and no. But mostly, it's just rude." She tried to dodge the line of questioning, not trusting where Sterling would take it.

Or how she'd handle it herself.

"So, he's not sure." Sterling wouldn't let go of the conversation.

Kessed walked around the couch, putting it between them, needing a buffer. "Not sure about what?" she asked, immediately regretting the question.

"Whether he has you or not. Did you…" Sterling winced slightly as he released the back of the chair and took a few tentative steps toward her. "Did you ever mention me? If so, he probably thought I had my head up my ass to not chase you down." He gave a humorless chuckle.

"Something like that," Kessed admitted, remembering the conversation that felt like a lifetime ago.

"So, you did talk about me." His expression changed into a confident grin.

Kessed glanced away, needing to keep her head clear, and it was so damn difficult with his cocky and sexy grin. But it was different; something had shifted, and while she was attracted to the grin, it didn't have that deeper effect that *moved* her. It was hard to explain yet tangible enough to feel.

Sterling persisted. "He was right. I've said as much before, but I get the feeling that there's this knife point, and you have to jump off one side or the other…." He started to walk around the couch, limping slightly, but Kessed could see the determined stride of a man on a mission.

Slowly, he reached for her hand, his warmth seeping through her fingers, and while one part of her fought against it, knowing it was the wrong hand, the wrong response, an older part of her resonated with the words he'd said, so she didn't pull away.

He was right. She was trying to walk a line that was impossible to navigate, and as much as she wished he wouldn't push the issue, someone needed to resolve it.

Leave it to Sterling to be the aggressive one.

"I have your history, Kess. I share it because a lot of it was mine too." His gray eyes sobered as he met her gaze. "And I was an ass."

Kessed couldn't help the giggle that had bubbled up. "Some things never change."

Sterling's answering chuckle made her grin widen. "I deserve that. And it's just one of the things I love about you. Yes. Love." He paused, waiting for the words to sink in. "You don't take my shit, and when I was too full of my own damn self, you didn't a write me off but were always there. And I don't want to lose that to some guy who recognized right away what I was too stupid to figure out until it was almost too late." Sterling took another step toward her, his bare toes only an inch away from hers as he reached up his other hand to grasp her waist. The scent of fresh soap and latex bandages clung to him, making a memory that instantly broke her heart.

As much as she wanted to say yes, to close the distance and kiss him like all the hundreds of times she'd dreamt of kissing him... it wasn't right.

Because while Sterling, the one man she'd always loved, was finally loving her back... her heart had found a home with someone else.

"Sterling." She whispered his name, feeling her brow furrow as she tried to formulate the words.

But he didn't give her a chance; rather, he closed the distance and met her lips.

Frozen, Kessed pulled back in surprise, only to hear the front door close.

Fear, shame, and confusion flowed over her like white water as she turned and met the familiar green gaze of Jasper.

His expression froze as he took a deep breath. "Laken accidently took your phone. She handed it to me as she came back to the ranch to drop off..." He spoke slowly.

"Thanks," Sterling answered for her, his voice shaking her from her frozen position.

Stepping from Sterling's arm at her waist, she watched as he quickly shifted his weight to balance himself on his good leg. His gaze flashed with pain, but not the kind that came from his injury.

The kind that came from a broken heart.

"Jasper, wait." Kessed glanced to him, taking a few steps toward the front door.

He took a step backward, dropping his chin, lowering his gaze to the hardwood floor. "It's on the table." He set her phone down and turned to the door.

Kessed twisted her lips. "Okay, cowboy, outside." She strode past him, opened the front door, and waited, pursing her lips. *Damn it all, this is going to be fixed and fixed right now.*

Jasper's eyes narrowed slightly, but he walked out the door. His shoulders had straightened, as if expecting a blow.

Kessed nodded toward the barn and waited for him to catch up then faced him, thinking through all the things she wanted to say.

His green eyes flashed with familiar fire that immediately resonated deep in her heart. "Kess, I've already laid it on the line for you. I'm not... I'm not the kind of man who can pretend something he doesn't feel. I don't have it in me. But what I need to know is if you're that kind of woman?

Because if this"—he pointed between the two of them —"isn't enough, then don't pretend it is. Don't string me along." He kicked the dirt with his boot. "I—"

"Hold up." He raised a hand, and she closed her lips, waiting.

"I want it to be enough," Jasper whispered then lifted his gaze, meeting hers. "I want it so damn much it hurts. And I don't know what the hell that was in there, but it looked like goodbye. I just wish I would have heard it, rather than seen it." He breathed out a long exhale.

"Are you done yet?" Kessed asked, arching a brow.

Jasper frowned slightly, clearly confused as he nodded once.

"Finally," Kessed replied a moment before grabbing his white T-shirt and pulling him close, catching him by surprise as she met his lips.

He immediately returned her kiss then backed off, as if remembering their conversation and still not sure as to the conclusion.

"Not you," she whispered against his lips.

His shoulders tensed as the words sank in.

"Goodbye… but not to you. Never to you."

Jasper's shoulders flexed under her hands as she reached up and pulled him closer.

He immediately grasped her hips and pressed her in tightly then lifted her from the ground as he met her lips, kiss for kiss.

"Why didn't you just say so?" he asked between pulling at her lower lip and nibbling at the corner of her mouth.

"My man of few words decided to overcommunicate." Kessed pulled away, grinning wildly as she saw the tension, fear, and indecision melt from Jasper's gaze.

"I'll stick to one-word answers from now on," he replied, splaying his hand across her back as he nuzzled her neck.

Kessed sighed happily. "Maybe not all the time."

Jasper chuckled then slowly set her down, his expression puzzled yet not concerned. "Would you mind setting the record straight, Kess? What exactly did happen in there?"

Kessed took a deep breath, knowing this was important, yet wishing she could simply leave it in the past.

But that was not how life worked.

The past had a direct effect on the present. Sterling wasn't an exception to the rule, but not in the way she would have ever guessed.

Rather than stealing her heart away from Jasper, he'd set her free to give it away fully.

THE COURAGE OF A COWBOY

And she told Jasper as much. "He wanted to know where my heart was, and rather than confuse me... which I'll admit totally happened at first... it just made the decision clearer. Because while Sterling had my attention, you stole my heart and ended up with both."

Jasper smiled, his full lips showing off his white teeth. "You made me work for it," he taunted.

"Don't think the work is done." She winked. "I fully expect to keep you on your toes when you're seventy-five and deaf. And I expect flowers every anniversary and red boots every few years."

"You expecting to keep me that long?" Jasper regarded her with something swirling in his green eyes that fascinated her, yet was unreadable.

"I'm not the kind of girl"—she paused, arching a brow—"who can say things she doesn't feel." She turned his words around.

"Touché." Jasper chuckled as she heard a car pull up in the drive and then another close behind.

"Laken and Cyler." Kessed nodded to the two vehicles as the dust settled. "They must have just picked up take-out."

"Since they are here, you want to come home with me? I have something for you." Jasper laced his fingers through hers.

Kessed glanced to the house then back to Jasper. "Wouldn't miss it, but I need five minutes."

Jasper twisted his mouth. "Sterling."

Kessed nodded. "He deserves to hear it from me, though I'm sure he already knows."

"You want me to come with you?" Jasper offered.

Kessed paused. "I think I need to do this on my own." She squeezed his hand.

"Then I'll be waiting out here. Give you some space." He reached out and kissed her forehead, lingering a moment before releasing her.

"Thanks." Kessed stepped from his nearness, immediately missing the close contact.

Laken and Cyler waved as she approached. Cyler broke off and headed in Jasper's direction while Laken walked toward her friend. "What's up?" Laken glanced between her and Jasper.

"The long and short is that... Sterling kissed me, Jasper saw it, and I just fixed everything but your brother's broken heart, and now I'm going to try and salvage that by letting him down easy." Kessed blew out a tense breath.

"I was only gone for a little while." Laken blinked, lifting a sack of Chinese take out, proving her point.

"Apparently, an hour was long enough," Kessed replied. "Can you give me a few minutes to talk with Sterling?"

"Sure. I'll join you in a little while." Laken squeezed her friend's arm. "Take it easy on him." She gave a sympathetic smile.

"As easy as I can." Kessed took a deep breath and walked to the house. "Sterling?" she asked as she opened the door.

"In here!" Sterling called from the living room.

As she walked down the hall and into the room, she didn't see him but heard his breathing.

"Uh, where?" Kessed glanced around the room, again.

A hand lifted from the couch, and Kessed walked closer, leaning over the back and meeting Sterling's resigned expression.

"Taking a nap?" she asked, moving around the couch and sitting on the arm.

"Band-Aid. Rip it off." Sterling sighed, waiting.

"It's not you. It's me." Kessed nodded sagely.

"Bullshit," Sterling answered, then a grin broke out on his face. "Seriously, that's all you've got?"

"It made you smile, didn't it?" Kessed asked, grinning.

"Damn it all." Sterling shook his head and slowly sat up. "At least it wasn't the *friends* talk."

Kessed nodded. "Hey, Sterling?"

He met her eyes.

"I really don't want to screw up our friendship by being more. Let's just stay friends."

"You're killin' me, Smalls." Sterling groaned, but his smile didn't fade. "I want to hate you right now, but I can't because you're you, and I kinda like your brand of pain-in-the-ass."

"Sweet nothings." Kessed sighed dramatically.

Sterling regarded her, biting his lower lip. "So, Jasper?" he asked after a moment.

"You'll like him." Kessed nodded.

"That doesn't make this easier," Sterling assured her.

"Nope. But it will be in the long run."

"Maybe."

"Trust me." She patted his leg gently. "Sterling?"

"What?" he asked, narrowing his eyes.

"Don't make this awkward."

Sterling chuckled, shaking his head. "You're certifiably crazy. But it's part of your charm." He took a deep breath. "Jasper, he knows that, right? Both that you're bat-shit crazy, but also one of a kind?"

Kessed glanced down, smiling widely as she even thought about his name. "Yeah, he does. It works for us." She glanced up to Sterling.

"Good. Then I guess I can be the bigger man and step aside. You gotta admit, I gave it a good shot, though."

Kessed stood from the couch. "More than you know. Now don't be a jerk to Laken. She's probably going to be all worried about your emotional stability."

"Being emotionally stable is overrated."

"Clearly," Kessed teased. "I'll see you soon."

"But maybe... not too soon. Give a guy some time to emotionally stabilize." Sterling gave her a brave smile, but she could see the disappointment deep within his eyes.

"I got it."

"Thanks, Kess." Sterling slowly lay back down on the couch. "You can tell my sister I'm distressed enough to need vanilla ice cream. It's the only thing that heals a broken heart." He closed his eyes.

"I'll pass along the message," she murmured and walked to the door. As she closed it softly behind her, her face split into a grin seeing Jasper and Laken across the drive.

"You ready?" she asked, tilting her head.

"Thirty more seconds, and I was going to come in and kidnap you." Jasper arched a brow, striding forward and giving her a quick, enthusiastic kiss.

"How's Sterling?" Laken asked.

Kessed turned to her, noting her friend's concerned expression. "He says that vanilla ice cream is the only thing that will mend his broken heart. Pretty sure you need to send Cyler to the store."

"He's fine, apparently." Laken shook her head, amused.

"He will be." Kessed returned her grin then tugged on Jasper's hand. "C'mon."

Jasper followed her willingly as they headed to his pickup. He opened the passenger side door for her and gave her a quick kiss before closing it.

As the engine rumbled to life, he grasped her hand.

Reminding her that home wasn't always a place.

Sometimes it was a person.

# CHAPTER TWENTY

"Do I finally get to meet Rake?" Kessed asked as Jasper pulled into the drive.

"He can wait." He grinned as he killed the engine. "I want you all to myself, and I'm pretty sure once you meet him, he'll have you wrapped around his little hoof."

Kessed shook her head, an amused grin on her beautiful face.

Jasper's relief in this whole situation was palpable. Once she had kissed him, he'd dared to hope. Leave it to her to blindside him just when he was sure he'd lost her for good.

That had been the longest three minutes of his life. As he clasped her hand and walked to the house, he inwardly winced at the memory of her in Sterling's arms, even though he now realized she'd been pulling away from the kiss rather than toward it.

He bit back a wave of jealousy.

It was one kiss that he wouldn't have of hers, and damn it all, he wanted to own every last one.

"You're quiet," Kessed noted as he opened the screen door to his home.

He gave her a small grin. "As opposed to my normal chatty self?" he teased.

"Valid point. Let me rephrase. You're thinking. What are you thinking about?" She gave him a sassy grin.

"You," he answered honestly. "And how glad I am that you're here... with me. I, uh..." Heat flooded his face at the realization. "I'm a bit more possessive than I realized."

"Ah." Kessed nodded. "Still working through it." She squeezed his hand.

"It kinda traumatized me to think I lost you," he answered honestly, laying his heart out there again.

Apparently, he couldn't stop if he wanted to.

"I'm sorry." Kessed glanced to his hands, twining her fingers through them softly as she lifted them to her lips.

"Nothing to apologize for." Jasper snaked his arm around her waist, pulling her in close, inhaling the sweet scent of her hair as he kissed her head.

"Am I interrupting?" Harper's voice broke through the moment, and Jasper felt a flare of irritation with his sister.

"Always." He softened his words with a grin.

"Just doing my job," she replied. "Good to see you, Kessed. He's been a wreck. Take it easy on his heart. He's not as young as he used to be." She gave a quick wink and walked to the door.

"Thanks, sis."

Harper turned around. "I got your back." She gave a quick salute. "Hey, did you talk to Cyler about therapy for Sterling?" she asked, pausing by the door.

"Therapy?" Kessed asked.

"Yeah, I had a few moments before we headed over, and he said that it sounded like a good idea. He's going to talk about it with Laken and then get in contact with you. Which reminds me..." Jasper fished out his phone and opened the messenger app. "I'm texting him your contact info. And I'll send you a text with his so you don't have a random number showing up."

"Safety first," Harper nodded sagely and a little bit mockingly.

"You can leave now." Jasper pointed toward the door.

"I'm gone." Harper lifted her hands in surrender. "I'll be in the barn all night with Rake. He sleeps better when I take the loft. So..." She eyed the two of them. "Yeah, I'll just go now." She ducked out the door but not before Jasper noted a pink tinge to her cheeks.

"Hey, you never answered my question. What therapy?" Kessed asked, bringing his attention back.

"Horse therapy. Basically, because of the nature of his injury, Sterling could benefit from the kind of movement that you perform when riding a horse. Harper had the idea, and I told Cyler. You get the picture."

"Oh. Well, that sounds promising, except for one thing."

"What?" Jasper asked, tilting his head, growing more and more distracted by the way Kessed's lips moved.

"Sterling hates horses," Kessed answered.

Jasper reached down and tasted her lips, unable to resist any longer. He pulled away only enough to answer. "Harper has a way of making everyone love horses. She'll be up to the challenge."

Kessed leaned in, finally reaching behind his neck and tugging him close for another searchingly sweet kiss. "I have a feeling the therapy sessions will be entertaining to watch, for more than one reason, just saying. Now, enough talking...."

Kessed met his lips once more, her tongue darting out to caress his lower lip, and every other thought Jasper had just flew away.

Impatient hands tugged at his shirt, lifting it from his filthy jeans. It was on his lips to protest, but her hand slid across his stomach, navigating the ridges of his abs and then tracing lower to his waistband. His hands squeezed her as he slid down to feel the shape of her, loving the way her warm body stepped into his, fitting perfectly, just as he remembered. Clothes or no clothes, they fit.

Gently, he pushed her back toward his room, only breaking the kiss long enough to sweep her into his arms to navigate the living room and hall with quick and impatient steps.

Kessed used the time to knead his shoulders with her palms, nipping at his ear with her teeth, sucking on his earlobe and driving him crazy with desperate need.

Jasper kicked his bedroom door closed, fleetingly thankful that Harper was staying in the barn loft.

As if emphasizing his point, Kessed gasped loudly as he grabbed her ass, flicking his tongue on her exposed neck as she arched slightly.

As soon as Jasper set her down on the floor, her hands were tugging on his jeans. He stepped out and kicked them into a corner, returning the favor and undressing Kessed from the waist up. His hands slid over her olive-toned stomach, his breath coming in short pants as he admired the way her breasts fit her lacy black bra. It was almost too much, yet he pressed on, melding into her, needing to feel her body without any space between them.

Yet at the same time, he wanted to go slow, to memorize the moment, to truly live in it. It was a sweet torture to have her hands trace down to his boxers then slide them over his arousal, caressing him along the way. He hissed in a breath, unable to think beyond the pleasure of the sweet demand of his body.

Her light giggle had him opening his eyes to give her a mock glare.

"Your turn," Jasper muttered then picked her up and tossed her onto his queen-size bed, earning a fake glower as she did a quick bounce before righting herself.

"Turnabout's fair play," Jasper murmured as he towered over her, kissing her lips, arching into her, and then pulling away, chuckling as she followed him with her body.

"Not yet," he whispered, reminding himself of the same thing.

Slowly, he kissed her neck, keeping his hips strategically above hers, enough to tease, not enough to satisfy. As he kissed down the delicate flesh of her neck, he inhaled the sweet fragrance of her skin, damn near worshiping her with his mouth as he trailed kisses lower till he felt the soft swell of her breast with his sensitive lips.

He reached under her back and reading his intent, she arched to give Jasper access. He tried to flip the hook of her bra, but failed. He kissed the delicate swell of her breast and nudged aside the distractingly sexy fabric with his nose, kissing farther down as he tried the unhooking motion again.

Failing miserably.

"Need help?" Kessed asked, her tone carrying a hint of laughter.

"Yes." Jasper growled, biting her softly and earning a gasp as she reached behind to unfasten the offending garment.

As it sailed across the room, Jasper took in the beautiful view. "God couldn't have created anyone more perfect than you, Kess. I swear." He placed a kiss to each breast, relishing in her gasp of pleasure before searing his words on her lips, devouring her response. He pulled away slightly only to say the three words that had burned in his mind from the very beginning. "I love you." He breathed them into her, giving them life as he sealed them with a kiss.

Kessed broke away, and he tried to follow but she placed a finger on his lips, and he regarded her with his drunken gaze. "I love you more."

And then the dam broke.

All the tension, the fear, and reservations he'd experienced over the past week melted away like a spring flood and swept him over the edge. No longer could he play it safe, much less slow.

Kessed responded in kind, and when she pressed into him, he didn't— couldn't—pull away. With frenzied efforts, he removed the last of their barriers of clothing and lost himself in the only woman who had ever stolen his heart.

*Who am I kidding? I gave it away on a silver platter.*

The best damn choice he'd ever made.

With each stroke, he found home.

Each breath she breathed, he inhaled and made his own.

And as she gave her final cry, he met her in sweet release.

When she finally caught her breath, he wanted to steal it away again and again, making every part of her somehow a part of him.

His heartbeat slowed, and he rested on his arm, using his free hand to sweep her dark hair from her face, learning every hint of color that came from being thoroughly loved.

Kessed traced the outline of his lips then reached up and placed the softest of kisses on his mouth.

He closed his eyes against the sweet onslaught of emotion that welled within. "Hold that thought." He twisted away, his body already acutely aware of the separation and demanding that he close the distance immediately.

But he had more important plans.

He'd wanted her to come here for a reason.

Well, so maybe more than one reason. He grinned as he pulled open his top dresser drawer and lifted out a wooden box.

He heard the rustle of sheets as Kessed sat up. It was a powerfully arousing sight, yet he forced himself to focus.

"What's that?" she asked as he set the old box on the bed.

"I have something for you." He took a deep breath, not of uncertainty, but of levity.

This wasn't a small moment....

Rather, one that would define a million more.

"This"—He held out a delicate ring in the palm of his hand, one that brought a thousand memories to mind with one glance—"was my grandmother's."

Memories of love, loss, loyalty, and blood lived in the circular piece of jewelry.

Kessed picked it up from his hand and studied it, her chocolate-brown eyes studying the ring with careful attention, realization and anticipation illuminating their dark depths.

"And now, I'd like it to be yours." Jasper spoke with rugged emotion. Slowly, he knelt by the bed, not once taking his eyes from the beautiful woman who had just shared it with him. "From the first time I met you, I wanted you. Not just for a season, but forever. From day one, I risked my heart, hoping to be rewarded with the greatest prize of all... your love. Kessed... will you marry me?"

Jasper held his breath as a single tear trickled down her cheek a moment before she nodded, then whispered, "Yes."

Before he could react, she leapt from the bed and tackled him to the floor. Her lips met his with an enthusiastic passion. Then she quickly rolled over and placed the ring on the fourth finger of her left hand, tears glistening in her eyes as she flicked her gaze from the circle to him and back.

"It's perfect," she whispered in wonder.

Jasper sat up and settled her on his lap.

She rested her head against his shoulder as they gazed at the ring together. The larger diamond was framed by several others, creating the snowflake design he remembered from his childhood.

"My grandparents had an amazing marriage, Kess. They're one of the reasons I didn't hold back when I chased you... and one of the reasons I was scared shitless to lose you at the same time. Love like that only comes around once." He shrugged.

"Once. But once is enough," Kessed whispered, meeting his lips in a kiss.

"Once is more than enough," Jasper affirmed, pursuing her lips as she leaned away.

When he opened his eyes, she had a small frown on her face.

"What?" he asked, yet the fear that had been present before had completely melted away.

She was his.

"What about Harper? I mean, if it was your grandmother's..." Her dismay seemed to deepen as she glanced to the ring and then fisted her hand as if determined not to let it go.

Jasper chuckled and gently encouraged her hand to relax. "Harper has my father's ring. Someday, Lord willing, she'll be able to give that to someone worthy of wearing it. This one"—he lifted her hand and caressed her fourth finger—"belongs to no one but you."

He placed the ring to his lips and kissed the symbol that forever represented their ties together. Body, soul, and everything in between.

And as Kessed tilted his chin up and whispered, "I love you," once again, Jasper couldn't help but be thankful he'd had the courage to chase her heart.

True love was worth the risk.

Every. Damn. Time.

# EPILOGUE

"You know, for an assistant, you sure are bossy." Jasper leaned against the doorway to the kitchen, grinning at Kessed as she held up a hand to silence him as she answered the phone.

"Yes, I'll get you all scheduled. Of course. Bye." She set the phone down, typed quickly into the laptop on the new kitchen table, and then gave him a glare. "Seriously. You should know by now that I can't concentrate when you're standing there naked." She gave a quick onceover to his body and bit her lip.

"You're the one who jumped out of bed to answer the phone."

"I wasn't in bed yet, and my boss is a pain in the ass who demands perfection." She grinned.

"Yeah, sure. The boss just wants to get laid by his almost-wife." Jasper closed the distance and slid a hand over Kessed's shoulder.

"Are you sure Harper's fine in the loft? I swear, she never comes in the house anymore."

"She's too obsessed with Spartan and Rake. She's always been better with horses than people." Jasper shrugged as he tugged on Kessed's hand, guiding her toward their bedroom.

Their. Bedroom.

It hadn't taken long for them to set the date—exactly three months from today—and finalize all the details. As Kessed had said, she didn't want to waste one moment of the future she finally had.

He couldn't have agreed more.

Harper had accepted Kessed right away, and the two had become closer than he'd even hoped. Of course, that was when Kessed could steal Harper's attention from her new horse, Spartan.

Kessed still gave Sterling a wide berth, and Jasper didn't hold it against him. But Sterling had made other progress, and Harper had been instrumental. She'd taken over his therapy when he made quick improvement with only a few horse-therapy sessions—much to the chagrin of Sterling who, indeed, did not like horses.

But Jasper had the distinct suspicion that he did like Harper.

It would be interesting to watch it play out.

As he all but tackled Kessed to the bed, he couldn't imagine the pain of losing her, of not having her love every moment.

Kessed nipped at his ear, train-wrecking his thoughts and diverting his attention away from all but her.

"I love you," she whispered as she walked her fingers along his chest.

"Guess what?" Jasper teased, reaching around her waist and pulling her on top of him.

"Hmm?" She kissed down his neck, setting his body on fire.

He splayed his palms on her back and hauled her in tight. "I love you more."

"Keep trying," Kessed all but moaned back.

"Every day, Kess." He nipped at her lips. "Every damn day."

Coming in August 2018,

Don't miss the next book in the Elk Heights Ranch
series,

**THE COWGIRL MEETS HER MATCH**

by Kristin Vayden

Harper and Sterling get together and the

sparks fly!

Available at your favorite e-retailer.

# About the Author

**Kristin Vayden** is the author of twenty books and anthologies. She is an acquisitions Editor for a Boutique publishing house, and helps mentor new authors. Her passion for writing started young, but it was only after her sister encouraged her to write did she fully realize the joy and exhilaration of writing a book. Her books have been featured in many places, including the Hallmark Channel's Home and Family show.

You can find Kristin at her website, http://kristinvayden.weebly.com, on FB as www.facebook.com/kristinvaydenauthor or on Twitter: @ KristinVayden.

Printed in the United States
by Baker & Taylor Publisher Services